WINTERTIDE

BY LINNEA SINCLAIR

GOLD IMPRINT

June 2004
Published by Medallion Press, Inc.
225 Seabreeze Ave.
Palm Beach, FL 33480

ISBN 1-932815-07-4

Printed in the United States of America

For more great books visit www.medallionpress.com.

PROLOGUE

It was well past midwinter. The deep snows had thinned, their ice-crusted shells sparkling in the bright, morning sun. Already a few green shoots poked brazenly through the ground. Yet, the healer felt a chill in her bones as she walked down the rutted path into the village. She drew the embroidered shawl more tightly around her shoulders and scanned the familiar horizon for the baneful shape of a black crow. She saw nothing. Only smoke rising hopefully from chimneys into a clear blue sky.

Just my old bones, she chided herself. Old bones, weary from winters spent in the damp cold of Cirrus Cove. Ninety winters of tending to minor ills and life passings, and ninety summers of harvest blessings and plague wardings. Healer's work. But watching, ever cautious, for things beyond the ken of an ordinary healer.

In the small square that was the center of the coveside village, cart ponies plodded steadily, hauling their burdens for the first time without their woolen blankets. She touched their essences as she passed. Dark magic wore many disguises. But all seemed to be as it should.

Miles to the south, hoofs pounded. The ominous thunder of their approach was still distant, and the healer heard nothing but the shrill cry of sea-fowl.

She followed the wheeling birds toward the pier. The Covemen were out in their square-rigged boats seeking the first harvest. Tradition demanded the healer greet their return, sprinkle their catch with herbs specially chosen for the First Harvest Blessing. She had a few hours yet. The healer drew in a deep breath of the pungent sea air and felt, as always, the presence of Merkara, God of the Sea. It was his blessing she would seek, though not without a prayer of thanks to the sky goddess, Ixari, for a mild and uneventful winter. Storms had been few.

Though a last one might yet be on its way. That wouldn't be unusual for Wintertide. Perhaps that's what she felt in the sharpness of the air, what she glimpsed in the murky shadings darting through the waves. It was still a winter sea: muddy-gray and crested with white foam. The air was crisp; the healer could imagine the shouts of the Covemen framed by frost. They'd be working their nets with frozen fingers, anticipating warm ale brewing for tonight's hearthside celebration.

More than ale would soon spill across the carefully polished, wooden floors of their cottages. But the healer saw only the pattern of the sails splashed across the horizon like clusters of low-lying clouds.

A young woman in a long, yellow dress stood at the far end of the beach, watching the largest boat swing gracefully about. The healer recognized Drucilla, the captain's daughter. The wind was shifting. The colorful ribbons on her dress fluttered in the same direction as the sails. Drucilla brought her hands to her hair, pushing it out of her face as she turned toward the pier. The healer was about to raise her hand in greeting, when a searing pain shot through her thin body. She doubled over, gasping.

From across the frozen marshlands came a deafening rumble, steady and relentless. It echoed through the icy pines. Snow cascaded from branches; icicles dropped like daggers, tearing slender wounds in the whiteness below.

The healer leaned unsteadily against a rope-bound piling, its pine-tar coating sticky against her skin. Bile rose in her throat. She blinked forcibly, focused on the thundering sound and saw them coming, saw the dark-clothed men on dark horses, raised swords glinting hard and cold in the Wintertide sun. She cried out to Drucilla in warning, but the young woman, blinded by fear, was already running toward the dunes. Her long dress whipped out behind her, its brilliant ribbons contrasting sharply with the sand and snow under her feet. She clutched her short woolen cape against her breast. Her boots dug a desperate trail into the sand.

A group of riders broke away, wheeling their horses after Drucilla. The healer watched with sickening certainty as they quickly closed the short distance. The rest continued toward the village, shouting oaths, yelling wardings. The mystic words were clearer now. The healer understood them.

Trying to stand, she pushed against the piling. Tar-coated splinters raked down her hands. But something far more heinous burned her soul, tried to strip her of her essence.

Then the sound of screams filled the air, mixing with the acrid smell of burning timber and canvas. And something else. The thick, cloying scent of dark magic that only the healer could smell. She cried out against the pain, thrust her hand into the amulet pouch threaded to her belt. Stiff fingers trembled over the stones. She palmed two, knowing their essences as she touched them. She struggled to stand.

"Tal tay Raheira!" The healer drew strength from the ancient words, felt her essence generate its own protective fire. Heat against heat scorched at the magics. Then the air cleared. Haltingly she stepped back from the piling and cast a worried glance down the beach. The horses were riderless. She was too late.

She stumbled off the pier and ran for the village. Her destination was solely practical. She could save dozens there. Behind her she could no longer save even one.

❃ ❃ ❃

Far out to sea, the Covemen perceived a blackish tinge on the horizon. But it wasn't until the red glow of the flames crested like scarlet breakers against the deep blue of the winter sky, that the captain shouted the order to return to port.

4

They found Drucilla, the captain's daughter, at the far end of the frozen beach. Her colorful dress torn, her porcelain complexion mottled with bruises. The bright ribbons still fluttered in the biting wind, streaming over the snow and sand. She lay in a pool of blood from the wound in her shoulder—a gash that crossed toward her right breast, now bared from where her blouse had been ripped from her body. She'd been beaten and raped by the Raiders, the Hill people from the West. But she was alive.

The village itself was a mass of smoldering rubble. The gusting wind wailed through the charred timbers as if the dwellings mourned their occupants, many now dead. Abused and mutilated bodies littered the cart paths and rutted roadway.

The burly Covemen cried out in anger, shouting oaths to their gods. Their anguished voices echoed, broke. Then in the silence that followed, the first of the children who'd escaped crept silently out of hiding from the thickness of the forest's edge. It would be days before the eldest—a lanky lad of twelve—would be able to relate, hesitantly, those things he'd seen. The bright glitter of silver daggers slitting flesh like butter, the intense crimson of the flames that licked through the shattered windows of the small, thatched houses. Many would never be able to voice those atrocities. But they'd hear forever in their nightmares the sickening thud of Hill stallions' hoofs on the lifeless bodies of their friends and kinsmen.

Other children stumbled forth, ten in all, some clinging to the skirts of their mothers. The Covemen rushed forward. Tears of joy ran down faces taut with grief.

The last child was a toddler, his hand grasped firmly by the healer.

The grizzled captain, his bushy, white hair stiff with salt spray, scooped his small nephew into his arms. "Why, healer? Why now?" In the forty years he'd ruled the village, the Hill people had never attacked in Wintertide; the ground was too slippery and treacherous for their slim-hoofed stallions.

The old Raheiran woman met his gaze levelly, but her fingers trembled as she traced the ancient rune signs embroidered into her shawl. "Come to my cave, at moonrise. I will have answers for you, then."

The captain suppressed a shudder as she walked quickly away, amulet pouches swinging from her belt. Hearthside legends told of times when the mysterious Raheira had ruled the Land, altering its form and enchanting it with spells. But now they were few, and many villages no longer used the services of a healer. Or cared to, for the Raheira were viewed with equal amounts of distrust and suspicion, as well as respect.

But at moonrise the captain found himself at the cave in the foothills, where the green and gold of the dunes intermingled with the browns and grays of the mountains.

Three times Bronya the Healer cast the stones into the mage circle scratched in the sandy surface of her cave. And three times she shook her head and told the despondent captain there was no choice. It had to be.

The old man clutched his short hunting knife and struck out at the heavens, daring the sea god, Merkara, to explain these actions. But neither the god, nor the healer, had anything further to say.

✳ ✳ ✳

In late summer, the captain brought Drucilla, swollen with child, to the cave of the healer. Again, stones were cast into the mage circle.

"I won't tolerate a halfling in my house!" The old man's dark eyes blazed.

Drucilla said nothing, her face ashen even in the rosy glow of the fire.

Bronya retrieved the round objects. "If the child is to be who the stones say she will, it's best I raise her. She will live with me."

A low rumble of distant thunder penetrated the stillness of the cave and echoed off mossy gray walls. The healer's gaze darted around the room, as if searching for something she didn't want to see.

The captain toyed nervously with his blade, his expression softening. "Well, perhaps a girl child should be raised in a house, healer. I wasn't thinking the child would be a girl. The foothills are too . . ."

"I will raise her." Bronya's voice held a note of anger. "The stones say this is the chosen child. The child he will want. Your village offers no protection to such a child."

Thunder resounded, sounding closer this time. The old woman stood abruptly, knocking the smooth stones out of her lap and onto the floor. She shook a gnarled fist toward the heavens, her metal bracelets clanging almost as loudly as the approaching storm.

"This time, she will be mine, do you hear me?"

A wind whipped through the cave extinguishing the fire, chilling the occupants of the dark hole. The captain grabbed his daughter's arm and quickly guided her toward the entrance into the failing daylight.

"We'll send word when it's her time!" His voice echoed back into the darkness. Wrapping his long cape around his trembling daughter, he carefully led her away from the mountains to the safety of their own gathering on the dunes.

Bronya stared defiantly into the storm, her coarse, green dress buffeted about in the winds.

"She will be mine!"

Suddenly all was quiet. The yellow light of the night sky cast an eerie glow into the cave of the healer. She followed its shaft to the floor. The outlines of the circle, now covered in dust, were barely discernible. The stones were as they had fallen from her lap. Their pattern was unmistakable.

The Sorcerer claimed the unborn child for himself.

❋ ❋ ❋

The thin, dark-haired, young boy scurried through the foothills to the cave of the healer. Mounds of gold and orange leaves, crisp from autumn's influence, swirled in his passing. Drucilla's time was near.

"Aye, Tavis. This I know. Everything's ready." She ruffled the hair of the smith's only son then sent him careening back through the leaves with word of her arrival.

The healer carefully patted the bags of herbs and medicines she wore around her waist, tied to the knotted string belt. More than the usual birthing herbs were needed with this one. Strong wards would be necessary to keep him out. She couldn't let him interfere.

Not yet. Not until the child knew of her powers and could choose her own destiny, as was her right, by Ixari, the Goddess of the Heavens. Merkara and Tarkir were not the only powers in the Land.

The afternoon sun blazed overhead. It was warm for mid-autumn. But the healer saw the clouds rolling in from the south. Heavy clouds, full of rain and wind and lightning.

The sea already churned as she entered the gates of the village. Strong winds whistled through the freshly thatched roofs around her. The boats in the Cove strained at their moorings. The spray dampened her face and the air smelled of salt, and something else. She squinted into the wind, narrowing her gray brows, the lines on her face deepening. The smell, the scent came from the storm clouds.

The smell of magic, the scent of power.

She quickened her steps to the center of the village, to the captain's house with its white-shingled sides and heavy, oak door.

The child, with hair as pale as the lightning that slashed the sky, was born at the height of the hurricane, a maelstrom from the south. The old woman cradled the infant in her arms. Gale winds buffeted about the house, screeching through the cracks in the timbers.

"She's mine!" she cried into the hot, damp winds. She wrapped a garland of herbs and gemstones about the child's small form.

When she moved for the door, the white-haired captain sprang from his chair by the hearth.

"You're mad, healer. Surely you can't take the child out in this?"

"It's either that or suffer the chance of this house being destroyed. There's no wind that can level my cave."

"Then go!" The captain thrust his hand toward the door, his arm shaking. "And take this madness with you!"

He slammed the large, oak door behind the hunched form. The healer's clothing darkened as it absorbed the slashing rain. Her head bent protectively over the small bundle she clutched to her breast, wrapped in a bolt of bright cloth that she'd spent hours embroidering with the symbols of the deities.

The child neither cried nor whimpered, in spite of the harsh sounds and flashes of light. Her large eyes, now blue, now gray, now green, watched with intense curiosity at the events around her.

The healer staggered into her cave and placed the child into the wooden cradle; its sides, too, were decorated with the signs and symbols of her craft. She shivered and added wood to the fire, unaware that the storm outside had subsided.

"We are home, Khamsin," she whispered to the sleeping child, whose small hand curled around the edge of the blanket. "He did not get you, this time."

CIRRUS COVE

CHAPTER ONE

Orange tongues of flame licked at the stout logs on the hearth. But the fire was more for light than heat. The last, warm breath of summer still drifted over the Land though it was a month into the autumn season.

The stone floor of the cave echoed a coolness drawn from the dark green forest. Khamsin folded a small rug into a cushion and decided that this was the perfect spot to finish the chain of brightpinks she'd started earlier.

She intertwined the long, green stems, keeping the blossoms to the outside. It was a silly thing, a brightpink chain. Tanta Bron told her it had no real magic to offer. But the village girls thought otherwise. They made them every summer, to call their lovers to them.

"A flower bright I take to thee, a flower bright brings thee to me." Khamsin recited the words softly, as she carefully bent the slender stem in a half circle. "A flower bright . . ."

The sound of a wooden chair scraping against the floor stilled her whispered song. Quickly she thrust the half-formed chain under an edge of the rug. She turned as Tanta Bron drew back the embroidered curtain covering the archway to her bedchamber.

"Finished your chores, child?"

"Yes, Tanta."

"But not your studies." Bronya knelt in front of the young girl and placed a leather-bound book on the gray stone floor. "Now. Time grows short."

A petulant frown creased Khamsin's face. *Time grows short; time grows short, for what?* "But I'm so tired, Tanta Bron . . ."

"Tired? Chasing that cat all day in the woods again. That's play. This is different."

Khamsin opened the book with a resigned sigh. Its thin, dusty pages had a sweet, powdery odor. "It wasn't all play. Nixa hears me now. Even when I'm not touching her."

At the mention of her name, the gray cat, curled in front of the large hearth, blinked opened her golden eyes. A soft Nixa-tinged sensation filtered into Khamsin's mind as their awareness linked briefly. She saw her own image from the cat's viewpoint: a slender sixteen-year-old girl, clad in boy's tan breeches and white overshirt, sitting cross-legged on the floor. But it was Khamsin's pale hair, in a long braid that reached past her waist, which caught the cat's attention. She shook her head. The ribbons binding the end fluttered. Nixa's playful interest rippled over her.

"And I can sometimes even see what she sees. Like now. She's . . ."

"Visions of ribbons to play with won't be able to protect you, when the time comes. Start here." Bronya tapped her finger at the start of a series of dark slashes and curlicues in the middle of the page.

Khamsin squinted at the shapes. They shifted, becoming words in her mind. Though not really words. She knew words, letters Tavis had taught her. She could write her own name and his. And simple sentences like, "I will buy this horse for two pigs."

But the rune signs in the healer's book didn't pertain to such mundane things. They pertained to spells: incantations, callings, and divinations. They had to be memorized, practiced over and over again until Khamsin could say them without hesitation. They had to be imbedded in her mind, inscribed on her soul.

"Now, this is . . ." Bronya prompted.

"Ixari's Third Blessing for Rain." Khamsin closed her eyes, called the rune signs from memory. "*T'cai l'heira, Ixari* . . ." she said softly, remembering to touch her lips with the side of her index finger as she said the goddess's name. The rest of the odd-sounding words flowed easily. She'd recited this incantation many times before. Weather blessings were the least difficult. She knew Tanta Bron had her repeat them only to relax her mind.

More difficult ones followed. The spell to stop the flow of water in a stream. The spell to stop the flow of blood from a wound. The spell to make lifesweet from leaves and flowers, if no food can be found. The spell

15

to make firestones, for warmth and protection.

"And the supplications, child?"

Khamsin opened her eyes. Saying her supplications signaled the lesson's end. She wiggled her right foot. Her ankle was stiff from sitting cross-legged for so long.

"To Merkara, God of the Sea. And Ixari, Goddess of the Sky. For protection, I beseech you. For guidance, I entreat you. In all . . ." And she yawned, then grinned sheepishly at the healer. "Sorry."

Nixa yawned, too, stretching her paws toward the fire. "Finish, Khamsin."

"In all things, mystic and mundane, in all realms and all planes. Let your powers now guide me. Your blessings, beside me. From harm you will hide me. I live in the light of your names."

Bronya pulled herself to her feet. "Good." She rummaged in the deep pockets of her long skirt. "I'll place the warding stones. No, don't turn around. Tell me first if they're right."

Khamsin closed her eyes again. A new image popped into her mind: Tanta Bron's bent figure in her long blue and green skirts and blue shawl. Her dark hair, pulled so carefully and so tightly back into a bun early this morning, now unraveled in wispy strands.

No, Nixa, Khamsin admonished gently. *You can't help. That's cheating.*

"Do you sense the spell lines?"

"Ummm. Yes. But the Ladri stone's in the wrong place." She felt the discordant hum of the stones' energy. "It's too close to the Khal."

16

"Then why didn't you say the Khal was in the wrong place? I've told you time and time again. You *must* look for Tarkir's stone before all others. Tarkir's stone must be your power point for all wardings.

"Yes, ma'am I know, but . . ."

"No buts, Khamsin. Now, tell me again."

A ripple of energy told Khamsin that Tanta Bron moved the warding stones.

"The Khal is centered in primary," she said. "Ladri and Vedri are balanced. But Nevri is . . ." She tightened her mental focus slightly. "Nevri is in opposition to Ladri. Nevri must be reversed."

There was a soft sound as Bronya turned the warding stone.

"Better?"

Bronya's approval washed over Khamsin even before she answered. "Better!"

"Much better. Now, come, come. Up off the floor. We'll have some moonpetal tea, and then it's off to bed with you."

Khamsin snuggled under her blankets and breathed in the sweet aroma of the moonpetal tea still in the air. She heard soft snoring sounds filtering through the embroidered curtain covering Tanta Bron's alcove.

The curtain across Khamsin's own small alcove was open. She saw Nixa sitting in front of the fireplace, her small form outlined by the weak, orange glow of the embers. The cat industriously washed her whiskers, pleased at having found a small piece of cheese on the table.

Behind Nixa, the folded rug was still where Khamsin left it. A tangle of brightpinks peeked out from under one corner.

At the mouth of the cave, where rough-hewn timbers and large boulders laced to form her home's front wall, Khamsin saw the flicker of the warding stones in the darkness.

Ladri. Vedri. Nevri. She touched each one with her mind. The warding stones responded, flaring briefly with a small spark.

Then she touched the Khal. Tarkir's stone. The God of the Land and the Underworld. The most powerful of all the warding stones. The most powerful of all the deities.

It pulsed a bright blue-white, startling Nixa. The cat scampered into Khamsin's alcove, leaped onto the bed and turned around three times before settling into a fold in the blankets.

Khamsin pulled the cat up against her and, with a small sigh, closed her eyes.

❋ ❋ ❋

That winter Bronya took ill for the first time that Khamsin could remember. The old woman lay on her narrow featherbed for days. Her thin body trembled as the cold, north winds shook the branches of the great pines outside, flinging clumps of crusted snow to the frozen ground. Her brittle cough echoed off the rocky walls. Khamsin kept the fire stoked until she could no longer stand the dry heat and sought solace at the entrance of the cave.

She was aware of Tavis's approach even before Nixa bounded through the deep snow with the news.

She gathered her long, layered skirts about her and trudged out into the small clearing. Nixa trotted after her, sniffing the drifting snowflakes.

"Bronya said the compounds would be ready today. But a wagon repair kept me working late." Tavis nodded to the slight figure silhouetted by the stark whiteness around her. The droplets of melting snow in his dark beard and tousled, curly, brown hair glistened like gems in the light of the full moons overhead.

"I've everything in a box for you. Come inside, out of the cold."

Khamsin took his cape and, while he peeled off a bulky, woolen outer-tunic, poured a steaming cup of jasmine tea for the broad-shouldered, young smith. She could tell he'd come straight from his forge. His wide face was still sweat-streaked in spite of the chill outside. She held the earthenware mug out to him. He accepted it gratefully and glanced at the slatted box on the table's edge.

She touched the cloth pouches stacked inside. They contained blessing and warding herbs used by generations of smiths. "Three red for your forge fires, two blue for metals for the boats. Two yellow for horseshoes and cart metals."

Tavis seemed surprised. "I thought with Bronya being ill . . ."

"Bronya didn't make these. I did." She didn't try to keep the pride from her voice.

"You? You're not a healer."

"I've been learning."

Tavis fingered the pouches again, and Khamsin reined in her desire to defend her skills. Bronya's dark eyes and, at one time, dark hair bespoke of her Raheiran heritage. Khamsin's light coloring didn't, and she sensed the smith's small tinge of dissatisfaction at his wares having been prepared by someone less than an "expert."

"How is she?" He cautiously sipped at the sweet liquid, his bushy brows drawn into a frown.

"A little better." Khamsin motioned him to the table then brought over a plate of sliced, honey bread. At least Tavis had no qualms about accepting her baking. "And the more I can do of her work, the more she's able to rest."

"It's good you're able to help her, I suppose. With the simple things. Until she's well again."

"I hope to learn more than the simple things."

"That's not for the likes of you, Kammi." There was a note of alarm in Tavis's voice. "Clean and cook, as a daughter or a niece would, yes. But a healer's workings are not for ordinary folk like us."

He patted her hand. "You look tired. Why don't you think about bringing Bronya to the village, at least until First Thaw? My sister said she'd be glad to help."

"No, really. But thank you."

"It would be easier for you. With Mowrina's help. And mine."

20

Khamsin waved her hand toward the rows of shelves on the far wall. "Everything she needs, everything I need is here. All her herbs, her powders, her teas." And her potions, her amulets, and charms. And the warding stones. No, Khamsin knew, staying at Mowrina's house wouldn't be easier.

Though the villagers were grateful for the lives Bronya had saved from the Hill Raiders, they still remembered the many who died. In the same way, they accepted Tanta Bron's moonpetal tea for sleep and her brightmint salve for infection, but were openly mistrustful of her rune stones and amulets. And equally as mistrustful of Khamsin and her cat. Tavis and his sister were the only friends she had in the village.

"Perhaps if I brought Mowrina here?"

"Who'll take care of Aric and the children?" She smiled. "You're a smith, Tav. Changing diapers and feeding babies might soften those big hands of yours!"

"Aye, well, that's true. And then Aric and I would get to playing cards, and nothing would get done at all."

Is that Tavis? Khamsin felt Tanta Bron awaken.

Yes, Tanta.

I wish to speak to him.

We'll come in and sit with you.

No, child. I need to speak to him, alone.

Before Khamsin could ask why, Bronya's weak voice called through the curtain. "Tavis? Young man, is that you?"

Tavis's mug stopped halfway to his lips. He put it back on the table. "Aye, lady. Did we disturb you?"

"No. Please." Bronya coughed. It was a thin, wheezing sound. "Come here."

Tavis looked at Khamsin and she nodded. "Bring her this." She handed him a hot mug of tea. "Maybe she'll drink it if you ask her."

Khamsin waited in the large outer chamber and played disinterestedly with Nixa. The deep rumblings of Tavis's voice could be heard now and then, punctuated by the high whine of Bronya's worsening cough. She couldn't hear their words, though she knew a spell to eavesdrop on their conversation, if she wanted to. But she allowed them their privacy, trusting that if anything said was pertinent to her, she'd learn of it shortly.

Finally Tavis emerged. He sat down on the wide, wooden bench by the fire, taking Khamsin's small hands into his callused ones. His touch was surprisingly chilled. He seemed clearly uncomfortable, almost shaken.

"Her time draws near, Kammi."

She guessed as much, but had been holding her sadness in check, knowing Tanta Bron might feel burdened by her grief. Now, at Tavis's words, sorrow flooded through her. She turned toward the hearth fire and drew a deep breath.

Tavis squeezed her fingers. "She's an old, old woman. Seen over one hundred summers, if not more. Her only thoughts have been centered on you. You're so young, yet . . ."

"But I'm not a child. I'll be seventeen after Summertide."

"True. That's why she asked me to take care of you, now. She said the runes show danger, in the next year especially."

Tanta's runes had long shown danger. But never before had the healer discussed that with anyone other than Khamsin. And even those discussions had been maddeningly sparse, frustratingly cryptic. Her seventeenth year, was all that Bronya would say. If danger were to come it would be then.

"Did she say what kind of danger?"

"No. But she asked that I keep you safe." He hesitated. "She won't be around to watch after you very much longer."

Khamsin swallowed the lump in her throat. "When?" Her voice was soft. "Did she say when?"

"She said before Wintertide."

That was just two months away.

She stood suddenly, folded her hands and held them against her chest, as if she could keep the hurt inside from escaping. The empty mugs and remnants of honey bread were still on the table. She cleared them away because she needed something, anything to do.

"I'm sure Tanta Bron just wanted to thank you for your friendship. To tell you how important it is to her. And to me too. You and Mowrina have been very good friends, Tavis." She stacked the mugs in the water basin.

Tavis came to stand beside her. He took her trembling hands in his own. "She asks that I be more than that now."

"You'll always be one of my dearest friends . . ."

23

"Bronya wants me to take you as my wife."

"Wife?" She tensed, startled at the word. She knew it was common for a girl to marry around her sixteenth year; one of the village girls, still an infant when the Wintertide raid took place, wed last Summertide.

And Tavis was a bachelor who had a large, three-room house and a prosperous smithing business. He was more than eligible. But she, Khamsin, a wife? The possibility never occurred to her.

Besides, marriage meant love. And she wasn't in love with Tavis.

She stared at the bearded man. "Why would Tanta Bron want us to marry?"

"So that I can take care of you."

"I can take care of myself!"

Nixa, curled on her hearthside pillow, slitted her eyes open at Khamsin's exclamation.

Tavis glanced away from her, and at first Khamsin thought she had hurt him by her declaration. But his gaze, she noted, touched on Bronya's braided ribbons and cloth banners painted with cryptic runes that hung around the room. Then moved to the shelves lined with jars filled with herbs and powders. Things not found in a smithy.

"Tanta Bron has taught me much about healing work. She would want me to stay, to help the villagers. And for you to continue to tell me when the villagers need help. Just as you've always done."

"That's not what she said to me, Kammi." He shook his head slowly. "It's Bronya's wish to see us wed. For you to be a wife. Not a healer."

You must marry, child. Bronya's words were weak in her mind. *The runes, the runes tell me this now.*

The runes say I must marry Tavis?

Khamsin felt the old woman's tiredness. Then a sigh. *That has not been clear. So much isn't clear anymore. But who else? There's no one else in the village who accepts what you are. That has been shown to me.*

A torrent of conflicting emotions surged through Khamsin. She tamped them down quickly, lest her frail Tanta be hurt by her confusion. She had no desire to see Tanta Bron hurt. She knew all the old healer had done for her, how she'd risked her life just to raise her. She owed Tanta so much. But to marry! And to someone not of her choosing. Even the girls in the village were permitted to choose.

But she had no choice. Even if she wanted to choose a husband, there were none in Cirrus who'd have her: Khamsin, child of the maelstrom, with Hill Raider's blood in her veins.

None but Tavis the Smith.

She didn't love Tavis. But she did like him. They'd been friends since she was little, though there was a nine-year difference in their ages.

She glanced at him and felt his concern flood over her like a moon tide. He was worried about her. She felt his devotion to Tanta Bron. And then, surprisingly, a flicker of desire for herself. That was unexpected and only added to her own confused state.

"Kammi?"

She brought her face up to meet his. The old

woman's wheezing was audible even over the moaning of the winds outside. Tanta Bron was dying. If marrying Tavis would bring her peace . . .

Khamsin raised her voice so that she was sure Bronya could hear her answer.

"I understand your offer and thank you," she replied evenly to the man who, sixteen years before, had run to the healer's cave with the news of her impending birth. "And I would be honored to be your wife."

Tavis smiled warmly, clasped her small hands in his large, callused ones. "You're doing the right thing. You'll see. We'll be happy together. I promise you."

The flames in the hearth fire behind him flickered as a sudden torrent of icy wind flowed down from the north. The bitter cold grazed Khamsin's cheek, and she shivered.

Tavis draped his arm over her shoulder. "Wind's picking up again. Be a cold walk back. Perhaps a cup of tea before I leave?"

"Of course." Khamsin stepped away from him and headed for the cupboard. Her hands shook slightly as she reached for the cups.

"If you'll get the kettle?"

She put the cups on the wide, wooden table. Steam rose in fragrant clouds as Tavis poured.

She sipped her tea immediately, trying to quell the sudden chill. But Tavis raised his cup first and touched it to hers.

"To my future wife."

A large pine not far from Bronya's cave trembled, then split in half. Cleaved as if by lightning in winter.

CHAPTER TWO

The bonding ceremony took place in the large main room of the smith's white-shingled house. Only Mowrina, Tavis's older sister, attended. The young, village captain glanced uneasily at the girl standing before him, amulets dangling from her waist, her skirt embroidered with strange curling symbols. He kept the ceremony brief. Donning his heavy cape and muffler, he nodded only the barest congratulations to the bride and groom. He scurried out into the light drifting of snowflakes that had been falling steadily since the early morning.

Rina, her dark hair as curly and unruly as her brother's, shook her head in disapproval as the captain quickly departed. She accepted her own cloak from Tavis.

"Aric is waiting for his supper. You know how Lissa, Cavell, and the baby get when I'm not there." She planted a light kiss on her brother's cheek then took Khamsin's small hands in her own.

"Don't let the village nosy-bodies disturb you. They can say what they like. But Tav chose you, so that's good enough for me."

Khamsin returned the older woman's warm smile. "I feel blessed to have you both."

"You have all of us, really. We're family now. Aric and I will have you both over for dinner as soon as First Thaw begins. Myself, I'll be glad when Wintertide's over. Too many memories creep up this time of year."

This will be another one, Khamsin knew, as the heavy, oak door shut behind Rina's retreating figure. First the Wintertide raid. Then, when she was six, the poisoned harvest. She was ten when the floods from the fast melting snows claimed the lives of four Covemen and two villagers. Twelve when another early thaw brought South Land Hill Raiders into the village at Wintertide. But the toll that year had been less. The villagers took to making weapons as well as fishing nets, and Tavis's smithy had forged swords.

Then in the Wintertide between her sixteenth and seventeenth year, Tanta Bron died. And Khamsin, the child of the mistral winds, became the wife of Tavis the Smith.

❈ ❈ ❈

Tavis made love to her carefully that first night. Khamsin, who thought she knew much of all there was to know about life, found she knew very little about men.

For all the water-sprites and elementals she could conjure, the forest animals she could converse with, and herbals she could blend into magical potions, she knew nothing of the basic human condition. It was several weeks before she comfortably accepted the sweating nakedness of her husband surrounding her own body and invading it. She learned to view his physical intrusions with a detached curiosity. Though she was pleased that she was able to provide him with something he viewed as pleasurable.

He was a good man and a good husband, she told herself. Grudgingly, he even permitted her to grow and mix the healing herbs that Bronya had dispensed in the village. Someone, he agreed, had to do that, until another healer could be found.

He was less than comfortable with the few items Khamsin had brought into his house from Bronya's cave. He insisted they be kept in a special cupboard with a lock. He forged the key with his own hand and destroyed the mold afterward. For safety's sake, he said.

Khamsin waited until he was busy at the forge one morning, then lined the cupboard's shelves with scented flax soaked in magic oils. She placed Bronya's book and the tools of her craft inside. Its small cabinets, of which there were three, held the more powerful herbs and roots. A long drawer held the warding stones and the cloth stenciled with rune signs.

Khamsin's own cradle carved with protective wardings sat by the hearth. But after a year of marriage, it remained empty.

Tavis's sister now carried her fourth. Khamsin knocked on Rina's back door, a newly quilted blanket folded over her arm. Six-year-old Lissa answered, her rag doll tucked under one arm.

"Tanta Kammi! Mama! Mama! Tanta Kammi's here!"

Rina rose awkwardly from the bench at the kitchen table, smoothing her apron over her swollen belly as Khamsin stepped inside. The sweet aroma of spice cakes baking wafted in the air.

"Mama's teaching me to bake," Lissa announced. "So I can help after the new baby comes."

Khamsin ruffled Lissa's reddish curls. "I'm sure you're a big help already." She handed Rina the brightly patterned quilt. "I thought you might need a new one."

"Oh, it's lovely, Kammi. And yes, we do, especially after the two boys."

Rina glanced down at her daughter. "Isn't it time for Dolly's nap?"

Lissa nodded sagely. "Oh, yes, Mama! I'd almost forgotten."

As the child disappeared through the curtained door-way, Rina touched Khamsin lightly on the arm. "You can tell me, can't you? Like Bronya used to?"

Of all the villagers, only Rina knew that Khamsin could do more than dispense herb teas and minor blessings. Even Tavis didn't know. But then, Khamsin had always been closer to Mowrina.

"Yes, of course. I brought the stones." She pulled the amulets from her pouch, cast them three times on the tabletop. A boy child. Another little brother for Lissa.

Rina sighed loudly, but was smiling. "Well, Aric will be pleased, but I'm not sure about Lissa."

"Not sure about what, Mama?" asked a small voice from the doorway.

"Not sure if I remember where I put that basket we made for Tanta Kammi."

"Granna put it in the dining room. So Taric and Cavell couldn't get it." Lissa ducked back through the curtains.

"Aric's mother's been a wonderful help with the boys." Rina held the curtain back and motioned Khamsin into the front of the house.

Khamsin could hear the older woman's soft voice coming from one of the back bedrooms. "How long will she be staying with you?"

"Until after the baby's born. But she has to be back in Dram before the snows start."

"If you need help after that, just ask."

"I'll help, too, Mama!"

"Of course." Rina smiled as Lissa reached for a basket of ripe vegetables on the table. "We've had a plentiful summer. You know how Tav likes these. Besides, you brought us those beautiful apples last time."

"I grow the fruit and you raise the vegetables. And the children," Khamsin added as Taric toddled in from the front porch and held his chubby arms up toward his mother.

"And you and Tav?"

"When the gods say it's my time to have children, I'm sure I will."

But the gods had told her very little since her marriage to Tavis, though she'd dutifully kept up with her supplications, even the basic divinations, while her husband worked at his forge. Without them, she'd no way of knowing what blessings were needed by the harvest and crops, what weather awaited the Covemen.

Khamsin walked slowly back through the village, Rina's basket on her arm. She smiled absently at the village children who darted out of her way, then stopped and stared at her with curious eyes.

Weather and harvest blessings weren't her problem. No, it was in her personal life that the gods gave her very little guidance at all.

She watched the children scurry off after a brightly decorated cart jostling on its way out of the village. It was the tinker's cart; its pace was just quick enough to be out of the reach of the children's hands. They lunged and jumped, laughing as they tried to grab some bright piece of cloth or string of braided belts from the merchandise piled in the back.

In the same way, Khamsin felt much of what she needed to know about her life now evaded her, in spite of all the divinations that Bronya had taught her. Answers dangled just out of her reach, with something or someone preventing her from gaining the knowledge.

But what could be so powerful as to interfere with the workings of the deities themselves?

The sky darkened as a large, black cloud crossed in front of the sun. In spite of the intense heat of the late summer's day, Khamsin shivered, and was still shivering when the cloud cleared.

She had just passed the sailmaker's shop, when a figure loomed out in front of her.

"Aye, lady. A kindly word, if I may." The old man's voice was slurred, and he smelled as strongly of fish as he did of rum.

Khamsin stepped back, clutching the basket to her chest. She knew all of the Covemen and many of the traveling merchants. This man was unfamiliar, and his long, dark cloak concealed whatever profession his manner of clothing might have revealed.

"You're seeking someone, sir?" Her voice was steadier than her rapidly beating heart.

His laugh was low and cruel. "That I am, lady. That I am."

"If you're a sailor, then Donal inside is the one to help you." She nodded to the sailmaker's closed door. "The captain's not yet returned . . ."

"I seek no man." A scarred hand darted out from beneath the folds of his cloak, missed her arm by inches as she twisted away. "Just a pretty girl for a good time."

"Sir! I . . ."

"Khamsin?"

She turned and almost stumbled into Aric's arms, as he exited through the sailmaker's door. A coil of rope was draped over one shoulder, and he placed himself between Khamsin and the old man.

"Khamsin?" he asked again, but when he turned the old man was already scurrying away. "Did the old drunk harm you?"

Khamsin shook her head hurriedly. "No. Just startled me."

Her brother-in-law motioned to the sagging pile of stained sails and tangled nets next to the shop. "He was probably sleeping off a bottle or two. You must've surprised him."

She let out the breath she didn't realize she'd been holding and forced a smile. "He probably knew these vegetables came from Rina's garden and wanted his share."

Aric laughed good-naturedly. "Shall I walk you to your door?"

"These are my vegetables. Your wife has more waiting for you at home," she teased from over her shoulder as she walked away.

By the time she reached her front steps, she'd dismissed her fearful misgivings about the old man as nothing more than an instinctual reaction to a very bad smell. Rotting fish and sour rum

She pulled the latch on the front door and walked to the pantry in the rear of the house. She placed Rina's offerings on the shelf. She could hear the sound of Tavis's anvil ringing with a steady rhythm. In a sudden wave of compassion, she left her meal preparations for the moment and drew a pitcher of cool, fresh water from the well.

Tavis greeted his wife's appearance in his smithy

with a wide smile. He wiped a soot-blackened arm across his sweat-bathed forehead.

"Ah, you're a real love." He gulped at the water then took the pitcher and dumped the remainder of the contents over his head.

Khamsin laughed until her sides ached. "Oh, Tav!" She reached behind him for a clean cloth and threw it playfully in his face.

He mopped his brow. Then he twisted the long cloth between his large hands, snapped it out in her direction like a whip. It caught the edge of her skirt.

She placed her hands on her hips, her eyes sparkling. "And I felt sorry for you because you were so hot and tired!"

"But I was, little Kammi!" He held his arms out to her. "The sight of your sweet face was enough to restore me to full strength!"

She pointed to the metal rods left glowing in the fire. "Then I'd best be leaving you to your work. Strong as you are, you'll be finished in no time. And I've beans to prepare."

The clanging of his hammer followed her as she crossed the small backyard. She finished emptying the basket, leaving it on a chair by the front door. She'd ask Tav to take it back to Rina tomorrow.

The thin curtains fluttered languidly in the front windows, wafting as high as the tabletop, as an occasional offshore gust blew through the village. Khamsin noticed the overturned vase on the table, the brightpinks scattered across it and onto the bare, wooden floor. No wonder she hadn't seen Nixa in her favorite spot on the back stoop. The gray feline had been up to her usual mischief. Khamsin knelt down to retrieve the last of the blossoms, and her eyes came to rest on the locked doors of her cupboard.

They were open. The lock swung in its hinges with an unnatural, mechanical rhythm. Soundlessly.

She stared, a cry strangling in her throat.

Slowly, she crawled across the floor until she sat in front of the cupboard. It radiated . . . something. She held her hands out before her, palms open. The glow of the enchantment flooded painfully into her mind. She gasped out loud, feeling the intense emanations of power. And whatever it was that touched the lock was no longer even there.

With shaking hands, she eased the doors back, careful to avoid the spell-charged metal. Bronya's book was moved forward on the shelf. It lay open.

She closed her eyes and whispered a small, protective spell. In her skirt pocket she felt around for the four amulets she needed. She put them on the floor by her knees.

Then carefully she reached into the cupboard and grasped the edges of the leather-bound volume with the tips of her fingers. Slowly, she pulled it off the shelf. She laid it on the floor then moved the amulets to surround it.

She cleared her mind again, leaned forward, and scanned the runes. Her breath quickened as she read the ancient words.

It was the spell of an assignation, an unalterable command for a meeting. The incantation was usually copied onto a parchment. It was forbidden to write in the book itself.

But someone had. Someone had inserted the symbols that Bronya taught her to be her *real name*. The name that *he* would call her by.

She was called to an assignation. And the assignation was commanded by the Sorcerer.

❆ ❆ ❆

When Tavis stomped his heavy boots on the steps of the back porch and didn't smell the pungent aroma of vegetable stew, he suspected something was wrong. Even Nixa, usually looking for handouts at mealtime, was missing. Perhaps a fevered child in the village required his wife's specials teas. Though out of habit they sought out the smith first. The villagers' fear of Khamsin was still strong enough that they disliked dealing directly with her.

Nothing prepared him for the sight that met his eyes, as he crossed into the wide living room in search of a pipe to help pass the time until Khamsin returned. The small form kneeling, trancelike, in front of the cupboard seemed barely aware of his approach.

He hesitated before touching her. Something about the open cupboard, and its contents, revolted him. Something about her unnatural stillness chilled his blood.

"K-Kammi?" he said finally, stuttering her name.

The name wafted in the moist, evening breeze that filtered through the gauze curtains and lifted the tendrils of hair that clung to her damp face. She stirred but didn't turn to face him.

He glanced at the open book. It was gibberish to him. Then his eyes caught the movement of the lock. No natural force was causing the metal to sway evenly, rhythmically, back and forth, back and forth. Khamsin's gaze followed the movement.

Tavis snatched the empty vase from the table behind him. He threw it with all his might against the open doors of the cupboard. The ceramic piece shattered with an earsplitting crash.

The lock stopped moving.

"Kammi?"

She turned in his arms, her eyes blinking rapidly. "Tavis? Oh, Tavis!" She clung to him, trembling.

❋ ❋ ❋

He knew the tea was not as pungent as Kammi would have made it. He was a smith. The kitchen was not his domain. But the hot liquid seemed to have the desired effect, in spite of its lack of flavor. Her hands stopped shaking, and some of the sparkle returned to his wife's eyes.

Nixa, too, had returned. She wove anxiously in and out of her mistress's ankles as Khamsin and Tavis sat in the high-backed chairs at the kitchen table.

He patted her hand. Things seemed to be getting back to normal. He wanted things to be normal. "It was probably nothing. A prank."

"No, it *was* something. Not a prank."

"You don't know that."

"I do. An assignation is not a prank."

"An assignation? Isn't that like a spell?"

"It's not like a spell, Tavis. It is a spell. A calling."

Her certainty disturbed him and offended him at the same time. "You do healing work, Kammi. You tend to the sick and birth babes. Healing work isn't assignations. Bronya never talked of those things, and she was a true healer. Spells are for the priests or their witches."

"Tanta Bron did talk of those things. She warned us this might happen."

He remembered sitting in the ailing healer's small alcove. She'd clutched his hand, whispered her fears about Kammi's seventeenth year. He thought perhaps the Raiders would return, claim the girl as one of their own. He hadn't considered the threat might entail magic.

"You must be wrong. She'd not have asked me to keep you safe from spells or witch-workings. If that was the danger she saw, she'd have sent you to Noviiya, to the temple priests there."

"I'm certain that was the danger she saw. She and I talked not long before she died about what needed to be done, if an assignation was placed on my name."

His eyes narrowed. The chill returned to his blood. "What needs to be done?"

"We talked about a sword. She said to ask you to make me a sword."

"A sword?" He laughed harshly. "Do you intend to defend the village from pranksters by yourself? You used to play make believe all the time with my old wooden one."

"More than make believe. Your father taught me quite well . . ."

"Aye, he did." He smiled. "I'm not saying you would trip over your feet. Father said you were strong for your size. Graceful. But a sword? Khamsin!"

"It's a different kind of sword. It must be small enough that I can wield it properly."

"I can do that. But . . ."

"And forged under my direction. For the metal must be able to hold incantations. The hilt must have amulets embedded in specific order. Rune signs must be inscribed, then forged into the metal."

Tavis sat back in his chair and pulled on his beard. This sounded less and less like healing and more and more like witch-working. The word sat cold and ugly in his mind.

But if it had been Bronya's idea? Bronya had saved his life, brought him back from a high fever when he was a small child.

"Bronya drew a sketch. With instructions," Khamsin persisted.

Well, if Bronya had designed it, perhaps he should consider it.

She brought him the sketch, unrolling it across the

table, securing one end with her mug. He sucked on his tea and studied it. The curling symbols on the page told him nothing. But the carefully drawn diagrams of the sword did.

He shook his head wearily, knowing what the task required. And knowing he couldn't refuse her.

But there was more.

"If there's to be an assignation, then let it be at my command, not his."

Tavis almost dropped his mug. "Surely, you're not in a position to dictate to some wizard!"

She hesitated. "The assignation comes from the Sorcerer."

"No! You must be wrong." Tavis's fingers clutched the mug tightly.

"I know what I saw written in the book." Her voice was soft, almost apologetic.

"You're wrong. We've no means here to stop the Sorcerer. You misread. You're not a healer, like Bronya. Those runes are hard to read. It must've said something else." He repeated his excuses as if the very act of speaking could dissolve the spell.

She laid one hand on top of the sketch. "Doesn't this tell you what I read is true?"

The arcane rune signs seemed to glow against the parchment. For the first time since the Hill Raiders attacked his village, Tavis the Smith was afraid.

"Kammi . . ." There was a pleading tone in his voice. "What if we leave? In two more months you'll be eighteen. Seventeenth year, Tanta Bron said. If the contact isn't made during your seventeenth year, this assignation would end. Isn't that true?"

"Yes, it's true," she admitted slowly. "But he's already tried to contact me. Perhaps even claim me."

"He tried to claim you? You saw him? Why didn't you say . . ."

"I saw an old man, earlier today. An old drunk. That may be all he truly was. Or he might've been more. But in any case, I do know that he's come here to our village, to our house. The writing in the book is proof of that."

The thought of a being as powerful as the Sorcerer in his house made Tavis's stomach clench. "We'll move. To Dram."

"Then those people could be in danger. I may be whom he seeks, but since when have the powers worried about the innocents when they've carved their trails of destruction? The raids, the poisoned harvests. It's been said that there were one or two who displeased the gods, yet scores perished. No, I have to go back to the cave, take up my studies, and pray that Ixari will send some guidance this time."

"Studies?" Tavis frowned.

"There are other things I must learn, ways to sharpen my mind and my senses, divinations to—"

"No. I forbid it." Tavis wiped his hand over his face, then turned from her. "There's nothing more to discuss. Nothing." His voice was gruff. He pushed himself abruptly to his feet and strode for the kitchen door, slamming it as he headed back to the smithy.

❄ ❄ ❄

She left that night, taking a small pack and some fruit with her. With Nixa in tow, she set out into the humid darkness for the foothills of the mountains, and her first home.

Tavis stood in the doorway, empty pipe still in hand. He watched as she slipped away into the shadows toward something as foreign and fearful to a mere smith as hell itself. And he began to hate those powers that were the very essence of Khamsin.

CHAPTER THREE

She spent two days in the cave kneeling over the mage circle, searching for wisdom in the ancient etchings. She sifted through compounds made of flax and feathers and seeds, recognizing patterns. She ate very little and slept almost not at all.

It wasn't until late in the afternoon, as she trudged down the rut-filled, dusty road back toward the village, that her lack of sleep and food caught up with her. She knew of a small spring off to the side, where wild berries grew through the rocks. She grabbed a few handfuls, rinsing them in the cool water. Then she splashed her face and arms to remove the dust.

A flash of color to her left caught her eye. Brightpinks, growing with wild abandon. She plucked a few, sat on a large fallen log, and started to twine a chain. And for a moment, she was a child again, carefree, with only her chores and her cat to consider.

But she was no longer a carefree child. And her cat waited for her, at the edge of the dusty road. She tucked the unfinished chain in her apron pocket and pushed herself to her feet.

Nixa, whose interest in the occult was none at all and who had a natural ability to fend for herself, had fared much better over the past two days. She pranced happily alongside her mistress as they returned to the road. To the cat, the days at the cave were a grand adventure in the forest and nothing more.

Khamsin shoved the long sleeves of her blouse up over her elbows. She regretted she hadn't thought to dampen a cloth at the spring. There was no wind from the sea, and the earth under her feet baked in the summer sun. If only the cool winds common to late summer would appear again. Daily she asked Ixari for blessings in that regard. The humidity was unbearable; her thin blouse clung to her damp form, and her skirts caught heavily between her bare legs. She thought again of the days when she ran about the forest in boy's breeches and a light vest.

There were spells in her book created to alter the weather, but they were to be performed only by a temple priest or a priestess. She was a healer, a benefactress for her village. She aided or advised; she didn't alter. A healer, as Tavis had reminded her, could question the gods but not countermand them.

The symbols she sought within the circle were for these purposes only. Though the knowledge she gained this time in Bronya's cave weighed as heavily on her mind as the oppressive weather. It was a cloudy knowledge, unlike the clear blue of the sky overhead. Everything pointed to the necessity of her continuing her training, but nothing explained why. As Tavis had said, why weren't her herbals sufficient?

But they weren't, and she wondered why Tavis didn't accept her need to continue learning. She—and Tanta Bron—thought that he would.

Again and again, the symbols for knowledge and experience appeared in her divinations and less and less, the symbols of benedictions and healing. She understood that some of this knowledge would come as a result of a journey, though by land or by water was not made clear. For when she consulted the circle for specifics, the answers were again vague.

It was as if there were a power struggle being waged amongst the deities themselves, and Khamsin's queries only served as a further irritation. She was beginning to suspect that there was more than just the power of the Sorcerer to fear.

But a tired mind easily finds misinterpretations. So she headed for home seeking, if not knowledge, then comfort and rest.

The narrow road wound around a grove of old trees. Khamsin's tracks cut even wider as she stepped aside to avoid a fresh deposit of dung. Nixa sniffed at the manure warily, identifying it for herself and Khamsin as *horse*. That meant there was a traveler up ahead with a small cart, judging from the marks in the dust on the road as well. She yearned to ask for a ride.

She caught up with the horse cart sooner than expected. The rider, tall and dark-haired, had dismounted and walked slowly. Khamsin recognized the mottled-gray mare and the red-stenciled cart as belonging to the tinker. It was laden with pots and pans and odd pieces of cloth and lace.

She hailed him by his name, which was his title and the same for all of those who plied the trade.

"Ho, Tinker!"

The man stopped and turned, his lean face registering surprise.

"Lady Khamsin! And what brings you out for a walk on this beastly afternoon?" He ran his hand wearily through his dark hair, pulling it away from where it clung to the dampness of his face and the back of his neck. His jacket and vest were absent, and his linen shirt was partially unlaced.

"Just on my way home." She drew up next to him. The gray mare whinnied and shook her head. Khamsin touched the animal's neck, and her mind registered the pain.

"You have trouble?" She noticed a slight swelling on the mare's front leg.

The tinker nodded. The small, gold star in his left ear glinted in the late afternoon sun. "She picked up a stone. When she went to put her weight on it, twisted something. I pulled up immediately, but I'm afraid the damage is done."

Khamsin cleared her mind of her troublesome thoughts and bent down to touch the mare's leg.

"It's just a slight muscle pull. Nothing serious, fortunately." She reached for the bag of oiled, crushed berries at her waist. She applied a small amount of the salve to the affected area. "There now, sweet one, this should feel better very soon."

"You dropped this," the tinker said, kneeling down to retrieve a tumble of pink at his feet.

Khamsin patted her apron pocket. The brightpink chain must have fallen out when she reached for the bag of berry salve.

"It's nothing. Just a silly . . ."

"Lover's chain?" He grinned back at her. "But it's not finished. It won't work unless you finish it." He twisted the stem on the end, deftly forming a loop.

"You do that well. You must have had lots of practice."

"But not patience. I've yet to finish one. But maybe this time, with your help, I'll succeed."

They walked slowly, so as not to strain the mare further. Nixa elected to ride in the overstuffed cart, settling her sleek form comfortably on top of a bolt of bright muslin. Khamsin kept pace to the tinker's shortened stride, looking now and then at his hands as they twisted the long, green stems.

He was taller than Tavis, she noted, for the top of her head reached her husband's chin. Walking beside the tinker, her height barely reached the man's shoulder.

"Lady Khamsin, the village has had a prosperous summer, I trust?"

"We've been fortunate," she replied.

"There's not been good news elsewhere, I'm afraid. Though I'm pleased your village has done well." He handed her the chain, with three more blossoms added.

She took it and fished out another brightpink from her pocket. "We heard there was a raid . . ."

"Two. Hill Raiders have come into Bright's Cove and Wallow's since Summertide."

She suppressed a shudder. "Isn't that unusual?"

"There are many unusual things in the Land right now. You know of the plague in Dram?"

"No! Tavis gets most of his metal from their mines." Alarm showed in her eyes. The tinker slowed, touching her lightly on the arm.

"There was nothing you could've done. It came and went so quickly. There wasn't even enough time to send for a healer."

She gazed back up into eyes as pale as the mist from the moons. "But I should've felt, should've heard something!" She thought back to unnatural gaps in her divinations.

"Perhaps there was nothing to tell."

"But there would have been a *need*. At least if I couldn't heal, there're always the offerings to Ixari, for safe passage through Tarkir's realm. I should have known. I should have been there." A knot of emotion caught in her voice. She looked down at her hands. The brightpinks were trembling.

The tinker squeezed her arm in compassion. She slowed her pace, stopping when he turned to her.

"You have so much to give, my Lady Khamsin," he

said softly. "You want so badly to offer blessings. Yet I fear so few offer blessings to you in return."

"The villagers have not been unkind," she protested.

"But have they been welcoming? No, don't answer. You see only their needs, even at the expense of your own."

He grasped her wrist lightly and took the brightpinks from her fingers. He draped the short chain around her wrist and wove the end stems into place. Then he raised her fingers to his lips, brushing her knuckles with a light kiss. "I offer you my blessing, then. Will you accept that, in place of your worries?"

His unexpected kindness touched a deep, lonely place inside Khamsin. Something warm sparkled inside her, and for a moment, it was as if all the Land stood still, waiting for her answer.

"Thank you kindly. And your blessing is welcome, and accepted."

The breeze ruffled through the trees again, and the Land settled back within itself with a sigh.

❋ ❋ ❋

Khamsin spotted her husband standing in the wide door of the smithy, wiping his hands on his stained apron. He seemed not the least bit surprised to find her in the company of the traveling tinker. He grunted a short greeting to both of them, then turned his attention immediately to the lame mare.

Khamsin stroked the animal's soft nose as Tavis

inspected the damaged hoof. "Nothing to worry overmuch about," he said, and set about repairing the broken shoe.

Only later when the tinker agreed with much gratitude to join them for dinner, did Khamsin notice Tavis showing more than a polite interest in the stranger. And only, it seemed, because of the news he brought about the troubles in the South.

"That explains much." He wiped the crust of Rina's freshly baked bread around the inside of his dinner bowl. "Seems we've been luckier than most, right here."

"Legends often say that the village of a healer is a village of luck," the tinker replied, and in the waning evening light his gaze caught Khamsin's. She again saw the gentle acceptance he'd shown her earlier. And felt his smile before it appeared.

"Won't catch the Covemen or the villagers here saying that." Tavis let his ale mug slip to the table with a bang.

Khamsin jumped, not sure if she was more startled by the noise or the bitterness she heard for the first time in her husband's words. It was such a sharp contrast to the tinker's.

"People often don't say what they feel," the tinker replied smoothly, as Khamsin stood quickly to mop up the splattered ale with her napkin.

She chanced a look at Tavis, but his mug was raised, hiding his face. His broad fingers grasped the handle tightly. Puzzled, she glanced at the tinker. He, too, wore a strange expression. His earlier nonchalance was gone; his brow furrowed in irritation. She felt a stab of anxiety and then he brought his gaze to hers, and his expression changed.

A warm breeze touched her cheek, the fragrance of the moonpetals sweet in the evening air.

She stepped to the window and pulled back the curtains, needing to put some space between herself and the emotions misting across the table. She breathed deeply of the flowers' scent. A wave of calmness passed over her.

When she turned, the tension at the table was gone.

Tavis raised his empty mug. "More of this ale, Khamsin?"

"Of course." She hurried to the kitchen.

The deep rumbling of the men's voices followed her. Talk was of horses and trade. She returned with a full pitcher, which Tavis took from her. He filled the tinker's mug and his own, once again the affable lord of his own manor.

Khamsin sat and, while the men debated the bloodlines of various horses, peeled an apple she brought from the kitchen. She listened halfheartedly but watched with more interest.

The tinker was so different from any of the Covemen she knew. And it was not just the fluidity of his conversation, the timbre of his voice, or his acceptance of her as a healer.

Yet he was also familiar. He, or one of his trade, had always been in the village, bearing trinkets from far-off lands. Or equally as interesting stories. Perhaps that's what it was that she found so curious about the man.

The Covemen were so much like the Cove, but the tinker was a little bit of every place he had been.

She glanced at her husband as he rummaged in his pockets for his tobacco pouch. The tinker was older than Tavis, though not by much. Perhaps five or six years. And his general appearance was similar to the men of her village and other Cove towns. But Tavis's hair was dark brown. The tinker's hair and mustache were black, glossy black, like the color of a moonless night.

Tavis offered the tinker a pipe, but he declined and pulled a thin cigar from an inside pocket of his suede vest. This he held out to the smith. Tavis accepted it, sniffing the mahogany-colored tobacco appreciatively.

"Don't find this quality often around here. You've been to the city, then?"

The tinker nodded as he lit his own cigar.

"You have a name? You know me as Tavis."

The tinker took a few short puffs, releasing a billowing cloud of pungent, blue smoke from his mouth. He leaned back in his chair. "I have more names than I care to remember. And most of them can't be repeated in polite company." A wry smile accompanied his words.

Tavis chuckled. "Well?"

"Rylan. The name's Rylan. Rylan the Tinker. It's as good as any, for now."

Khamsin picked up the empty pitcher and stood, expecting her husband to bring the meal and the visit to a close. It was late. She hadn't seen him in three days, and they had parted with harsh words between them.

Even so, she assumed he would be as anxious to hear about her findings as she was about the telling of them. Therefore, she was caught off-guard when her husband seemed reluctant to let their guest depart.

"Then tell me, Rylan. Do you play cards?"

She shot a confused glance in Tavis's direction. But he avoided her eyes, reaching instead for the dog-eared deck of playing cards on the small table behind him.

"Of course I play," she heard the tinker reply. "For what is life, but a game?"

Suddenly, she felt alone and discarded. She cleared the dishes from the table and fed the scraps to Nixa, while the men played cards. The fire in the kitchen hearth softened to an orange glow, but still the men played on. Their laughter and gruff voices followed her as she walked down the short hallway at the back of the house. And went to bed that night, alone.

❋ ❋ ❋

The morning after the tinker's visit, Khamsin sat Tavis down in the main room and made him listen to what she'd learned in her two days at the cave, knowing by the reaction on his wide face that he didn't like what he heard.

"This is not for the likes of a healer." He didn't look at her but ruffled the dog-eared deck of cards through his fingers. He hadn't even looked at her over their tea that morning. Khamsin sighed.

"I can't be sure of that."

"Because you say these signs aren't clear. As if something's disturbing them. Something powerful."

"Yes, but . . ."

"It's too dangerous." He slanted a glance at her then looked away. "You don't know what may come of this. Best to stop asking these questions. Best to do nothing at all."

She folded her hands tightly in her lap as if doing so could contain her growing anger. "And then what, Tavis? More raids? More plagues? Are you asking me to just ignore everything I've been taught and let that happen?"

"Yes! That's exactly what I'm asking."

"But if I could prevent it, if I could give warning . . ."

"We've not asked for your help, have we?" He tossed the cards into a basket under the window with a quick thrust, then pushed himself to his feet and glared down at her. "You're not to go back there, Khamsin, do you hear me? You're not to go back to the cave."

But that's my home, she almost said and was startled by her own thought. Bronya's cave was not her home anymore. This house, Tavis's house, was her home.

"Promise me you won't go back! And promise me you won't be using that book of yours anymore, except for aches and pains and healin' stuff."

She unclenched her fists and shoved them under her apron. "I won't go back," she told him as she carefully crossed her fingers. "And I will use the book and my stones only for healing. I promise."

She kept her promise for three days. But by the

fourth she could no longer fight the call of the stones. The headaches and inexplicable chills wearied her resolve. She felt the powers shifting, felt magic burrowing out of the very bones of the Land. So she slipped out of their bed in the wee hours of the morning, while her husband snored heavily in his sleep.

Sitting cross-legged on the pantry floor, with the book propped before her, she slowly resumed the practice of her spells and incantations. Pitchers and goblets danced gaily around the stone floor of the kitchen, much to Nixa's amusement. Whiskers twitching, she stalked the prancing tableware.

But that was child's play, and Khamsin knew it. She also knew she couldn't further her skills without returning to the cave. Only there did she have the solitude so necessary for her concentration. And only there did she have a real mage circle carved deeply into the rocky earth, its runes aged and timeworn. The chalk-scribed symbols on her kitchen floor were not the same.

She and Tavis stumbled upon more disagreements. For the fourth time in as many days, Tavis stormed out of the kitchen in a foul mood, slamming the door behind him. Her early morning sessions made her more tired than usual and perhaps also a bit more touchy. And the decreasing supply of metals from Dram put Tavis into a bind with some of the Covemen.

He snapped at her when she didn't respond to his questions at once. And when she did, he was critical of her answers, even of the way she answered. He jumped nervously if she walked into his forge and once accused her of following him; then later, of avoiding him.

He sat up late most nights, smoking his pipe, staring at the hearth fire. And some nights he came to bed not at all.

Khamsin accepted they were both under a strain. The approach of her eighteenth birthday didn't help matters at all. She studied the faces of the villagers now as she walked daily to Rina's, or to the market for fish. The old man in his long, black cape never reappeared. Twice she thought she sensed a discomforting scrutiny, but when she turned, no one was there.

The day before Reverence she stopped at the candle maker's, seeking an Honorsbane votive as an offering. A well-dressed man, his fair hair pulled neatly back at the nape of his neck, held the rough-hewn door for her as she entered and sketched a bow. His behavior, so gallant, so out of place in Cirrus Cove, was almost comical. Save for the chill that ran through her when he touched her arm.

"Perhaps you can assist me, lady? I seek Mirtad the Tailor."

Mirtad? The name was unfamiliar, especially to her shaken senses. And a tailor? Here? But then her memory thawed. Mirtad. Didn't Gilby the Oarsman have a cousin, a tailor named Mirtad? From Flume? She directed the stranger to Gilby's lodgings and, calmer now, busied herself among the scented candles.

Then two days before her birthday it was as if a dam broke. Tavis called her into his smithy early that afternoon, pulling her away from slicing beans. Wiping her hands on her apron, she followed, barely able to keep up with his long stride.

It was there, gleaming and bright and about the size of the long ladle. Her sword, forged to perfection. Her hands flew to her mouth and then out to the silver object, touching it gently, almost reverently. It felt smooth to her touch, yet open. She could enchant it. He followed her instructions to the letter.

"Oh, Tav." There were tears of joy in her eyes.

He draped one arm across her shoulders. "Pretty proud of myself, too, if you don't mind me saying so."

He made love to her that night for the first time in many months. Though she would have been content just to hold him, treasuring him truly as one of the finest friends she had ever had.

The morning, however, brought dark clouds on the horizon and an argument in the kitchen.

"But I won't be going back to learn anything," she pleaded for the fifth time. "It's just that I can't do the proper incantations for the sword anyplace else!"

Tavis glared at her over his breakfast. "No. I won't hear of it any more."

"But . . ."

"Khamsin!" He slammed a heavy fist down on the table, rattling the mug and pitcher. "I will not tolerate any witch-working!"

"Witch-working!" She rose to her feet. Nixa dashed across the kitchen and out the back door. "How dare you call it witch-working! I'm a healer, as was Tanta and . . . "

"But Tanta is not my wife!"

"You knew what I was before you married me."

"I knew you were a healer. Not a witch. I would never have agreed to marry a witch. Not even to honor a life debt."

Khamsin felt his admission as if he'd slapped her. She knew Tanta Bron had saved Tavis's life many years ago. But that she'd used that to coerce the smith to marry her shook her deeply.

She started to reply but he stood, his wide hands splayed on the table and towered over her.

"A healer doesn't meddle with such things as concern the gods. She heals, tends with her herbs. She offers charms and benedictions. I watched Bronya, remember? I knew her longer than you. She didn't do as you do."

"We're all different." Khamsin's voice was quieter now. "Tanta Bron practiced as she felt best. Some things she could do better; some things I can. That's all."

"Is it?" The burly man turned swiftly.

"Then why did you make me the sword?" she called out to him as he headed for the half-open door.

He stopped, hand on the latch, and turned a cold face to her. "Damned if I know." And he stomped heavily down the back steps.

When he returned for his midday meal, Khamsin, Nixa, and the sword were gone.

CHAPTER FOUR

She didn't hear the howling of the winds or the hard tapping of the rain against the trees, so intent was Khamsin upon her incantations. She knelt before the ancient circle on the floor of Bronya's cave. She could sense a power in the stones beneath her. She could feel it in her blood. She was raised here and nurtured on it.

Nixa sat impassively on all four paws and watched the rain as cats often do. The twitching of her long tail was the only sign of her discomfort with the elements. Her large, yellow eyes stared, now at the twirling, wet leaves on the edge of the clearing, then back at her mistress, solemn and motionless as she had been since their arrival at the cave this afternoon. Finally, feigning boredom, she stretched out her front paws and yawned, letting her head come slowly down to rest against her own softness.

The storm died, and the two moons rose full before

Khamsin sat back with a sigh and ran her hands through her hair. It had been a lengthy preparation, an elaborate entry but she was there. She could feel it. The sword hung in midair before her as if suspended by invisible strings, as proof of her expertise. It was also a safe, stopping place for she was tired. And tired minds could make mistakes.

She curled up onto her straw bed and felt the weight of Nixa against her, as she found a comfortable place to share the night. Nixa never came to bed when Tavis was there.

Tavis. She had left him in such turmoil. She hoped the short note tucked into his tobacco jar would suffice until she came home. He would have to understand that things such as these were things she had to do, just as he had to work with his anvil. A craftsman, he often called himself. A practitioner of an art. Well, she was a craftsman, too, and one whose skill only increased with knowledge.

She rose before the sun the next morning, disappointed to hear the light tapping of rain on the trees outside. She had wished, only weeks before, for cooler weather. And now all they seemed to get was rain.

She let herself slip into a trance. She recited the incantations again, feeling her mind more in control that she had ever felt it before. Her extra sessions in the kitchen pantry paid off. The ancient spells rolled off her tongue with an easy fluidity. The sword glowed with blue pulsations as the words were uttered, given life. Then there was a bright flash of light, and she was finished. The spell for her sword was complete.

She looked around the large room for Nixa, feeling guilty at perhaps startling the little feline with all her pyrotechnics. Nixa had no mystical talents herself, no more than any average feline. It took Khamsin several years before the small cat willingly accepted their shared mental contact. And only lately was she willing to sit quietly by as Khamsin worked her mage circle and rune stones.

Seeing no sign of her cat, Khamsin stood a bit shakily and walked toward the entrance of the cave. The light outside was dim for mid-afternoon, which her inner sense told her it must be. She listened to the sounds of a distant storm. Thunder rumbled, though she saw no lightning.

But she did see something gray slink and pause, slink and pause, through the underbrush. Nixa, stalking . . . Khamsin lightly touched the cat's mind. A cricket.

She shook her head, a small smile on her face, and went back inside the cave. There was still one more thing she had to do.

She dusted off the mage circle and drew a new one, this time with her sword at the center. Bronya had been insistent about the creation of the sword. Khamsin felt sure part of the reason was that it would become a source of magic on which she could draw.

Closing her eyes, she reached mentally for her warding stones, and a bolt of light flashed painfully into her mind.

She cried out. And in that brief moment of intense pain, she knew she was too late. More than a week too late. The tampering of her cupboard had been the first warning, the first sign. Others had followed, but she had kept her promise to Tavis and not returned to the cave, or to the powerful mage circle etched in its floor.

While she contented herself with twirling crockery, unspeakable evil advanced toward the village.

She shot to her feet and ran for the entrance of the cave.

"Nixa!" she called, her voice filled with terror. The cat streaked from the underbrush, already deeply shadowed by the dark sky overhead.

But it wasn't a sky darkened by any natural storm. And the sounds that met Khamsin's ears were not the rumblings of thunder, or the howl of the winds, but the crackling of burning timber and the screams of people in terror.

She stood frozen at the entrance. The sky was black with smoke, the air acrid. Then she bolted and ran wildly through the forest toward the village. Thorns and brambles tore at her skirts and ankles, ripping her flesh. Branches, still wet from the morning's light shower, whipped at her back. She stumbled once, twice, over half-buried boulders slippery with moss but continued onward, her hands out before her, a strangled cry in her throat.

She burst out of the woods into the clearing just before the village. She slowed in her steps as the horror of the scene lay before her. Everywhere things burned, smoldering. Thatched roofs caved in and timbers jutted awkwardly through broken walls. She passed by an upended cart, nets trailing from beneath its shattered boards. Dead fish, with white, bloated bellies lay in a pool of watery blood.

She saw no one, nothing alive.

She quickened her steps toward a familiar, stone fence. Its wooden gate hung at a crooked angle. She thrust it aside as she entered, calling out Rina's name and the names of the children.

She found Aric slumped over the large table in the main room, a spear in his back, his lifeless hands reaching out toward . . .

Shaken, she glanced at the end of the table. Nothing was there, at least, not anymore. By the hearth were the bodies of Cavell and Lissa, their throats slit, their dark eyes staring into eternity. A gasp of horror escaped her lips, and Khamsin felt her knees buckle. She reached down to gently close the children's unseeing eyes with a touch, and her hand trembled uncontrollably. Her voice was strained as she whispered a departing prayer to Ixari.

Rina and Taric she found in the kitchen, huddled together in the corner. Taric's throat, too, was slit. The shaft of a spear protruded from Rina's chest. Her white apron, painstakingly embroidered only weeks before, was stained a deep red from the flow of thick blood that drained into her lap. Her left hand still held her son's life-less ones; her right, a long scrap of dark fabric, bordered in red. Colors worn by South Land Hill Raiders.

The new baby's cradle lay nearby. It was empty, its quilted coverlet that Khamsin had made discarded on the floor. Hill Raiders often stole infants and raised them as their own.

Khamsin touched the edge of the cradle and suddenly sobbed in great gulps. She clasped her hands over her mouth, unable to contain the emotions within. She lunged for the back door, her only thought now that of her own home. And of Tavis.

The smithy burned fiercely as she approached the front door of her house. A sudden gust of heat almost sent her reeling backward, but she pushed against the heavy, oak partition, crying out at the top of her lungs.

"Tav-is!" She ran to the kitchen. Her cupboards were stripped and emptied. She rushed back to the main room and into their bedroom. The bed linens were torn off, and the mattress was slashed with great, long strikes as though someone had been looking for hidden gems. But other than that, the room was empty.

She raced down the short hall, stopping only when she reached her cupboard. The book was with her, as well as the divining cloth and several of her potions. All she left behind were some minor amulets and charms. She was surprised to see that they were still there, the cupboard intact. The Hill Raiders, too, had their superstitions.

She heard the creaking and groaning of the burning timber outside as the forge began to crumble. There was a great crash just as she exited through her front door. She watched, dazed, as the entire back wall of the smithy caved in, sending a shower of flames and sparks high into the air. If Tavis was in there . . .

The thought was too horrible for her even to imagine. She leaned weakly against the low stone wall in front of the house. He couldn't have been. He was strong, one of the strongest men in the village. Surely, he fought the Raiders successfully or found some way to escape. She forced herself to stand and head back to the center of the village.

She was only a few houses away from the burning smithy when a scuffling noise behind her caused her to stop and turn. She recognized Enar, one of the Covemen. His pale face was covered with soot and blood, and in one hand he clutched a short dagger.

"Witch!" He limped toward her. "Have you come back, witch, to see if we all died? Where's that cat of yours? Or was she one of the demons you sent to us?"

Khamsin stood, horrified. "Enar, it's me, Khamsin, Tavis's wife. Where is Tavis, Enar? Where is he?"

"Don't you know?" He flashed the blade before her. She stepped backward. "He's dead, like all the rest you abandoned. Look!" And he flung his arm out to the left, pointing toward the large trees near the dockyard. A body dangled from a rope tied to a high branch.

Choking back a cry, Khamsin ran toward the docks, recognizing the dark blue trousers, leather apron, and high leather boots of the smith. But before she could reach him, hands grappled out toward her, rough hands, smelling of salt and ashes and death. They clamped over her mouth and around her shoulders and waist.

She was dragged downward, and she landed on her back, small stones grinding into her skin.

"Witch!"

She heard the cry and recognized the faces of Gilby and Turpin and Enar, all Covemen. They tore roughly at her thin bodice and layered skirts.

She flailed at them, tried to push them away, then felt a presence burst into her mind: angry, frightened. Very close . . .

Nixa.

She balled her hands into fists, pummeled them against arms slick with blood. *Go!* she commanded the cat. The witch's demon cat. *Run! Safety! Be safe!*

A distorted view of herself, struggling on the ground flitted through her mind. Then greenery, scrub brush. Her contact with the cat faded.

Someone grabbed her by the hair, and she cried out in pain and fright. There was the flash of a knife and the pain on her scalp was gone, as was most of her hair. Another dull flash of silver and the blade turned toward her throat. It was only then she came to her senses and fought for her life.

Swiftly, she raised her knee up into Turpin's groin. He collapsed back against the stocky Enar. She rolled to one side as Enar reached over his groaning companion, but his grasp fell short. Her shorn head no longer provided the handhold it did before, when her hair fell almost to her waist.

In one movement, she was on her feet. She lashed out with her forearm at Gilby, fist closed, just as she had learned to many years ago in the mock battle-games she played as a child.

It was only the glare of Enar's dagger that at last quelled her desperate efforts.

She held her hands out before her, her breathing ragged. "Enar, this is madness."

"No, this is revenge for what you've brought upon us." He took the rope Gilby held out to him. "What the Hill people did to Tavis, we'll do to you."

"I'm not a witch, Enar!"

"No, even your husband knew that. Sorceress, he called you. Did you know that? He tried to warn us. Said you'd run off. To practice your sorcery. Then the Hill Raiders came from the South. We know it's Tarkir's spawn, the infernal Lucial, you pray to now."

"That's not true!"

A sound in the distance caused both men to hesitate and exchange glances. "Raiders. Coming back," Enar said in a hushed voice.

Gilby nodded. "For her."

"Then we'll give her to 'em."

Khamsin screamed as they grabbed her. She flung her arms wildly in an effort to break free of their hold, even if only for a short time. It was all she would need to summon an elemental, something she would never have done in the village before. But the village no longer existed. And the men who roughly held her small body had every intention of killing her.

Desperately she shoved against them. Gilby stumbled and her left hand was free. She cupped it against her chest quickly then flung it outward, screaming the incantation at the top of her lungs. Flames like fireflies danced on the ground around Gilby's boots. The thin Coveman tripped on his own feet as he scrambled backward.

"You filthy bitch!" Enar slapped her hard across the face, and this time it was Khamsin who stumbled, wrenching her arm as the stocky man still grasped her firmly. He threw her to the ground face down and clamped his boot hard against her back. He grabbed first one wrist, then another. She cried out as he forced her arms backward, almost pulling them out of their sockets.

"Scream, witch!" he bellowed, as he lashed her hands together. "Scream while you die!"

"Enar!" It was Gilby. He clawed at the older man's trouser leg. "They're almost here!"

The sound of hoof beats was getting closer.

The Coveman stood tensely for a moment, hatred glittering in his dark eyes. Then he spat on the ground. "Come on!" he ordered gruffly, grabbing Turpin by the scruff of his neck. "Gilby, take his arms. Let's get out of here." The men ran, dragging a limping Turpin between them.

CHAPTER FIVE

Khamsin lay sobbing in the dirt and stones, her arms aching. Her mouth tasted of dust and blood. She cried out for Tanta Bron, her voice like a child in pain. She'd lost her home, her husband and friends, her sister-in-law, and all that she cherished. She was beaten and accused of sorcery. Terrorized. Damned. And today was the day she was to turn eighteen years old.

She cried until her voice was hoarse and choking, and then cried some more. Her body was vaguely aware of the thudding of hoofs coming nearer. The riders that Enar had seen. Hill Raiders. *Let them kill me,* she pleaded inwardly. *Let them slash and mutilate my body. I have nothing, nothing. Am nothing, anymore.*

Tears spilled down her cheeks as she slitted open her eyes. The ground trembled beneath her face, and she saw the spindly but powerful legs of horses slashing through her field of vision. One horse drew nearer, no, two. Maybe more. She could no longer count the legs, make sense of what her stinging eyes told her. She tensed her body, the supplications to her goddess echoing through her mind in a senseless litany.

For protection, I beseech you.

For guidance, I entreat you.

For protection . . .

Someone shouted. It sounded like the Olde Language. Bronya had used those words. But when? Where? And who but a Raheiran would speak . . .

The Sorcerer. Raheiran was the language of all magicks. She would finally hear his voice, calling her true name.

But she heard nothing, save for her rasping breath and the distant crackle of burning timbers. Everything was silent again. If not for the pain coursing through her limbs, she would have thought she was dead.

Someone touched her, grabbed her shoulders. She no longer cared to fight. She let her body go limp and unyielding.

Let it be done. Let it be over with.

Her hands were untied but still she didn't move, didn't resist even when she was turned, slowly, onto her back. She let her head fall to one side. She hiccoughed spasmodically.

At the sound of her own name, she opened her eyes. "Khamsin? Lady Khamsin?"

She looked up, expecting for all the world to see the hideous countenance of the Sorcerer, or the fierce face of a South Land Hill Raider. And saw only the pale eyes of Rylan the Tinker. Her swollen lips mouthed his name.

He shook his head then murmured something she couldn't hear. She tried again to speak but he silenced her, his finger to his lips.

The last thing she remembered was being lifted into his arms.

Then cool water was placed against her face. She opened her eyes. A gaily striped awning formed a partial roof overhead, framed by brown, green, and golden leaves beyond. A faint glow of orange told her it was near morning. The tinker's face swam ethereally before her.

"Lady Khamsin." His voice sounded distant.

She blinked rapidly a few times and tried to speak. But nothing came out. She gasped, aware of a searing pain throughout her body.

"Hush, hush." The tinker placed his fingers lightly against her parched lips, his touch gentle, reassuring.

She closed her eyes and fell again into a merciful oblivion.

Toward midnight she tossed restlessly, waking and sleeping in small spurts. Her dreams were filled with the black of burning timbers, the bright red of blood. She saw Rina again, her throat slit. She saw the baby's empty cradle.

A low moan of terror escaped her lips. And then a touch on her face, and she sank into forgetfulness.

In moments of wakefulness, her eyes sought something recognizable in the dark shadows that surrounded her. She saw nothing and, fearing she was blinded, groped out into the darkness. Her fingers rested against cloth, warmth, and then stronger fingers were wound into hers. Her hand was held tightly. She tried to return the comforting grasp but failed.

Tears trailed down her cheeks in frustration. Then she heard a familiar sound. A soft, rumbling purr.

Nixa?

Warmth, comfort flooded through her.

She slept.

❄ ❄ ❄

The following morning she woke to find Nixa curled against her side. She whispered the cat's name, found her voice stronger and her throat less painful. She admonished the tinker, as he wiped her brow with a damp cloth.

"You shouldn't." Her voice cracked slightly. "They called me a witch, you know. They'll come back." She swallowed painfully. "They think Nixa's a demon." The tears began to flow again.

"Their grief drove them more than a little mad. You were simply a convenient object on which to vent their anger."

She cried anyway. Words had no meaning, not even the kind, sensible ones from the tinker. He held her, her head cradled in his arms until her sobs abated. Voice shaking, she asked for her medicine belt and pouches. He brought them to her, and with stiff fingers she sought what she needed; swallowing a pinch of this and a leaf of that; applying a touch of balm, ever-so-sparingly, here and there. Her hands came up to touch her head.

"They cut off my hair."

"A bit crookedly too. But when you're feeling better, I can fix that. Perhaps we'll start a new fashion."

And so it went, as she lay in the tinker's tent in the wooded grove, healing her body with her herbs, while the tinker countered any despondent statements she would make with his light comments and witty retorts. It was as if it were all a great joke to him. Finally she sat up in anger, her eyes blazing like pale lightning. She accused him of being an insensitive, shallow, arrogant bore.

"Good. Get angry. That's healthy. It means you're feeling better." He poured more tea into the mug they shared and held it out to her.

She let her head fall forward onto her knees. "I'm sorry. I didn't mean that. I just . . ."

"I know, my lady," he replied softly, nudging her hand with the warm mug. "Drink. You'll feel better."

She drank and wondered just how long it would be before she would ever be able to feel anything, again.

❋ ❋ ❋

The fifth morning after the raid, she awakened very early; the sunrise was still a vague promise on the horizon. There was a slight chill in the air. Nixa was already off stalking breakfast.

Khamsin tugged at the blanket that had slipped down around her waist during the night. She could hear the steady breathing of the tinker who lay nearby. She turned slightly on her side and studied the man who had rescued her only days before.

Only days? The aching in her body felt as if it had been there for weeks. Though through her herbal balms and the tinker's gentle touch, most of the pain had subsided.

It was replaced, however, with a new and more disturbing sensation. One she suspected was tied directly to the man that lay sleeping, just out of her reach.

Gratitude, she advised herself. She drifted back to sleep again, the warmth of the blanket soaking into her shoulders. She was grateful. That was all.

❊ ❊ ❊

When she was strong enough to walk, the tinker followed her to Bronya's cave, though she forbade him entry. She hadn't been back since the day Cirrus was attacked, and Tavis and Rina were killed. Her oldest and strongest memories still lay inside, and she stood on the worn, rag rug in front of the empty hearth for a few moments, trembling. She couldn't yet face her old bed, or Bronya's curtained alcove.

Then slowly, methodically, she gathered up her belongings, and her memories. Tanta Bron's embroidered shawl and curtain. A set of carved spoons. Other items she'd never needed in Tavis's well-stocked house. She rolled as much as she could inside the braided rug. That had always been Nixa's favorite sleeping spot.

The tinker didn't question her need for solitude but waited outside. He took the small bundles from her as she exited and wisely left her the sheathed sword she carried in her right hand. In exchange, she sat quietly on the backboard of his red cart, while he snipped and trimmed her hair until, at least to her hand, it felt better. He rummaged around inside a large trunk, disturbing a sleeping Nixa. He produced an oval looking-glass, which he offered to her without comment.

She took it, equally without comment, and appraised her reflection. The swelling on her face had subsided, and save for a small purplish bruise on her cheek, the beating she received at the hands of the Covemen was now just a bad memory. Her new haircut fell wispily to the middle of her neck, framing her face, just brushing the tops of her eyebrows. It made her already large eyes appear even larger, and she wrinkled her nose.

"I look like a ten-year-old boy in a dress." Her comment was wistful. She wondered why she suddenly was concerned over her appearance. It never mattered much before.

"I can take care of that too." The tinker produced a worn, but clean shirt with full sleeves and bib-front, along with a vest and matching chamois breeches. "It'd be safer, if you intend to travel."

"I do." She accepted the clothing and returned to the cave.

Minutes later, she reappeared barefoot with stockings in hand. "We forgot one thing."

The tinker pointed to a woven basket at the front of the cart. "Find what fits and they're yours."

She pulled on a pair of mid-calf high boots. "How can I thank you?"

"You already have, my lady." He smiled, adding, "You healed my horse and fed and entertained me."

"You saved my life. Surely that far outweighs one meal and some herbal balms."

"Perhaps." He hoisted the basket back into the front of the cart. "Where will you go now?"

Khamsin started to gather her belongings, shoving her short hunting knife and then the sword through the loops on her belt. She hesitated, and her eyes wandered in the direction of the village. Tendrils of dark smoke curled over the treetops.

"I don't know. I could return to the village. Perhaps there's some way I could help . . ." The image of Tavis's lifeless body came to her mind, and her throat constricted. Surely, someone had cut him down, had buried him and the others. "Blessing rites . . ."

"Were said. A journeying priest, I believe." He reached out and touched her shoulder briefly. "It's all been taken care of. You needn't go back."

"But the survivors would want to rebuild. I could help."

"They've left. The village is deserted."

This news startled her. "You're sure?"

"I traveled there on a few afternoons while you slept.

There's nothing for you to go back to. And even if there were, I would advise against it."

Enar and Gilby were probably some of the survivors. Khamsin hadn't forgotten their hate, their anger.

"There's nothing there for you to go back to," the tinker repeated.

Khamsin picked up Nixa and stroked the cat's soft head. The village of Cirrus Cove and the cave in the foothills were the only homes she'd ever known. Where else could she possibly go?

And then the omens in the mage circle swam before her eyes. A journey. She had been directed to start a journey.

"I'll go to the city, to Noviiya perhaps," she said, surprised at the conviction in her voice. But the words felt right, even as she said them. The Temples of Ixari and Merkara were there. She could spend time in prayer and meditation.

She released Nixa, and the cat jumped nimbly into the tinker's cart. "Yes, to the city. My learning here is finished, that much I know, that much I found out, that day that . . ." Her voice drifted off into a whisper.

"I'm headed there myself, if you care for company."

"I can't burden you any longer. You've been far too kind. To be honest, what I seek is dangerous."

"So I noticed." He touched the bruise on her cheek. His fingers were warm, gentle. She fought the desire to rest her face against his hand.

"But still, I'm going that way, and as your cat has no qualms about accepting my offer, I suggest you take her advice and do the same."

Khamsin sighed and allowed her bundles to be taken from her. "I'll repay you. Somehow."

"Can you cook? Well, yes, of course you can. I've had your stew. Very fine." He pursed his lips and blew a short whistle as Khamsin climbed into the cart beside him. The gray mare started into a trot. "Get tired of eating my own cooking, you know. That's why I sell pots and pans. Never make it in this world as an innkeeper."

He slapped at the reins, and Khamsin was sure she glimpsed a mischievous smile underneath his mustache.

CHAPTER SIX

For two days they traveled northward on the seacoast road, leaving Cirrus Cove far behind. They crossed the Fohn River. The road rose sharply into a rocky hillside. The soft gold of the dunes disappeared into the harsher grays and browns of the uneven landscape. The pines here were thicker, their bark a deep brownish-black. Their needles were coarser, unlike the silken foliage of those that grew in the coveside meadows.

Khamsin had never traveled north. She went south only once with Tavis to the village of Dram, shortly after they were married. That had been a two-day, hard ride from Cirrus Cove. There had never been the need to leave her birthplace before.

She commented on the starker landscape when they stopped for the second night, noticing that the tinker had trouble finding a plot of ground free of rocks and stones for his bedroll. Her own bedroll was in small space under the tent-like awning that extended from the side of his cart. She felt guilty of depriving him of the more comfortable lodgings.

He waved away her concern with an air of indifference and concentrated on building a small fire.

She hadn't told him what she was running from or why, and he hadn't asked. That plagued her mind, as she peeled the thick outer skin from the wild potatoes she discovered growing in abundance near the campsite of the previous night. He seemed satisfied just to have someone to talk to. And talk he did, about all manner of things he saw or heard in his travels to the various towns and villages that dotted the countryside. Yet, she couldn't believe he was totally without curiosity as to herself.

But what if he viewed her as the Covemen and Tavis had? Long ago she had hardened herself to others' criticisms; even her husband's disapproval was taken in stride. But the tinker was somehow different. She didn't know how she'd handle his viewing her as a creature to be feared, suspected. A woman-child linked to the powerful Sorcerer by command of an assignation.

An assignation that never took place.

The last thought so startled Khamsin that she dropped the potato she was peeling into the small pot, splashing herself with water.

She was eighteen years old now, eighteen. The dreaded seventeenth year had passed, and though it brought much pain and suffering, the contact, the crucial contact, had never been made. Though he must have tried—she thought of the old man by the sailmaker's, the young gallant in the candle shop, perhaps even those faceless riders in the raid—he hadn't claimed her! Even during her enchantment of the sword, she hadn't felt his presence as she had many times before. She was free. Whatever her life portended, it wouldn't involve the whims of the Sorcerer.

Oh, and there was so much to do now! With an increased energy, she finished peeling the last of the vegetables and, plopping them into the pot, placed them over the fire.

The tinker looked up from the wineskin he was mending, as she tugged at one of her small bundles stuffed into the back of his cart.

"Need something, my lady?"

"No, no, that's all right. I can manage, thank you." She rummaged around in the deep canvas bag until her hand found the hard binding of the book. "I've something to attend to. I won't be gone long."

She glanced over her shoulder as she slipped into the shadows of the tall pines. The tinker smiled, then returned to his wineskin.

Her short hunting knife trembled as she scratched the lines of the mage circle into a mossy patch of earth. With a breathless intensity, she voiced her incantations. Then she bowed her head, closed her eyes, and waited for the feeling of weightlessness to come over her as she descended into a light trance. She chose three stones from the small pouch she wore around her waist and touched them to her forehead, lips, and throat before casting them into the rough circle.

Nine times she threw the stones, and nine times the answer came back, without variation. She'd crossed a milestone in her life and now must expand her knowledge, increase her sphere of experience. And all signs led her to the city.

The exultation she felt at the clarity of the symbols in the dust and the strength emanating from her circle overrode even the dull, painful ache she had carried in her heart since she'd left Cirrus Cove. Had she more time, had supper not been boiling away and the tinker not been aware of her absence, she might pursue her investigations, requesting specifics. Where should she go in the city, and whom should she see? Was there still danger? The rapidity and ease with which the few answers came back to her restored her faith in her powers that, for over a year, had lagged and been vague. Still, they were a few days ride from the bustling trade center built on the north cliffs, overlooking the sea. There was time for her to divine other information later.

For now, the aroma of potatoes and leeks wafted in the air. She whispered the spell that would un-enchant the small patch of moss and rose, never bothering to look back to see if the ground recovered its formerly unbroken surface. As indeed it did.

The tinker stirred the potatoes with a long-handled wooden spoon. She bent over the pot, sniffing appreciatively.

"Smells good."

"Better than I ever made it."

"You survived well enough on your own cooking before now."

He plucked at the front of his shirt. "I was on the verge of emaciation until you took over."

Khamsin's laughter hid the slight flush on her cheeks. She remembered the feel of his strong, hard body against hers, when she was weak and trembling. There was nothing emaciated about the man at all.

They finished the meal with light conversation, dotted with stretches of comfortable silence. At last, when the fire reduced itself to a pale orange glow, Khamsin sighed and leaned back against the wheel of the cart, stretching her legs out before her.

"You seem contented, my lady." His voice was soft but carried easily over the night sounds of crickets.

She couldn't see his face in the darkness, but the earring in his ear reflected the dim light of the glowing coals. She didn't need to see his face anyway. She knew every line by heart. The sight of him that first morning after the burning of the village etched him indelibly into her mind.

"Things are better, yes," she replied, ignoring the direction her thoughts again traveled. She was a widow, she reminded herself. A widow, and when the tinker touched her, it was only to heal her wounds. Her outer wounds. Not the tear in her heart.

"They were bad." His words held no judgment, or pity.

"Could have been much worse."

"That is true of most things."

Then they were silent for a while. The sound of the

wind playing through the leaves around them was the only interruption to their thoughts. Khamsin's drifted back to Cirrus Cove, to what she had been and what she could become. She thought of Tanta Bron, practicing her herbals and spells and marveled that the old woman never chose to further her own education in the occult. She seemed content to live her days out in the cave. Khamsin knew now that even if the raid on the village hadn't happened, she would have left Cirrus Cove before Wintertide. With or without her husband. But her reasons, then, would have been different.

"Haven't you wondered, Tinker, why I was willing to leave my home?"

She heard the rustle of clothing as he stirred and could envision his now-familiar, noncommittal shrug in the dark.

"Besides the obvious, you mean, with the destruction of the village and the death of your husband?"

The words still carried pain, though not as much. "Yes," she said.

"Did you love him?"

His question caught her by surprise. She didn't reply.

"Your husband, Lady Khamsin. Did you love him?"

"Tavis was my friend," she said finally. "So I suppose I did love him."

"As a friend."

"Yes."

"But not as a lover."

"Tinker, I . . ." Though she knew the answer, it was

difficult to voice, even in the dark.

"I know. It's not my place to ask such things. But it matters, you see."

"Why?" For a moment, her heart inexplicably skipped a beat.

He cleared his throat. "For one, it would help me understand why you left Cirrus."

She forgot that that was her original question to him and so felt obliged to answer it.

"No, I didn't love him, as you said, as a lover."

"You're sure?"

She caught a movement in the dim light, as he leaned closer to her. "I'm sure. But . . ." and she hesitated, wondering if his questions uncovered yet another flaw in her character. That of a stingy, selfish wife. "But I never refused him. I did care about him."

"I see." He was quiet. When he spoke again, his voice carried a slight hesitation she had never heard before. "Tell me. That is, have you ever been in love, Khamsin?"

She thought a long while. Love was something that grew over time, over a sharing of mutual experiences. It was deeper than just a physical attraction. She wondered if that was what was happening to her. But perhaps the tinker was a symbol of strength and reassurance only because he was present at a particular place at a particular time. Her rescuer could've been anyone. Even a Hill Raider. Shaking that disturbing thought from her mind, she answered his question.

"No. I don't believe so."

"Well. You have much to learn then."

She heard the smile return to his voice, and she relaxed. It was so easy to talk to him, easy to voice things she wouldn't have been able to say to herself a week ago.

"Even before . . . the raid, I had begun to wonder if I belonged in the village," she told him, turning her thoughts to more practical matters. "You know I'm a healer. I've also practiced the magic arts." She waited for his reaction, wishing she could see his face.

"The villagers didn't approve."

"They didn't understand. Perhaps if they had, they would've approved." She tugged on a blade of grass poking through the rocky ground. "But that's all past, now."

"So you leave, seeking what?"

She sighed. "Knowledge. Experience. There was only so much Tanta Bron could teach me. And only so much I can learn on my own. It's as if I've come as far as I can go by myself. New surroundings should provide increased knowledge."

"That sounds like something from a book of prophecies."

"It is." She pulled up one knee and rested her elbow on it, toying with the short thickness of her hair.

"Why didn't you leave Cirrus sooner?"

"Because . . . an assignation was placed on my name. But since it never occurred, I'm now free."

"An assignation?"

"I was claimed as a child. Though Tanta Bron—

87

Bronya the Healer—raised me, it was with the knowledge that I'd been marked at birth. But there was a time limit: The assignation had to take place before my eighteenth birthday. I turned eighteen the day the village was raided."

"Do you know who placed the claiming mark on you?"

Khamsin hesitated, the silence filled with the hollow cry of an owl. "The Sorcerer," she admitted finally.

"That's serious business." The tinker shifted position with a rustling of clothing. "And not one to be taken lightly."

"I'm aware of that. That's why I'm cautious about maintaining your company. For your sake, you understand. And that's also why, though I view you as a friend, we must part when we reach the city."

There was a spark from a tinderbox, then the sweet, heavy smell of tobacco as the tinker lit a thin cigar. Khamsin could hear the hushed sound of the smoke as he blew it between his lips.

"To be honest, I've not thought much past tomorrow. Never do, you know. Learned a long time ago it doesn't pay." He twirled the cigar between his fingers for a moment. "But what I do know is this: We have an early start and a long ride ahead of us, if I'm to make it to Browner's Grove. I have some business there that must be attended to. So, my friend, Lady Khamsin, it's my suggestion you take to your blankets and get some sleep."

❖ ❖ ❖

She didn't accompany the tinker into the small, inland town of Browner's Grove but remained on a grassy hillside by a winding stream with Nixa for company. The thatched roofs of the town were just barely visible in the distance. It was a clear autumn day. The sun was warm and there was a pleasant, light chill to the air. The leaves of the trees were already turning the deeper shades of gold and orange. Only the pines remained green.

She walked along the stream, her light woolen cape open, Nixa tagging by her side. She carried the small satchel containing the book and her amulets. In the few hours the tinker would be absent she could accomplish much, if she set her mind to it.

But her mind wasn't on her divinations at the moment, but rather on horseback, following the tall man down the rutted road to the town. She wondered what drew him there. Though he dragged the red cart behind, she had the feeling his purpose in Browner's Grove had little to do with his trade or his merchandise. Did he have family there? A wife and children, perhaps, who might not look with understanding at his traveling with a young widow?

If he had children, she mused, settling against the flat top of a large boulder, they might very well be closer in age to herself than she was to the tinker. She asked his age, just in conversation, over their small dinner at the first campsite. And he replied, in his usual offhand way, that the last birthday he counted was number thirty-three. His children, if he had any, could have counted a dozen birthdays by now.

She refused to let herself speculate about his supposed wife.

But there she was being a nosy-body, as Rina would say. The thought of the curly-haired woman caused a painful tightness in her throat. She sighed raggedly, reminding herself of her purpose. Which wasn't to pry into the tinker's private life. Tomorrow they should reach the city and then go their own ways. It would be best, for both of them.

She scraped a section of the rock free of litter with her short hunting knife and laid a handful of tinder on top. To this she added some roots from one of her medicine pouches, laying them carefully in specific spots. Then she took a small vial from another pouch and let two drops of an amber liquid fall into the center of the pile. She closed her eyes, murmured a few words, and a sharp popping sound heralded the start of her fire.

She read the patterns in the smoke as it spiraled upward. Then, with a sharp wave of her left hand, she extinguished the blaze and looked for a message in the charred twigs and grasses.

For the first time, she saw the sign for revenge along with the symbols for power. And the symbol of the dark god, Tarkir. She shuddered as the atrocities of the Hill Raiders came into mind.

So. That was the purpose of her education. It began to make sense now. It was remarked in the Cove towns that the Hill people were in league with the Sorcerer, currying favor with the darker powers. Had the assignation been completed, had she been taken to the

Sorcerer's lair at Traakhal-Armin, then there would be no one to stand between him and his quest for power.

For over three hundred years he had ruled, become stronger. Villages, cities, even kingdoms were said to fall under his hand.

He could command the beasts of the forest, the winds and the tides, all on a whim. The early thaw the year the Hill Raiders charged through Cirrus Cove at Wintertide could very well have been his handiwork. As could the storm that preceded their latest attack. He could render men sightless with a look, speechless with a touch.

And he so feared one small babe born in the midst of a maelstrom, that he placed an assignation on her, in his name.

But it was an empty threat, for he never called her, never appeared before her mage circle in his billowing black robes, embroidered, it was said, with threads spun of the finest white gold, forged with the blood of virgins.

But how could she, Khamsin, possibly hope to confront the tremendous powers of the Sorcerer? She was just a healer, in truth, who dabbled in white magic. A few spells, here and there, and some incantations. She could never use her abilities to attack, only defend. As she did the day Enar, Turpin, and Gilby grabbed her.

She passed her hand over the charred embers again, and the answer came back, again. Knowledge. Experience.

But where was her teacher?

NOVIIYA

CHAPTER SEVEN

The city was called Noviiya. It was set on a high finger of land that jutted out into a churning sea—a sea darker blue than Khamsin had ever seen. White-frothed waves slammed against the bare escarpments, while flocks of gray sea-fowl circled in the spray. Even the sky was darker, the clouds wispier.

Khamsin and the tinker jostled their way up the wide road in their red cart. The late afternoon sun slipped behind a cloud, plunging the travelers into the shadow of the city. Khamsin shivered in spite of the cloak draped around her shoulders.

They passed underneath a large, arched gateway, one of three such gateways in the walled city. The one they used opened to the south; the two others, to the west and north. The great sea itself lay to the east.

❋ ❋ ❋

Suddenly, Khamsin found herself in the center of a commotion. Chickens and pigeons squawked and cooed, children cried, and vendors called out praises of their wares along with damnations of their competitors. A thin brown dog darted in front of the cart, barking. The gray mare skittered.

"We should walk." The tinker offered her his hand as she stepped down from the high seat. He, like herself, wore a cloak, though his was a dark blue, while hers was a light tan. It fastened at his throat and trailed to mid-calf. Standing next to him, Khamsin was once again aware of his height. Though he moved with an easy grace, he could seem imposing. As they walked down the cobblestone street, even the shifty-eyed gutter-thieves gave them wide berth.

The tinker held Khamsin's hand in one of his, the mare's reins in the other, keeping a firm grip on both as if concerned that some unexpected occurrence would set them both to flying off in different directions. Even Nixa, a master at the art of the indifference, sat upright in her basket, ears flicking warily, tail tapping a constant rhythm.

They followed a street that paralleled the progress of the high stone wall. It was ringed on both sides with colorfully decorated signs labeling the establishments as stables. Even a Cove-dweller like Khamsin understood why. In a city as congested as Noviiya, horses and carts stayed on the outskirts, for reasons of space as well as sanitation. Only the very wealthy were allowed to bring their steeds onto the main thoroughfares. And only if they paid for the services of a dung-keeper.

The tinker stopped before the seventh stable, by Khamsin's count, and led the gray mare inside. The animal seemed at ease with her surroundings, obviously having spent time here before. The stable hand, a young boy of perhaps fourteen, called her by a name: "Friya," he crooned, stroking the soft nose before relieving her of the burden of the tinker's red cart.

Khamsin took the satchel the tinker instructed her to pack the night before. It contained a change of clothing and her belongings. It, along with the sheathed sword strapped to her side, was all that she owned. The clothing was a gift, the tinker insisted, but she pressed into his palm her favorite amulet for luck. He seemed touched by her offering and used its silver chain to thread it through his belt.

"It's good-bye, then." She ignored the lump forming in her throat and held her free hand out toward him. Nixa jumped down by her side.

The tinker secured his merchandise in his cart. At her words he turned, facing her. He frowned.

"And where do you intend to go from here, my lady? LeCarra Street has some reasonable lodgings, or if you wish, I could recommend a small inn at Courten's Square. But then, those names mean nothing to you, do they?"

She let her hand drop as the realization came upon her that Noviiya wasn't like her village, with its one main road and one small tavern. It was a city, a huge city with thousands of occupants. And she knew neither a street nor a soul. Save for the one who stood before her.

"I'm aware that I'm at a disadvantage." Her

independent nature came to the fore. "But strangers have traveled through the city before and found their way. You must have had your first time here alone too."

"Ah, but it was a much smaller place then." He reached for her hand and held it. "I don't doubt that you're well capable of finding your way. I'm sure many would offer assistance, as you have a face that has that effect on men. But I've been coming to Noviiya for so many years now that I feel that it's almost my home. And it would please me greatly to show you some of the finer sights of the city."

She blushed self-consciously at his words, withdrawing her hand from his. "The only men who would find me pleasing, tinker, are those who have an affection for ten-year-old boys!"

"Noviiya has its share of those too."

"It sounds like a very unusual place."

"It is." Ignoring her murmured protests, he grasped her satchel, then his, and threw both over his shoulder. "I suggest you carry your cat. There are also those in Noviiya who would consider her supper."

❊ ❊ ❊

As night approached, he led her straight to the small inn on Courten's Square, which wasn't square at all but round with a small fountain in the center. The buildings that ringed it were made of the same gray stone as the wall around the city and reached up three stories high. Their façades were decorated with placards bearing the insignia of their trade. There was a candle shop, a carpenter's shop, a small bakery, and a sign that read simply "Jarman and Son." The inn was wedged in between the carpenter's and the bakery. Like most of the other buildings, it seemed to be well kept, but unimposing. Courten's Square was not an affluent address, but it wasn't the slums, either.

The great room of the inn had a large hearth at one end. Long, wooden tables filled the opposite side of the room. Several patrons lounged on the benches, sipping at froth-topped ale mugs. Khamsin could smell the tart aroma of bread baking and wondered if it came from the inn's own kitchen or the bakery next door. It also reminded her that she'd had nothing to eat since sunrise.

The innkeeper was a short, potbellied man, balding, with a full-jowled face and bright blue eyes. His white brows were as bushy as Nixa's whiskers, Khamsin noted, as the tinker strode toward the man leaning on the end of the small bar. Nixa heard her comment and disagreed. Her whiskers were bushier. And prettier.

"Aye, I've a room for you, sirrah, but not for the lad," Khamsin heard him say, as she waited patiently in front of the great hearth. There was a good-sized fire going inside it. The heat penetrated her clothing. She turned and removed her cloak.

"Well, then, what you have will do for us both," the tinker replied, as the innkeeper suddenly stared at something behind him. "I never go anywhere without my little cousin."

"I can see why," came the balding man's droll reply.

The tinker turned also and smiled. Khamsin smiled back in return, then stretched her arms up over her head as the warmth from the fire relaxed the tension in her body.

"And some people complain about their relatives," the tinker quipped, as he pressed the required coins into the innkeeper's soft palm. He was handed a heavy key in exchange.

"Just one room?" Khamsin stood before the large door as the tinker fit the key into the lock.

"It's all they have, my lady, and at this hour we're not about to go traipsing around the city in search for another. Besides, the price is reasonable, and the food won't kill you. And I trust Master Verney not to rob me blind if I happen to fall into a drunken stupor at one of his ale-room tables downstairs."

She followed him hesitantly into the room. There was a four-poster bed along the back wall with the smaller trundle adjacent to it. They camped together for night after night, but that was different. She was secure in her bedroll and he, in his. Though there were times she longed for a warmth that couldn't be provided by their small stone-ringed fire.

But the openness of their outdoor encampments kept her from pursuing her foolish whims, for that was all she considered them to be. Yet here, here was a room with walls. And a door that locked. She'd never been in a bed-room before with anyone other than her husband.

"Do you do that often, fall into a drunken stupor, that is?" It would make his presence more worrisome if he were in an inebriated condition.

He crossed to the window, drew back the curtains, and shoved the wooden panes outward. " 'Bout once in a blue moon, only."

She waited until he turned and was involved in unpacking his satchel before she sauntered by the open window and, with a quick glance upward, checked on the condition of the twin luminaries of the night sky. Both were half-full. And neither was blue.

She had little to unpack and found all she had, including her sword, fit nicely in a small cupboard in the corner. She hung her cloak on a nearby hook. Then, while the tinker went in search of a pitcher of fresh water, she touched all four corners of the cupboard door with a warding spell. She worried less about her meager wardrobe than she did about her sword.

They returned downstairs for a light supper. Khamsin said little, content just to listen to the tinker's recitation of various legends about Noviiya. She found his manner of speech fascinating, his precise choice of words enlivening his descriptions. She giggled unashamedly at his recounting of the antics of Noviiya's miserly merchants. Then stared, wide-eyed, when his deep voice dropped to a whisper as he described the secret treasure supposedly lost forever in the icy depths of the Great North Sea. She felt she could listen to the sound of his voice forever, and she forgot for a while her real purpose in the city. She let herself get lost in the fantasies he wove before her.

But reality was thrust upon her all too soon when, shortly after supper, she found herself back in their room with the tinker making preparations for the night.

She placed her cloak and vest carefully over the back of a chair. Then clutched the front of her half-unbuttoned shirt self-consciously.

The tinker regarded her with undisguised amusement from where he sat on the higher bed, tugging off his boots. "Would you prefer if I were to close my eyes?"

"Would be more proper," she murmured, hearing the foolishness in her statement. This was the man who tended to the bruises left on her body by the grief-maddened Covemen.

"Proper?" His voice was unexpectedly soft. She turned, surprised at the sound. "Nay, little one, would be more proper if I were to take you in my arms and . . . but I don't know if you're ready for that."

She felt her face grow hot. Was he aware of her attraction to him? Or did he expect her to be willing in repayment for his aid? "Sirrah! Surely you know I'm a widow and recently so. It's cruel of you to take advantage of . . ."

"But you're also a woman. There's much I could teach you, much we could share."

"I don't care for lessons of that sort!" She snatched at the vest she had discarded only moments before. "I thank you for your assistance, but it seems . . ."

"It seems we're both overly tired and wont to misconstrue. I mean no disrespect in my words." He leaned forward, his eyes dark with concern. "Have I hurt you in any way to this point, Lady Khamsin? Have I broken your faith in me?"

She fingered the softness of the vest distractedly and

avoided looking at him. "No," she admitted.

"Then have faith that now and forever, I mean you no harm. Judge me by your heart, my lady. It's wiser than you think."

Warily, she let herself stare into his eyes. They were a cool blue compared to the heat she felt emanating between them. She felt unsettled and ashamed. Not that he'd hurt her. But at what she feared she wanted.

"I can't."

"And I'm not asking. I'd never take anything from you that you weren't first willing to give. And I'd never force you to do, or be, anything. Other than what you want to be. In this, if in nothing else, you may place your faith."

He motioned to the trundle bed next to his own, with its warm coverlet and soft pillow. "Sleep, little one. You need your rest. We have busy times ahead of us."

Khamsin slipped out of her breeches and let her shirt fall from her arms onto the chair. She stood clad only in her camisole and underpinnings. Swiftly, she climbed under the reassuring weight of the coverlet.

The tinker cupped his hand around the bedside taper and blew softly, extinguishing the light.

Khamsin listened to him adjust his weight on the bed frame. Then shyly she reached up into the darkness and, finding his hand, clasped it for a moment in her own.

❊ ❊ ❊

The next morning they left Nixa behind and set out into the city. Khamsin felt refreshed after a good night's sleep, though where Nixa slept she didn't know. She found the gray cat perched on the windowsill in the morning, a haughty expression on her feline features.

"Surveying her kingdom," the tinker quipped, all the tension of the previous night now gone.

It was where Nixa still sat even now, as Khamsin and the tinker passed in front of the small fountain outside the inn. Khamsin turned, sending one more motherly reminder to the gray cat to "behave" until she returned.

The tinker led her down a confusing array of twisting cobblestone streets and alleyways, stopping here and there to point out some item of interest. Like the elegant tearoom where wealthy ladies, suspected of nobility, sipped steamy liquid from thin, porcelain cups. Khamsin watched in open-mouthed amazement as two young women about her own age were escorted by an elderly gentleman through the wide doorway. She had never seen dresses of the fine fabric they wore: polished muslins and rich brocades, trimmed with eyelets and laces. And all before noon!

"Those are the Princesses Adorna and Ordella, with their great-uncle Fazmir." The tinker guided her away with a light touch on her elbow.

"You know them?" Her amazement was genuine.

"Noviiya has an overabundance of princesses," he scoffed.

"Are there healers here, too?" They walked down a short flight of steps. She heard the pounding of the surf over the constant rumbling of the city.

"Some, though most are just fortune-tellers. Their

skills lie not in their ability to heal but in their ability to deceive their patrons. And deprive them of their coins."

"They get paid?" The thought shocked Khamsin.

The tinker chuckled and his eyes sparkled. "You do have much to learn."

They were clearly in the more affluent section of the city. The tinker explained the meticulously cared-for façades around them were residences, some of wealthy merchants, some of government officials. And some of what he called "old money." Wealthy land-barons with large estates to the north and west who maintained a city address as well. These were all things Khamsin never dreamed of, never knew about back in her small village by the Cove. She walked around in a haze of wonder and amazement.

There was also a museum, and farther down the street, a library. When the tinker explained what a library was, he had to physically restrain his young companion from dashing toward the gate and attempting to gain entry. Though her reading skills were rudimentary, the thought of endless knowledge beckoned to her like forbidden fruit. Only when he made it clear to her that the library was not open to the average citizen, but only to those who ruled in the business, government, or religious sectors of Noviiya, did Khamsin cease her pleading. She stood, forlornly, in front of the spear-tipped locked gate like a chastised child.

"Come, come. There's much yet to see." He chucked her affectionately under the chin.

She raised her eyes to his. "It's not fair that they

should keep all that wisdom locked away."

"Ah, but little one, some people say that knowledge is a dangerous thing."

The Sorcerer, she felt, would be one of those.

He drew her attention to the turrets of a tall building at the end of the street. "The governor's mansion."

"And that?" She pointed to a two-story building with colorful banners draped over its sides. Like the library it, too, was encircled by an iron gate but this one was more elaborate, with scrollwork and curlicues adorning its base. A high, arched window topped a wide, ornately carved, wooden door. A nattily attired, young man, hawk-faced, in a brocade jacket and braid-trimmed stockings, stood almost motionless, facing the street.

"That's the Games Palace." At her quizzical expression, he continued. "Another toy for the wealthy and the privileged. It contains many rooms, each relegated to a different game or amusement. There are card games in some, games of skill and chance in others. There's also a wrestling arena and a sword pit. And other things," he added, as they made a sharp right before reaching the building they were discussing. "For those who seek their entertainment on more intimate levels."

The street ended suddenly. Khamsin found herself clasping onto a railing on the cliff's edge. The dark surf pounded below her, the breakers licking hungrily at the rocks. The wind whistled through the railing. She drew a deep breath of salt and found, for the first time in her life, she was afraid of the sea.

"It's not like home," she said.

"No," the tinker agreed, his face serious. "No, the sea knows the difference, too."

She let the wind buffet her back. The edges of her cape flapped lightly, and she could feel her short hair dancing around her neck. "I'm keeping you from your business here."

"Today? No, not today. Today I set aside just for you."

"That's very kind of you, Tinker." The warmth in her words was real.

He tucked a trembling strand of hair around her ear. "Rylan. My name, Khamsin, is Rylan."

"Then I thank you, Rylan. You've shown more than an ordinary kindness to a stranger. It will not be forgotten."

"You talk as if I'm already a part of your past."

She shook her head. "No. It's just that you can't be part of my present. What I have to do breeds danger. It's something I must do alone. For all the help you've given me, my friend, this, I'm afraid is out of your realm of experience."

"What do you have to do?"

"Exactly, I'm not sure, which is part of the reason I had to come to Noviiya. The answer's here, somewhere. And it involves the incidents that we discussed that night at my house. About Dram, and other villages to the south. As well as the raids on my village that not only granted me my life, but my friends and husband, their death."

"You seek revenge, then?"

"Eventually. But for now I seek someone who can teach me what I need to know. You mentioned there were healers here in the city. Are there any of great reputation that could provide me with the training I need?"

"In Noviiya? Several, if you're willing to pay the price."

"Which is?"

He rubbed his fingers together, as if toying with coins.

"Then they're not healers, they're thieves!" She folded her arms across her chest in a defiant gesture.

"If it's knowledge you seek, then why don't you go to the one who's the keeper of the Orb of Knowledge? To Traakhal-Armin, to . . ."

"Rylan, surely you're mad!" She stepped toward him, her hands outstretched. "For he's the power behind everything that I oppose. He's the Sorcerer, the evil lord, the demon-keeper. He placed the spell of assignation upon me when I was born, and . . ."

"And perhaps he was trying to tell you something." He took her hands.

She shook her head violently. "No!"

Rylan started to speak but a flock of sea-fowl sped through the air, screeching. Khamsin twisted around to look at them, jarred by the sound. His hands clenched tightly over hers.

"Perhaps . . ." he said again.

When she turned back to him, she drew her mouth into a firm line. "I know you mean well. But what you suggest is impossible."

"Then, I don't know, Khamsin. I don't know how to help you."

CHAPTER EIGHT

Late that night, while Rylan slumbered under Nixa's watchful eye, Khamsin slipped down the back stairs of the inn to a small, private garden. In between the day's laundry hung out to dry and a collection of empty baskets littered with leaves of wilted lettuce and crusts of dry bread, she cleared a small area and set out her amulets as Tanta Bron had taught her. Then she cast her stones, again.

This time a name appeared in the dust. "Ciro," it read, in the runes of an ancient tongue.

"Ciro," she whispered out loud and in the distance heard the deep rumble of thunder.

❋ ❋ ❋

She woke to find Rylan already out of bed, his trousers on, a clean linen shirt in one hand. He held a darning needle awkwardly in the other. He winced as he pricked himself with the needle then silently mouthed a curse. She giggled when he placed his finger into his mouth.

"Wounded in battle," she teased, and he grinned back at her, holding his finger in her direction.

"This is your calling."

She rose from her bed clad in nothing but her camisole and underpinnings and grasped his wrist, holding his palm upward. She inspected the minor puncture and sighed.

"Well, we probably should contact a surgeon and have him amputate, but in the meantime . . ." She retrieved her braided belt of pouches and removed one dyed a deep dark red. "Hold still." She released his wrist and placed some balm on her fingertip. Gently, she touched the small wound.

"There. All better."

He wriggled his fingers in her face. "Good as new."

"Now, what were you trying to do?" She reached for the shirt he dropped onto the bed, but he caught hold of her arm.

"It's done, now. Just minor mending." His eyes searched her face. "I have to leave this afternoon, Khamsin. I have some business to attend to in the northern section of the city. Then I have to leave Noviiya for a week or two, maybe more."

Leave? She tensed at his words.

"Come with me." The plea was uttered quickly, as if he already knew she would refuse.

She thought of her divinations of the previous night.

There was so much ahead of her. So much to learn. Yet her heart still sank.

"Rylan, I can't."

"Why?"

She dropped her gaze. "There's someone here I have to find. We spoke of it yesterday. You know I have to find a healer."

He thought for a moment. "My business could wait until the morrow. And there are many healers. Not just in Noviiya."

"No." What she needed to learn couldn't be grasped in mere hours. "I must stay in Noviiya. Perhaps, if you return . . ."

"If you come with me, I won't have to return. We could search together for these answers you want." His hand tightened on her wrist. "Please come with me."

She shook her head, the ache in his voice matching the one growing in her chest.

"I belong here, right now. If you come back . . ."

"I promise you. I'll be back."

But would he? She looked up at him. Why would he return? For her, for Khamsin, for a mere slip of a girl that looked more like a young farm lad than the lady she was supposed to be? She thought of the princesses they saw only the day before, their elegance, their carefully tended beauty. She knew she could never be anything like them.

Oh, she could weave spells, she supposed, to make herself as elegant. But they'd be false, and somehow Rylan would know. Besides, why return for her when

Noviiya was full of reasons for him to stay? Perhaps that's where he was headed now. An attractive man such as Rylan the Tinker no doubt had more than one lovely tucked away in the city. As he did, she surmised, in Browner's Grove. She was just little Kammi, the young girl he rescued from the Hill Raiders. He no doubt felt compassion for her, but little more.

She pulled out of his grasp. "Leave word at the stables. I'll check there when I can." There was a sudden chill to her voice. "We can meet here for supper, if you like."

He frowned slightly. "You'll stay here. The room is paid for, for as long as you need it."

"I've availed myself of your charity far too long. There's no reason for you . . ."

"No?" He hesitated, then reached for her hand, pulling her back to him, twining his fingers into her own. His voice was soft, almost apologetic. "There's a very good reason. One I've been afraid to tell you. Tried to tell you last night. It's why I asked how you felt about your husband. I had to know if you still loved him. Before I could tell you what I feel. How much I love you."

It took several moments for his words to sink in, for the thousand bubbles that just exploded inside her to settle down into a mere fluttering of her heart.

"Me? That's not possible!"

He drew her hand to his lips. "Why?" He kissed her fingers lightly. "Khamsin, you're a beautiful woman. Kind, gentle but strong. You have a deep loyalty. A true intelligence. You're all I've sought for years, and more so.

"And this is the truth, with no falseness on my part. For if I were here only to seduce you, I could've done so in Cirrus Cove, the day you healed my horse. But I wasn't seeking seductions. Or love, if truth be known. So if my feelings surprise you, understand they surprise me doubly more."

"You don't know me, haven't known me long enough," she countered lamely.

"Haven't I?" His eyes glistened playfully now. "And what determines the proper time for love, little one? Is it written in one of your books?"

Khamsin started to speak, but he continued. "I'm no stranger to Cirrus. I've watched you for years. Watched you grow from a mischievous child to a lovely young woman. No, perhaps you weren't aware of me, as my passings through your village were oft-times infrequent. But, nevertheless, I've for a long time been aware of you."

Khamsin closed her eyes for a moment, thinking of the night the tinker sat across the dining room table from her. There was an unsettling sensation, an attraction she could not explain at the time.

A shiver ran up her spine. "Rylan, I . . ."

"Could you love me, Khamsin?"

She stared at the man whose lips brushed against her fingers, whose eyes stared into hers with an intensity that made her knees weak. She wished she could give him the answer he sought. But she couldn't.

She knew nothing about love, had never been interested in love. Her only thoughts were on her magic and her healing. Those were the only important things. For love, for a man to love to come into her life now . . . No. Not now.

The stark reality of Rina's and Tavis's deaths grazed her conscience. She steeled herself. Now was not the time. There was too much she had to do. She knew when she was with Rylan, her thoughts were anywhere but her divinations. What she found herself feeling for Rylan she forced herself to dismiss as just a physical attraction, a remembrance from the past. A response to her loneliness. That was why she was unwilling to accept his departure.

"I wish I could but . . ."

He silenced her protestations by drawing her against him. He placed his mouth on hers. Khamsin found his lips warm, his kisses gentle and for now, undemanding. She struggled briefly, unconvincingly, until his hands caressed her face, his thumb traced her lips. She shivered in anticipation and leaned into his touch.

He kissed her lightly on the cheek where the bruise had been, only days before. His lips brushed her ear.

"Khamsin," he whispered, and the voice she heard wove itself inside her mind, mesmerizing her. She sighed raggedly and rested her head against his shoulder. He trailed kisses down her neck.

"Rylan, Rylan, please."

"Do you want me to let you go? Do you want me to leave?"

She fought at the turmoil within herself. And damned her own weaknesses when she answered him. "No, I don't want you to leave." She buried her face in his shoulder. "But, I shouldn't. I can't."

"Can't what, little one?"

She dug her face further into his neck as if to hide from the truth.

He stroked her hair, then nudged her face with his own until their lips met again. She could feel his breath, warm against her face, the roughness of his beard on her skin. Suddenly something inside her ached as if she were empty and he was the only one who could fill the void. Ignoring all the warnings in her mind she pressed against him, wrapping her arms around his neck. Her fingers locked into the thickness of his hair.

His hands explored the softness of her through the thin camisole. She felt his touch like fire inside her, a fire that trembled, shivered. Tavis had never done this. No one had ever touched her like this, so softly, yet so demandingly. Tavis had rarely held her, except in their marriage bed. And then it was to hold onto her shoulders or her waist, kissing her hard, only at the height of his passion.

But this . . . this was something she had never experienced. This yearning, this desire to be touched. To caress in return.

She leaned her head back. His mouth found the base of her throat, then the swell of her breasts where her camisole was unbuttoned. The rest of the buttons he attended to with gentle fingers and moist, warm kisses. He lifted her up and carried her onto the bed.

He stroked her, touching and tracing the lines of her body until she cried out in pleasure and reached for him, bringing him down on top of her. She kissed him with unrestrained passion this time, suddenly needing the taste of his mouth, the scent of his skin.

"Khamsin." He whispered her name in her ear. Whispered his longing, his love for her. His loneliness.

Her hands answered, for words for her were now impossible. Her fingers traveled down the length of his back, finding the hollow at the base of his spine. She splayed her hands, pressing the hardness of him against her.

But he had other ideas and pulled back slowly. His mouth retraced the trail his hands had burned earlier on her skin. Gently, his tongue teased the peaks of her nipples, then trailed kisses down her stomach. When he reached the softness between her thighs, her gasps of surprise turned into moans of pleasure.

When she could bear no more, when her breathing was rushed and ragged, he took her slowly, lovingly. Her passion built with his until it was only one heart beating, one touch knowing pleasure. One soul knowing love.

And then his arms closed around her once more, and he held her small body curled against his. He teased her eyelids with kisses.

"Look at me," he said, his voice hoarse with emotion. She opened her eyes. "Look at the one who loves you more than you can ever understand, loves you more than you can ever know . . ."

And she brought her fingers to his lips, silencing the words she felt she did not deserve.

※ ※ ※

It was after midday when they untangled themselves from the covers and rose from the large bed to dress. Rylan touched her as he gathered his belongings from around the room, as if he needed the warm contact of her skin. He adjusted her shirt, his fingers first smoothing her collar. His mouth planted kisses where his fingers had been.

He insisted on lacing her vest. She blushed, knowing what his inquisitive fingers would do there. But she let him, reveling in sensations just as sweet as they'd been hours before.

Then he combed her short hair with a tenderness she'd not experienced since she was a small child, in Tanta Bron's lap.

"You're spoiling me. I shall have to hire you as a lady's maid."

"I enjoy fussing over you." In words and actions he made sure she knew that, in spite of her farm lad's attire, she was very much a woman to him.

Finally, he fastened his own cloak and slung his satchel over his shoulder.

Khamsin's heart was torn between pain and pleasure.

"Lady," he said, tracing her jaw. "There is a matter I must handle before sunset."

"I remember." She remembered also he said he would leave, for a week or more. But that part she found she couldn't voice.

"I thought to head north immediately after that. But now I find myself very reluctant . . ."

Khamsin took a quick breath of anticipation.

". . . and if you're perhaps willing to share a late dinner with me, tonight? Will you wait up?"

"Yes, yes, of course!" The words tumbled from her lips.

He pulled her face toward his and kissed her softly, teasingly. Then suddenly he crushed her tightly against him. Khamsin felt a hot wave of passion surge through her.

He abruptly stepped back, though one hand still caressed her face.

"Tonight. Just after first moonrise."

"I'll be here."

She listened to the sound of his boots fade down the stairs. Nixa was perched on the edge of the small night table, and Khamsin reached for the gray cat and gathered her into her arms. She buried her face into the cat's soft fur.

Tonight. Though tomorrow he would depart, she still had Rylan for tonight. It was a small parcel of happiness, but she grabbed it willingly. It would be all she would have for a while.

Nixa had much less forbearance. Her plaintive meow drew Khamsin out of her reverie.

"Hungry?" She released the cat and grabbed her tan cloak. Nixa waited by the door, tail swishing.

"There's the baker next door. Or we could find a tea shop. Some cream, perhaps?"

Nixa tilted her head with interest at the word "cream."

"Cream and tea it is, then. And perhaps something more." She found she was hungry all of a sudden. Rylan's departure wasn't the only emptiness inside her.

Khamsin caught no glimpse of the innkeeper in the large main room. A thin barmaid scrubbed at the long table by the hearth.

"Aye, there's a few shops what have somethin' tasty near here." The barmaid wiped her hands on her checkered apron. "Take a right out the door, then three blocks. Short ones, not far. Copper Kettle's on the right. Across from that's the Silver Cow. But I'd be glad to make a pot here, if you like."

"Thanks, but no. I've not been to Noviiya before. I'd like to look around." She needed to walk, to feel the fresh air on her face, and fill her mind with new sights and sounds. She needed to think of anything other than two weeks without Rylan.

Nixa chose the Silver Cow. The shop was set farther back from the cobblestone street and had several tables on a small front porch. Thick vines with red and orange flowers covered the porch railing. Nixa finished her cream quickly then darted in and out of the foliage. She disrupted a nest of crickets and caught two for a snack.

Khamsin sipped her tea and watched the bustle of passersby. The tea shop was located on a busy corner not far from the entrance to the market. A stout woman hurried by, a squawking goose under one arm. Two small boys trotted after her, each carrying a basket laden with bright green and yellow vegetables. They almost collided with a bearded man pushing a red cart loaded with bolts of patterned cloth.

In her mind's eye she saw Rylan the Tinker, sitting on the high bench of his red cart, his night-black hair ruffled by the soft breezes of Cirrus Cove. She remembered the children chasing after his cart, snatching for the brightly colored ribbons trailing from the overstuffed baskets.

Perhaps some of his wares came from this same market.

She was leaving Rina's that day when she saw the children skipping happily, clutching small bits of lace and ribbon the tinker always gave them. The entire scene symbolized her problems with her divinations back then, a few short months ago.

She'd been grasping for answers without success, not even gaining the small scraps Rylan bestowed on the children. Then everything changed, for she returned home to find the vase of brightpinks on the floor. And the assignation imprinted in the book.

Everything had changed. The life she knew was gone. And her divinations, like the one late last night, now came with an almost urgent clarity.

She finished the last piece of nut bread on her plate, washing it down with the remains of her tea. There were several hours yet before sunset and first moonrise.

She called to Nixa. They had a healer named Ciro to find.

CHAPTER NINE

Khamsin always gathered her herbs in the forest, as Tanta Bron had taught her. But there were no forests within the walls of the city. A city healer, she surmised, might well utilize the market for such a purpose.

Several vegetable sellers had strings of herbs drying on the walls of their booths, but, she found as she fingered and sniffed the brittle leaves, they were mostly for cooking.

"Moonpetal powder?" The farmer pulled at the skin of his leathery chin. "Healin' stuff, that is. My wife grows 'em, but just for pretty.

"Try Crowson's, back yonder about five rows. He's got that blue awning atop his stall. Or maybe Fat Halba. She might know."

She threaded her way back toward the booth with the blue awning. It was growing late, and many merchants were starting to bring in their wares and lock their shutters.

Farmer Crowson greeted her arrival with interest. Until it was clear her purpose was not the purchase of vegetables.

He shrugged off her questions and went back to keeping the flies off his cabbages.

"Crowson wouldn't tell you e'en he did know." Fat Halba stripped the bright green husks off a long ear of corn with swift professionalism. "Used to carry some moonpetal powder meself. Years ago, when me granny was alive. Not a healer, no. But she knew some of that stuff. Now, them that carries it comes only once a month, during hearthmoon."

It was another two weeks, Khamsin knew, before both moons would rise full into a hearthmoon. About the same time Rylan would return.

"But I hear tell there's a small shop in the Old Quarter what stocks some stuff. In glass bottles. You might try there." Fat Halba shifted her considerable weight on the stool and reached into the basket for another ear of corn. "Kin of yours needs healin'?"

"No. Actually I'm looking for a healer called Ciro. I thought if I found where healers bought—"

"Ciro?" Halba's fingers stilled their movements, then started busily again. She ripped at the coarse husks.

"You know of him?"

"Ciro, you say? Thought you said Claro. Was a . . . baker named Claro. Years ago. Made a fine sweetcake, he did. No, don't know no . . . What'd you say his name was?"

"Ciro."

Halba sucked on her plump lips. "Sorry. Don't know the name."

"This herb shop in the Old Quarter, they might know?"

"They know the healers in the city," Halba replied. "Not much happens anywhere in the city what it don't get talked about in the Old Quarter. Just," and she looked Khamsin up and down, "just you don't go pokin' 'round there at night."

"Thank you, no. I've no intentions of that. I'm having dinner with a dear friend tonight." She felt the heat rise to her cheeks as she thought of returning to Rylan's arms, in only a few short hours.

A man and a woman brushed by Khamsin, pushing their way into Fat Halba's booth. "Still open, Halba?" The man's voice boomed in the small space. "Good! That Upland corn you got there?"

Khamsin's thanks were lost under the haggle of negotiations.

The market was almost deserted, shutters locked tightly in place for the approach of night. Nixa sauntered ahead. The translucent gold skin of a water-onion fluttered across the cat's path, and she pounced on it.

Torn bits of string littered the ground. The harsh bang of shutters punctuated the descending silence.

In the sky to the west, Khamsin saw the orange glow of the sunset over the high turrets of the city wall. She quickened her steps.

She felt it at the same time her cat did. A presence, a searing cold. She spun around. Nixa hissed, her fur prickling out from her small form.

A large black crow swooped out of the sky, screeching. Khamsin's small hunting knife was already in her right hand.

"Ixari!" She whispered the name of her goddess for protection. Then a second crow landed. And a third. The trio pecked fiercely at something on the ground.

Still grasping her knife, Khamsin stepped closer.

A remnant of a crusty, meat pie. The crows stabbed their beaks into the ground and fluttered their wings. One glanced at her briefly, his dark eyes glittering in challenge.

She sheathed her knife. "No, I don't want your dinner." *And you*, she told Nixa with a light touch of her mind, *stay away from them. They're far too thin, and far too hungry, to be of interest to you.*

Nixa gave herself a brief shake and trotted away.

Khamsin looked over the row of closed stalls. Had that searing cold she'd felt just been the ravenous need of the hungry birds? She felt nothing now.

Shaking her head with a small movement not unlike her cat's, she resumed her pace. She passed under the arched market gate, leaving the crows and the puzzling sensation behind.

Shadows on the narrow streets were thicker now. Rylan was probably finishing his business and, within an hour or two, would return to the inn. Not enough time to launder and patch her one skirt and blouse, the ones ripped by the maddened Covemen.

And in spite of Rylan's reassurances that he found

her current attire quite charming, Khamsin wanted to present a more feminine picture. This would be their last night together for a fortnight.

A flash of pale green in an open doorway caught her eye. It was the entrance to a clothier's shop. And the flash of color was a dress hanging limply over the back of a chair.

She stepped inside. The shopkeeper peered over thick spectacles at her.

Khamsin plucked at the boy's trousers she wore. "My clothing trunk fell overboard. Had to borrow my cousin's things. How much do you want for the dress?"

"It's out of fashion," the shopkeeper said. "Was about to use the material for something else. Some aprons, perhaps. But if you want it, as is, won't cost you much."

She gave him the two small coins he requested.

❄ ❄ ❄

She heard the sounds of his boots on the stairs and rose from her seat by the open window. The night breezes, soft and tinged with a salty odor, ruffled the lace trim on her new dress. She smoothed her palms nervously over her skirt, then brought her hands back to her short hair.

The key scraped in the lock.

She wiggled her toes anxiously in her boots.

The tall figure stepped inside, his dark cloak swirling around him. He turned, and the light of the candles glinted off the gold star in his ear. He looked somehow taller, more imposing. Almost regal, Khamsin thought. There was something in the strong set of his shoulders, in the tilt of his head. Her heart fluttered.

A slow smile formed under his mustache. "My Lady Khamsin." The husky tones in his voice make her knees feel as if they were filled with jelly.

My lord, she almost replied, but caught herself. This was Rylan, the tinker. Embarrassed at her fanciful imaginings, she dropped her gaze.

"It's not very fancy, but . . ." She plucked at the skirt of her dress, then chanced a look at him again. "Do you like it?"

He shrugged out of his cape and tossed it onto the bed. "Beautiful." He clasped her elbows and drew her against him.

She brought her mouth hungrily up to his. She never wanted to kiss anyone more than she wanted to kiss Rylan at that moment.

Finally she pulled back from him, a bit breathless, her knees still far from steady.

"Miss me?" he whispered in her ear.

She nodded into his shoulder.

"But you've been busy, I see."

His large hand gently grasped her chin and tilted her face upward. He kissed her nose. "A new dress. Nothing for Nixa?"

"She had a few crickets. And almost got into a fight with some crows." The odd cold sensation still puzzled her.

Rylan brushed her cheek with his fingers. He frowned.

"They were after a piece of meat pie in the market," she explained. "They thought we wanted some too. It was nothing."

Rylan looked at the cat, sitting on her haunches in the windowsill. "Best not to tangle with city crows, Mistress Cat. They don't take kindly to sharing their meals."

Khamsin laced her fingers through his. "We're not from the city. And we'd be glad to share our meal with you."

He chuckled. "Your kindness overwhelms me. Especially since I spied a wonderful roast and some thick stew in the kitchen below. Will you join me, my lady?"

"With pleasure."

He tucked Khamsin's hand through the crook of his arm. She hesitated as he opened the door. "We'll send a small plate up for Nixa?"

He looked over her head at the cat in the window. "Stew or roast?"

Nixa blinked twice.

"Ah. Roast it is then."

Khamsin shot him a surprised glance. There was laughter in his eyes. There was no way he could hear Nixa's immediate affirmative to the word and image of "roast." Rylan's teasing response was nothing more than a lucky guess.

She never told him of her telepathic link to her cat. There would be time for many explanations when he returned, in two weeks. She hoped to have answers about the signs in her divinations and her search for a healer named Ciro by then.

But tonight was just for herself and Rylan. She wanted nothing of the past to intrude upon her future.

❊ ❊ ❊

She awoke in the morning to the light touch of Rylan's fingers on her face. She offered him a sleepy smile.

"Morning blessings." It seemed odd, yet so right, to have him to next her.

"Morning blessings to you, love. And you," he said, as Nixa nudged her nose against his hand.

"You'll be leaving this morning, or . . ."

"This morning." He kissed her gently. "But we have time for tea."

He was delaying his departure, and Khamsin knew it. The thought warmed her. At the same time, she knew she had to let him know she'd be fine until he returned.

"I'll probably go to the Old Quarter today," she said, as he bent over to retrieve his clothes from the floor.

He pulled on his pants. Khamsin rose from the tangle of covers and drew the soft sheet against her chest.

"The Old Quarter?" He threaded his leather belt through the loops. "Why there?"

"I heard of a shop, an herbal shop, that carries healers' wares." It was on the tip of her tongue to tell him about

Ciro, but so far the healer's name had elicited nothing but suspicious glances from everyone she spoke to. She didn't want Rylan to worry; he'd seemed worried enough when she mentioned the black crows in the market last night.

"I'm not sure where the Old Quarter is," she continued. "Is it far?"

"A bit north and west of this square. Ten maybe fifteen blocks. It's an old section of the city." He shook his head as if shaking off disturbing thoughts. "Some of it's not as well kept as perhaps it should be."

Halba had issued a similar warning.

"The herbal shop's on Windward Lane. Not far from the Street of Dreams, if my memory serves me correctly."

"I'm sure I'll find it." At the moment, finding her stockings was a more immediate concern. Her pants and tunic shirt were where she'd left them the night before. But her socks were nowhere to be found.

She glanced at Nixa, curled at the foot of the bed. The feline affected her most innocent look.

"Just don't tarry there, love. It's not a place I'd want you to visit after dark."

"Oh, I won't. Have you seen my socks?"

Five minutes later both socks were recovered from opposite corners of the room, where Nixa had hidden them during the night. Khamsin finished dressing and followed Rylan down the stairs for some tea and butter cakes. And for the next half hour, everything was fine. It was just a morning, like many mornings she hoped to share with him.

But then they were back in the room, and he was knotting the strings of his satchel. A feeling of intense loss washed over her.

He kissed her, tasting of tea and sweet butter. She clung to him.

He folded her into his arms and pressed his mouth against her ear. "I will return to you," he said softly.

She pulled back slightly and looked up at him. "Quickly?" It was a hope beyond hopes.

"As quickly as I can. Unless you change your mind and come . . ."

She laid her fingers on his mouth. "We both have things to do, things to settle. When you return, all that will be finished. And we'll have all our time for ourselves."

He nipped her fingers. "Such a wise woman!" he said as she drew them away.

She placed her hand over the amulet she'd given him when they arrived in the city. It dangled from a silver chain around his neck. "Where you go, I go with you."

"But do I go with you? Khamsin, promise me you won't forget me. Promise me you believe in what we have."

Khamsin stood on tiptoe and answered him with another kiss. It was a long, lingering kiss full of unspoken words. And all her promises.

CHAPTER TEN

Nixa seemed pleased. Her yellow eyes half-closed as Khamsin stroked her soft head. Together they watched the tall figure in the dark blue cloak move easily into the crowds meandering through Courten's Square. Something in Khamsin longed to run down the creaking stairs after him, to grab his hand, to say she had changed her mind. She would go with him, wherever he had to go.

But the part of her heart that ached with Rylan's departure also stung with the deaths of Rina, the children, and Aric and Tavis. And she knew if she let herself dwell on these sensations, it would tear her apart.

She waited until she could no longer see the top of his dark head before turning from the open window. She had to get out of the room. Rylan's presence was too strong here. If she sat, she would pine. Better to keep her mind busy. She had her own problems to solve before he returned.

Moments later, she strode past the bubbling fountain, scattering a flock of pigeons that had descended on a slim crust of bread. She headed for the Old Quarter and a street that was called the Street of Dreams.

The pavement was uneven, the cobblestones jutting at odd angles. She slowed her pace lest she stumble and turn her ankle. The governor's mansion was at her back. She viewed the neglected condition of the thin row houses around her and was relatively certain His Excellency rarely looked out of his northward windows.

It struck her also that there were no children in this section of the city. Everywhere else she and Rylan traveled, the shouts and giggles of youngsters at play resounded down the long alleyways; rag dolls were perched on open windowsills. But not here. It was as if the Old Quarter had come to embody what its name portended. Only the elderly ambled slowly down its streets.

An ancient woman, her frizzled, gray hair bound up in a dark yellow scarf, sat on a crumbling doorstep clasping a cane in her trembling hand. Rheumy eyes followed Khamsin's approach.

"Blessings upon you, Tanta." Khamsin spoke to the old crone, as she had been taught was proper.

Sagging jowls worked convulsively. "I'm not your Tanta, child!"

"I seek an herbal shop. On this street, perhaps? Is this Windward Lane?

"What street? Windward Lane? You're far from there. It's far away. Far away."

"Or a healer. Do you know of a healer called Ciro?

I've been told he can be found in the Old Quarter. Do you know of him?"

"No. Don't know. Don't know nothing."

"Perhaps if you could tell me of someone I could ask who—"

"No!" The ancient voice rasped. "Don't know. Don't know nothing. Now, go. Go!" And she struck out at Khamsin with her cane.

Khamsin jumped out of her way and stepped back. "Apologies, Tanta, for disturbing you. Blessings of the day." And she left.

A white-haired man and woman, arms laden with cloth-wrapped bundles, started to cross the narrow street just as Khamsin appeared from around a corner. They stopped upon spotting her and hurriedly retraced their steps. Their sunken eyes darted left and right as they blended back into the shadows.

A street sweeper finally pointed her in the right direction. "Windward's three blocks to yer right," he said gruffly. He pulled his knitted cap over his brow and turned away.

She almost missed the narrow alley. The small wooden street sign was warped and faded. The letters were gone; only a worn symbol for the wind remained. She stepped into the shadows. The lane sloped toward the sea. She passed a boot maker's, a tobacconist's, and a rug seller's. Then the lane turned slightly and widened. The narrow, stone buildings here had wooden porches, many with broken railings. Thin curtains fluttered in the windows. This row of buildings was residences, not merchant shops. She smelled the aroma of a vegetable stew. But she saw no one.

Another block and the shabby residences gave way to shuttered shops. A flicker of light on her left drew her. The sign above the door was a carving of a compass. The letters below it spelled out "map maker."

The heavy door was open. A thin man sat bent with his nose almost to the top of the table. Four candelabra on tall stands flanked the table. Their light filled the small shop and spilled out into the dim light of Windward Lane.

Khamsin cleared her throat. "Pardon, sirrah. But could you tell me if there's an herb seller's shop nearby?"

The long plume on the man's pen made short fluttering motions. "Sometimes," he replied, without looking up.

"Sometimes?"

"That's what I said. Sometimes. Sometime there is. Sometimes there's not."

"And when there is, where would this shop be?"

"Where it always is, whether it's there or not."

Khamsin hoped the man's maps were more precise than his answers. "And where is it always?"

"Across from Queenie's Tavern."

"On Windward Lane?"

"Fishbelly."

"Pardon?"

"Fishbelly." The feather plume jerked left and right. His face was still inches from the parchment covering the table. "Fishbelly Street."

"And how far is Fishbelly Street from here?"

"Thirty-seven strides. Or twice a dog run."

Strides? Dog run? The unfamiliar terms were less important than the fact that she wasn't far from her goal. She relayed her thanks to the top of the mapmaker's head, for he had yet to raise his eyes.

She returned to the rutted lane and began to count her steps.

Her strides, she decided at forty-four, must be shorter than the mapmaker's. At fifty-one she saw the sign for Fishbelly Street, and Queenie's Tavern on the corner. On opposite corners were other shops, but none purported to sell herbs.

She had just decided to enter the tavern and ask more questions, when she noticed a narrow door next to the cabinetmaker. A faded moonpetal blossom was stenciled on the front.

She pulled the latch. The door swung open. She stepped into a round, brick courtyard. An ornate metal bench sat next to a second door, directly in front of her.

A sign that read "Moonpetal Herbs and Healing Balms" was propped on the bench. Next to it was another sign. Closed.

She knocked on the door, just in case. There was no answer.

Closed. She'd come all this way, and the herb shop was closed. Perhaps that's what the mapmaker meant. Not that the shop changed locations, or disappeared. But that it was open on an irregular schedule.

She bit back a sigh of disappointment and left the courtyard.

Fishbelly was a wider, and brighter, street than Windward Lane. The sun was almost overhead, and Khamsin stood for a moment, arms folded over her chest, and tried to decide if she should ask more questions, or satisfy the rumblings just now starting in her stomach.

Or possibly, she thought as she stared at the squat corner building that housed Queenie's Tavern, she could do both.

The stone steps were crumbling and worn from the tread of many boots. She wondered briefly, as she stepped inside, if Rylan had ever been here. He'd known of the location of the herb shop. And Queenie's was the first tavern she'd seen on her long walk down Windward Lane.

She pulled a few, small, silver coins from her pocket and laid them on the scarred, wooden table. She hooked her right foot underneath, pulling the low bench toward her. The fieldstone floor beneath her boots was cracked and stained, and there was a pile of gray straw in one corner. She sat, the coins at her fingertips, and waited.

There were three other patrons in the low-ceilinged tavern. The thick, wooden beams were crusted with smoky cobwebs. They glanced disinterestedly at her arrival and she at them, though her appraisal was more thorough. She'd spent much of her life reading illusive messages in flickering elementals. Her eyes were trained to see and record.

Two men in grimy work shirts sat at the table in the corner; one was elderly, the other, a son or nephew, middle-aged. Both had round, flat faces and bulbous noses. The older man's face bore lines of age; the younger, a faint scar across his forehead.

The third man, who sat by himself near the small hearth, was neither middle-aged nor elderly, but somewhere in between. He appeared thin upon first glance, but his ebony-toned forearms were muscular and covered with curly, black hair; his hands were callused. His shoulders weren't hunched like the other two, and his back was straight. A knitted cap was pulled over his ears. He wore a streaked over-tunic, suggesting to Khamsin that he entered the tavern only moments before her and had not yet sufficiently lost the chill in his body to necessitate the removal of his garments. Though the temperature was mild in the city for late autumn, it would be much colder out on the Great Sea. The faint aroma of salt and fish that assailed her as she strode by him told her that was his previous location.

Finally, there was a noise from the back room. A fleshy, pink-faced woman, her gray-streaked hair pulled severely back into a bun, emerged through the dark green curtains. Her bright yellow dress was low-cut, edged in what once was an expensive lace. It showed off an ample amount of the woman's large bosom. A faded, patchwork apron wrapped around her thick waist, its pocket bulging with coin. The woman ambled over to Khamsin's table and leaned one hand on it as she spoke.

"What's yer interest, lad? Come on, I ain't got all day!"

As if it were she and not Khamsin who had been kept waiting for over ten minutes.

"A mug of hot tea and some bread and some cheese, if you have any, mistress."

The older woman leaned closer. "You ain't no lad

and you ain't from 'round here, that's for true."

"No," Khamsin agreed, meeting the dark eyes levelly. "But I'm hungry and would like something to eat."

"Hmpff! Well, pushy little lady, ain't ye now, missy?" But she waddled back to the kitchen, the sight of the coins on the table overriding any personal prejudices.

The tavern-keep brought a small plate and returned to the kitchen. Khamsin ate her small meal in silence. The bread was fresh, better than expected; and the cheese, aged, but with a mellow flavor. The tea, however, was weak and watery. Still, it was hot and felt good in her empty stomach.

She removed her cloak and sat, letting the steam from the mug filter past her face. There was a loud noise behind her, a scraping of a wooden bench backward. She turned to find the father-and-son pair stepping in her direction. She pulled her short hunting knife from its sheath by the time the younger one laid his greasy hand on her shoulder.

"Pardon, sirrah." She disliked his touch.

"Queenie's right. She is a lass!" He leered down at her, the line of his scar pink against his pale skin.

The older man squinted his eyes, deepening the lines on his leathery face. "So she is, so she is." Thin lips parted into a toothless grin.

"I don't see where I'm any concern of yours, sirrahs."

The two exchanged glances. "Don't get many like you in this part of the city," said scar-face, his hand still on her shoulder.

Khamsin tensed her body and suddenly sprang to her

feet. The younger man lost his grip on her. She held the short knife at waist level, not flashing or brandishing it but simply making its presence known.

"Don't play rough with me, girl!" Scar-face reached for her but stopped as a loud, grating voice filled the room.

"All right, all right, you two bastards!" Queenie stood in the doorway, hands on her pudgy hips. "Enough, now. Leave the little missy alone."

"Should've let you take 'em, lass," she added as the two men grumbled their way out the door. "But I just washed me floor, and I didn't want you to get it all dirty."

She plucked a grimy rag from beneath her apron and threw it at the man in the knitted cap, still seated at his table. "And what's wrong with you, captain, lettin' those two get out of hand like that? Where's your sense of kinship? She's Cove people. Can't you hear it in the way she talks?"

"I heard," the dark man replied, folding the towel neatly into a square. "That's why I didn't interfere. She can take care of herself."

Queenie patted Khamsin's head as if she were a stray mongrel. "Well, you can have your peace an' quiet an' privacy back now, lass. We won't be botherin' you. Whatever's brought you up to the city sure don't have nothing to do with the captain and myself."

"Wait." Khamsin took a step in Queenie's direction. "Perhaps you can help. I'm a stranger here, and I need some information. I'm looking for a healer. A man named Ciro. Have you ever heard of him?"

Queenie's dark gaze darted to the captain. "Ciro?

Ciro? Name's got a nice sound to it but I can't say for sure."

"What ails you that you seek a healer?" The captain studied Khamsin for any outward signs of an infirmity.

"Nothing. I'm a healer, myself. I've been instructed to seek him out."

"You?" Queenie's broad face registered surprise.

Khamsin nodded.

"And since when do healers travel as boys and carry knives?"

"Since Hill Raiders attacked my village and killed my husband."

Dark eyes softened. "Ach, lass, 'tis strange times we live in." Queenie's hands fluttered helplessly before her, and she turned, heading for the kitchen. "Let me get you a nice cup of hot tea."

Khamsin took her seat.

"May I join you, lady?" The captain removed his cap. His tightly curled black hair was dotted with silver.

"Please."

Queenie was back with the tea and set the mug before Khamsin. "So it's old Ciro you want, eh?"

"You know him?"

Again, the troubled exchange of glances. "Know *of* him."

"No one else seems to."

The captain dropped his voice. "Everyone knows. Few will admit."

"Where do I find him?"

"You don't. At least, there's no residence that bears

his name. But it's said that, sometimes late at night, he's been seen in the old bell tower at the end of the Street of Dreams. But as to when he will show up there?" The captain shrugged.

"You best not go lookin' for him, lass." It was Queenie. "They say he's quite mad, and you know that means trouble. A mad wizard." She shook her head.

"He's a wizard?"

"But I thought you knew?"

"No. I only knew that I had to find him. His sign was that, well, it wasn't an easy reading, you understand. But I thought I interpreted his sign as a healer. Though the signs are somewhat similar."

Queenie laid fleshy fingers against her lips. "He was a healer, once. But that was a long time ago. Some say he's even older than the Sorcerer."

Older than the Sorcerer. That thought ran through Khamsin's mind as she left Queenie's tavern, after blessing a few of the woman's favorite amulets. Her refusal of money for her services shocked both the tavern-keep and the captain, and Khamsin heard echoes of Rylan's opinion of local healers. But the blessing of minor charms or local healers' financial demands were not her main concerns. She was barely aware of Queenie's gushing thanks as she pulled her cloak about her and stepped out into the night.

Older than the Sorcerer. Then he would be the one who would know.

CHAPTER ELEVEN

The room seemed empty without Rylan. Khamsin sat in the window, watching the moons rise and found herself alternately filled with anticipation and sadness.

Anticipation over finding her teacher, Ciro. Or rather, finding a place where he'd often been seen.

But sadness over the losses that had filled the past year of her life. Tanta Bron, Tavis, Rina, Aric, and the children. And all the others she had known at Cirrus Cove. Familiar faces. Familiar times.

Everything here in Noviiya was distant and strange.

Some hours later, she heard the noises of the inn become muted, with only an occasional thump of a door, or clink of glass. The street below her window was deserted. The lamplighter had long come and gone.

She slipped down the back stairs again into the small garden and took out her amulets and warding stones. She wrote Ciro's name in the dust, then her own sign as a healer. It was more of an announcement than a spell. She wasn't even sure it would work. She'd never tried to contact another healer—or a wizard!—before. Tanta Bron said it was something Khamsin didn't need to know.

The runes for the open calling in the book were vague. Even as she inscribed them, they felt weak.

But perhaps that's because they were spell runes.

She waited. Something shifted over her mage circle, a pulsation of the palest blue. And then it was gone.

She bit back a sigh of disappointment. She'd have to look through the book again. Perhaps realign her warding stones. There was interference, she felt, from Tarkir's stone. It was too powerful, but Tanta Bron never permitted any other placement for Khamsin's circles. Tarkir's stone had to be the primary.

She waved her hand over the circle, and the dust settled back smoothly onto the ground. Amulets went back into her pockets, and the stones were carefully placed in their soft, velvet bags. She was just rising from her knees, when a gust of hot wind buffeted her face. She looked up quickly. The moons were gone. A large, dark shape plummeting toward her was all she could see.

She was on her feet, knife in her hand. Her throat was suddenly dry.

Then the moons appeared again, and the dark shape arced away and settled on the top of the low wall. There was the ruffle of feathers and the sharp scrabble of claws against stone.

A crow. A large black crow, larger than the one that had frightened her and Nixa at the market.

"Do you bring me a message?" she whispered. But the crow didn't answer, and she sensed no spellbinding as she sought his bird essence.

Yet there was something . . . almost a foul smell about the bird. No doubt it feasted on dead fish and carrion. The odor of rotting fish brought to mind the old man in a cape as dark as the crow's feathers, his claw-like hand reaching for her that day in Cirrus Cove. A lecherous drunk, filthy from sleeping in debris.

Or was he, like the crow, a well-disguised specter, a minion of a greater power?

She slipped her left hand into her pocket and rolled one of her amulets between her fingers. If there were magic here, perhaps the amulet would sense it, bring it to her by touch.

But the amulet resonated nothing. Not even crow essence. Nothing.

As if the crow wasn't really there.

"What do you want?" she asked it quietly.

It turned its large head from her and pecked at the round stones of the wall, as if seeking an insect or small hidden rodent.

Then it shook its feathers again, took two short hops, and sprang into the air. Its large wings beat furiously, and in seconds it was out of sight, lost in the shadows of the rooftops.

Khamsin brought her sword out of the cupboard when she returned to the room, and slept with it, and Nixa, by her side.

❆ ❆ ❆

She rose late after a night of fitful sleep. She brought a pot of tea back to the room and, making sure the door was secured, brought out the book and laid it on the floor.

She had a lot of studying to do.

She took supper in her room as well. It was just after sunset that she and Nixa left the inn and headed toward the Old Quarter.

Nixa bounded ahead and would have been lost in the thick shadows of the night but for the mental contact Khamsin kept with the gray cat. After a day of being confined, the feline needed the feel of the wind through her fur, and she scampered, halted, and scampered again, stopping only to sniff at an unfamiliar doorstep or a pile of dog dung.

Khamsin, too, kept up a brisk pace, no longer as interested in her surroundings as she was in her destination: the bell tower. At the end of the Street of Dreams.

The captain told her that the dilapidated structure was the tallest in the Old Quarter. Probably in Noviiya itself, save for the governor's mansion—which Rylan told her was six stories. The bell tower matched the height of the Temple of Merkara, which was five stories, and located at the end of Pier Street. But the bell tower had no stories, save for a ground floor and a top floor with a winding staircase connecting the two.

The view from the top floor was breathtaking even late at night. It was worth the treacherous climb up the crumbling stone steps that spiraled up the interior walls of the tower. To the north and northeast, the tower looked out over the Great North Sea and all the heavens. To the south and southwest, the city. A panorama of lights sparkled through patches of darkness. Khamsin stood for a moment, arms wrapped around her waist, and wished it were Rylan who held her, instead. Probably he'd seen this view a hundred times, or one just like it in his travels. Still she felt a need to share it with him. She promised herself she would, when he came back.

She walked slowly around the circular top floor that was punctured by a hole through which the bell ropes descended to the ground. The bells were gone. Khamsin stopped at the edge of the shaft, tilting her head back, and gazed straight up at the great cross beams above her. Their only occupants now were the city's pigeons.

A fine feast for Nixa, had she not been relegated to the duty of guard on the ground floor. The door to the tower was locked and bolted; though with its reputation as being haunted intruders were not a serious problem. Khamsin unlocked the door with the proper spell, securing it again after they entered. But felt safer with the night-eyed feline crouched at the foot of the stairs.

She stayed almost until dawn, watching, waiting, occasionally levitating a cluster of pigeon feathers for practice, swirling them in a circle or marching them in a line across the floor. It kept her mind occupied and kept thoughts of a dark-haired man from seeping through. She missed his company more than she thought she would and consoled herself with the stories they'd share when he returned.

If he returned, a small voice said. She pushed the thought away.

No one appeared to interrupt her reverie. Not even

the pigeons overhead seemed the least bit interested that the healer from Cirrus Cove was in the bell tower at the end of the Street of Dreams.

She and Nixa left at dawn accompanied by the clatter of chickens and the calling of voices through open windows in the early morn.

The next day was Reverence, the end of the week. It was the day when shops and stores traditionally shut down in observance with religious requirements, allowing Noviiyads to don their best and spend some time in prayer in the temple of their choosing. There were three temples in the city: the Temple of Merkara, the God of the Sea, appropriately enough on Pier Street; the Temple of Ixari, the Goddess of the Heavens, across from the governor's mansion; and the largest, Tarkir's Shrine, a few streets west of the Old Quarter, where those who recognized the great powers of the Land and the Underworld could pay homage. The god, Tarkir, was the husband/brother of Ixari and, just as the sky and the earth met, but never intertwined, the two religious factions coexisted. But just barely.

Khamsin chose to pay her respects to Merkara early in the morning, her heritage being that of the Cove and the Sea. Then at mid-morning she lit candles in Ixari's temple. One for Tanta Bron and one for Rylan. She prayed for the sky goddess to watch over them both.

She avoided Tarkir's Shrine, even though the powerful dark god was often favored by healers and others who worked with mystical realms. The deaths at Cirrus Cove still weighed too heavily upon her to ask for favors from the god the Hill Raiders also worshipped.

Then wrapping her tan cloak around her, for it was a chillier day than Noviiya had seen in a time, she and Nixa made their way toward the Street of Dreams.

But Reverence produced nothing more than the previous night and neither did the next three nights following into midweek, save for an aching back and a feeling of disorientation due to the disruption of her sleeping schedule. She took to catnapping, literally, with Nixa in the afternoons before stopping in to see Queenie and the captain. She either ate supper there or purchased it and took it back to the tower to share with Nixa and a pitifully thin brown dog they had recently befriended.

And so it went even past midweek, until Reverence was again only one sunrise away. The mad wizard Ciro was still nothing more than an illusive legend.

Rylan the Tinker, too, failed to reappear. She checked with Master Verney personally on several occasions. A week, the dark-haired man had said. Perhaps two. Well, she had now one week behind her. The loneliness hadn't diminished as the days went by. Neither had the memory of the warmth of his touch.

She stopped at the Temple of Merkara on her way back to the inn. She almost collided with the captain on the steps after the sunrise services.

"There are other healers," he advised, after commenting on the shadows under her eyes. "Why don't you seek them out instead?"

But Khamsin shook her head, knowing that what the runes instructed couldn't be altered. Ciro was the one.

Her dreams that afternoon were strangely troubling,

the strain on her body taking its toll. She tossed and turned in the soft bed in the room she had occupied with the tinker, disrupting Nixa. The cat sought the safety of the windowsill on which to snooze. Twice, she called out for Rylan as if her body remembered the magic his touch could work. Then she settled into a deep slumber.

Just as the shopkeepers filtered out into the streets, heading home for their evening meals, Khamsin awoke with a start, trembling and in a cold sweat. Danger. It was all she could remember of her dream, if a dream indeed it was. Danger. Terror. Darkness.

That night her sword hung from her belt as she and Nixa climbed the worn steps of the bell tower. Had she unsheathed it in the darkness, it would glow with a faint blue light of enchantment. But she kept it hidden for more reasons that just her lack of knowledge on how to use it. True, she'd given the instructions for its forging, and true, she placed the proper spells within its heart. But the power it now possessed was one that was far beyond her experience. She could call upon it. But wasn't quite sure what would happen when she did.

A light tap-tap-tap-tap interrupted her thoughts. She reached out to stroke the scruffy head of Nixa's new friend, the stray brown dog. His tail kept a private rhythm on the stone floor, his belly now pleasantly full from his share of cheese and bread. Unlike the odd crow, which never reappeared, the dog's animal essence was easy to read. Grateful emotions emanated from his mind into hers, and she smiled. He knew a soft heart when he saw one.

She had hoped, on the first day she had befriended

the animal, that he had had better bloodlines or training. A hunter or a retriever, perhaps, which could have been useful to her. Nixa's size did limit her capabilities, and Khamsin was reluctant to experiment with more advanced spells on the feline. But the dog's mind was simple, very simple, perhaps due to poor nutrition as a pup. She accepted his existence because he needed her. And because Nixa seemed to like him.

The dog stood and shook himself, his ears flapping rapidly. Nixa batted at him playfully, and he gave a small snort, then trotted down the stairs. The cat followed him part way then returned. The dog wasn't interested in playing, and Nixa preferred to stay with her mistress.

Khamsin broke the last of the bread into small pieces to feed to the feline. Nixa chewed delicately, and then sat and began her usual ritual of an after-meal bath.

Suddenly, the cat bolted. Too late, Khamsin became aware of a foul stench filling the air, surrounding her, choking her. She rose up on one knee, her hand on the hilt of her sword. There was a flash, a bright fiery light in the center of the room where the bell-cords once were. She fell backward, as if the light alone pushed her against the wall.

She was blinded, could see nothing but a diffuse orange glow. She groped for her sword, pulling it from its covering. The pale color of blue was added before her, pulsing almost as hard as her heart pounding in her chest.

Then, all was dark save for her sword and two red orbs that smoldered like embers above her, moving closer.

She struggled to her feet. "Name thyself!"

A hot wind whipped around her and closed upon her

face like a hand, smothering. She coughed, the stench almost unbearable. She brought the sword up higher between herself and the approaching red eyes.

"Name thyself!" Her hands trembled and not from the weight of the sword.

Then she saw it. It stepped into a shaft of moonlight. It took all her training to stifle the scream of terror rising in her throat. A demon. A hell-spawned creature bred for deformities, weaned on the sludge that oozed from the graveyards in the Black Swamp. It stood twice her size. Its face was a grotesque carving of a lidless and lipless creature: eye sockets vacant but burning; mouth, a cavern of sharp, yellowed fangs. Its tongue, slit and pointed like a snake's, dangled from between its teeth. A slimy mucus slid down it, sizzling as it impacted against the cold, stone floor.

Long arms covered with slime-matted hair reached out for her. Webbed-fingers flexed, beckoning. She angled the sword in its direction.

"Cease, creature of hell! By the powers of Ixari I command thee, that thine eyes that see and thine ears that hear, now obey. *"T'cahra fie diraheira."* She recited the ancient words. *"T'cahra fie diraheira, fie daremai!"*

The Beast wavered, but only slightly. For four heartbeats it stood, facing her, less than two sword-lengths away.

"I t'cahra chimour s'fai a raima, s'fai a fi." Khamsin began the chant that would unleash the power of the sword, her voice hushed to a whisper. *"I t'cahra . . ."* she started again but never finished. The demon lunged, its huge, hulking form suddenly all she saw.

CHAPTER TWELVE

It was mostly instinct; instinct and training from her childhood days at the Cove that made Khamsin drop to her knees. She folded herself into a ball and rolled to one side as the demon lunged for her. Its clawed hands barely missed her face. She felt the intense heat from its body as it plunged past her. Its stench was overpowering. Her stomach spasmed. She tasted bile, but fought to keep herself under control.

Instantly, she was on her feet again, her sword grasped securely as she faced the creature. It lashed out toward her with a frenzy. She countered its attack with the sword. The upper floor of the tower was showered in blue sparks every time the demon's claws grazed the spellbound metal. Again, it came at her, lunging lower this time, compensating for her diminutive stature. She struck out and down, feeling a sickening thump as metal met flesh. The demon screamed a terrifying, earsplitting shriek. It wrenched itself away, leaving a large clump of matted flesh dangling from the tip of her sword. She shook it free, disgust evident on her face.

But its wound was simply an irritation that healed before her eyes. It moved on all fours, swaying then darting, first to her left, then to her right. It tried to force her toward the rope shaft in the center of the room.

Khamsin longed for enough space, enough time to release one hand from the sword and barrage the demon with elementals. Not fire, but water, holy water gathered from the mists of the moons. But the creature gave her no peace, lunging with its powerful hind legs.

She backed up, very aware of her proximity to the shaft. She slashed out again. The demon skittered back. But only just short of her reach.

Then, she heard a word she'd heard only once before, in Tanta Bron's cave, heavily warded with spells of protection. A word she'd read only on one page of the book. And dreaded the next time it was spoken.

"Ki-a-sid-ir-a," the demon breathed.

Khamsin shuddered.

"No." She shook her head, as if she could deny the name *he* would call her by.

"Ki-a-sid-ir-a."

'No!" she screamed. She lashed out blindly with her sword. *He* would not get her, would not claim her, as long as there was a breath left in her body. She felt the sword strike something. For a moment all was still, frozen. Then, all was movement. The sword was ripped from her hands and sent plunging down the shaft, out of her reach. She fell backward, one leg caught beneath the other, her hands scraping raw against the rough stone floor.

The demon sprang. She closed her eyes and screamed.

Then there was silence. Only the sound of her own heartbeat in her ears told Khamsin she was still alive.

She opened her eyes. In the misty darkness that floats through the air just before dawn, she saw the smoldering ashes of the creature sprawled across the floor next to her, tendrils of acrid smoke curling white in the air.

"You should never have let go of the sword, young lady." A voice said. A man's voice, with the crackle and huskiness of age.

Khamsin sat upright. Her heart pounded, her skin cold and clammy. She stared into pale silver eyes set deeply into a thin, lined face. White hair curled in wispy ringlets to bony shoulders. Equally as bony elbows and knees poked through a dark red robe woven of a rich fabric. A gnarled hand held her sword. The old man sitting on the top step didn't look strong enough to make it up the stairs of the bell tower, let alone vanquish a demon. And he looked far too affable to be the Sorcerer. She took several breaths before speaking.

"What happened?" she stammered.

"It appears you had a rather unpleasant encounter with a demon."

"Unpleasant?" She was still gulping air. "And you killed it."

"Killed it? No, no, no, dear child. One does not *kill*

demons." He patted the floor then motioned for her to join him on the step. "One simply returns them to the nearest available hell."

"Yes, m'lord, I realize that." Cautiously, she joined him on the stairs. "But what I meant was . . ."

"I know. I know what you meant. Allow an old man his meanderings, will you?" He smiled, the tip of his long nose turning downward. "And this 'm'lord' business. 'Tis nonsense. The name's Ciro. Just Ciro. Been good enough for four hundred and fifty years. Should do fine now."

"Ciro!" His name burst from her lips with more exuberance than she'd intended. She blushed. "I'm, I'm sorry, m'lord. It's just that I've been looking for you!"

"Which is what I thought, but one can never be too sure." He waggled a knobby finger in her face.

"Then, why did you wait to send that thing," and she gestured toward the cooling pile of ashes, "back to where it came from? Was this some kind of test?"

"Do you mean did I conjure that demon? By love of Ixari, no! But had to make sure just whose side you're on. Your response to it gave me my answer."

"Whose side I'm on?"

"You've been asking questions about me in the Old Quarter. I have to be careful. Lots of trickery abounds now, these days. Tarkir's children are misbehaving again."

"I know. That's why I'm here. I'm a healer. I've been seeking a teacher. Your name appeared in my mage circle."

" 'Twas my name you saw, eh? I'm flattered, young lady . . . now, what did your fiery companion say your name was?"

"He called me, well, that's not my name. My name's Khamsin. Khamsin of Cirrus Cove."

The wizard stood and handed the sword back to her. He brushed invisible specks of dust from his long robes. "Come along, little Khamsin. We have much to accomplish. You couldn't have gotten here a little sooner, could you? I was about to die of starvation!"

"Starvation?"

"Of course! Can't survive on one meal a day of crusts of dry bread and some cheese, now can I?" He held his hands up comically before her in his best imitation of the bedraggled brown dog she'd befriended.

✳ ✳ ✳

Ciro's rooms were in the loft of a warehouse in the Old Quarter, not far from the bell tower. At one time, the warehouse was a luxurious residence, and he lived on the top floor as was befitting his status as high priest of the Temple of Ixari. But that was two hundred and fifty years ago, shortly after the Sorcerer was born, and Ciro and Ixari had quarreled. In fact, Ixari spoke to no one for a long time, and the temple fell to ruins.

So, in fact, did Ciro's residence. A wealthy land baron finally renovated it into a warehouse, and Ciro was forced to move into the attic. Much of the ornately carved furnishings that graced the chambers of his former residence were now crammed into the top floor that was sectioned off into three small chambers and one large great room. Paintings were stacked haphazardly in several corners; odd bits of statuary served as paperweights, bookmarks and, in the case of a particularly large piece depicting a forest animal with multi-flanged antlers, a clothes valet.

Interspersed with the artwork were jars and vials filled with brightly colored liquids, pouches of crumpled herbs, and several well-worn leather-bound volumes with gold runes etched in their bindings. A large mage circle was carved into the floor before the hearth with a solitary candle, unlit, at the center. The embers in the fireplace, however, still glowed warmly, diminishing the chill that threatened to seep in through the windows. A half-empty bottle of wine sat on the table nearby. Evidently, the fire was sometimes not enough to create the illusion of warmth.

The cold dampness that flowed over the Old Quarter from the Great Sea wasn't the only problem with Ciro's residence. There was the problem of gaining entry. The attic-loft of the warehouse was simply a space between the roof and the ceiling of the two-story building; there were no stairs leading up, as the building's sole occupant had no need for stairs. So Khamsin's first lesson involved dematerializing herself and her cat and reappearing in Ciro's attic.

She listened closely to his instructions and got it right on the first try.

"Flashy little trick. Comes in handy at boring

government parties." Ciro handed a slice of cheese to Khamsin, who had just appeared by the long table in the center of the room. "You seem to have an affinity for this stuff. Never cared either way, myself. All cheeses taste the same to me. Now, a meat pie . . ." He licked his thin lips, and suddenly a hurt expression crossed his face. "You never did bring me a meat pie, you know. Don't you know dogs like meat?"

Khamsin flipped her palm up, down, then up again and a small, brown-crusted pastry appeared. She handed it to Ciro. "Just baked."

"Where'd you steal this from?"

"The bakery across the street."

"Hmpf!" He nibbled on the crust, pulling off a piece to throw to Nixa, who was preening herself on top of a stack of books in the corner. "When you can pull this off the table of the governor himself, then I'll be impressed."

But all her lessons were not so frivolous or quite so easy. Ciro, for all his light retorts, was a stern taskmaster, stopping her in the middle of a complicated incantation, pulling her abruptly and painfully out of her trance because the inflection of one syllable in a word was not perfect.

"Not 'ay-neel-la la-sa-rah'!" he would bellow, his bushy white brows drawn into a frown. *"Le* sa-rah! *Le* sa-rah!"

Tired and aching, she had repeated the spell again.

Later, he handed her a glass of deep red wine. She sipped it slowly, and feeling its warmth throughout her body, she thought of Rylan the Tinker. It had been more than three weeks since he left. Fool's Eve had passed. She doubted now that she would see him again. Perhaps there was a wife waiting for him in Browner's Grove, though her discreet inquiries to Master Verney, when she informed the innkeeper she'd no longer need the room, revealed nothing. She left word with the balding man, though, lest the tinker return. He could contact her through Queenie, in the Old Quarter. She didn't think he'd believe her, if she said her new residence was in an abandoned warehouse.

Ciro rapped on the table with the pestle he used to grind herbs. It caught her attention, and she turned away from the west window.

"You're looking pensive, again. Thoughts, Khamsin?"

She shrugged. "Past."

"Hmpf. Too much in the present to worry about. Past. Past."

He explained the present to her during her first lessons, describing the ongoing battle. This "infernal, eternal war," he called it, between Tarkir's children, the man she called "the Sorcerer," who reigned from Traakhal-Armin, and his siblings: Lucial the Wizard and Melande the Witch. They were the ones meddling with the volatile Hill people, using them to steal infants from which to mold their armies of demons.

Khamsin shuddered and thought of Rina's last child, Willar, who she helped bring into the world. His cradle was empty.

Now, other questions came to mind.

"Ciro, why didn't Ixari summon the healers together when all this started happening, two hundred years ago? Surely, their combined magics could have halted this 'war'?"

"What, the more the merrier, Khamsin?" Ciro shook his head. "No, child. That's not the way it all works. A hundred healers casting the wrong spell are not more powerful than one healer casting the wrong spell. It's still the wrong spell."

She regarded him patiently. Ciro rarely answered any question with a simple "yes" or "no."

"Any more than a locked door can be better opened by one hundred of the wrong keys," he continued, pulling out another obscure example. "A handful of wrong keys is still a handful of wrong keys. But the right key, ah, that's the one! And only one. Do you understand?"

She stared out the window again for a long time before answering. In an odd way, she did. She heard echoes of Tanta Bron in Ciro's words. "Yes. But, is there only one proper key?"

"In this matter, yes. But it's one thing to be the proper key to the door. It's another to have the power to understand the knowledge that lies behind it. Then again . . ." and he shrugged. "I only know what the runes have foretold. That a girl child would be born in the midst of a storm. And that the signs upon her birth would confirm that she was a chosen one."

He looked at her, his gaze suddenly sharp and penetrating. "But then, I'm sure you've heard this before."

She took a sip of wine. Its warmth coated the slight frisson of fear that went through her at his words. She was raised with Tanta Bron's stories. With her warnings. But that was Tanta Bron, who was always telling her to be careful about this or that.

And the dreaded assignation. That never happened, did it? She was visited by much terror this past year, but not by the Sorcerer.

Yet here was Ciro, a stranger, albeit a wizard, saying the same words that Tanta Bron had. The child born in the midst of the storm. The child *he* would want.

"You know who I am?" she asked timidly.

He nodded. "I know what I've sensed in you from the first time we met. You've been marked by powers much greater than mine. The hand of Ixari lies surely upon your shoulders. But the strength of the Khal is there as well."

"Tanta Bron insisted I place Tarkir's stone as primary in all my circles."

"Wise woman. She protected you well. Well enough that even I couldn't discern who you are, Khamsin. Only that you walk a path that only a chosen one could walk."

She asked one of the questions Tanta Bron never answered. "Why, Ciro? Why me? Is it because I'm a halfling, because my father was a Hill Raider?"

"Your father wasn't a Hill Raider."

Khamsin turned, shocked. "But the raid! My mother was raped during the raid!"

"That may very well be, child, but the blood in your

veins is pure Raheiran. Witch-blood, if you like. Look in the mirror, Khamsin, and tell me every time your eyes change color that you're not Raheiran. Hmpf!"

Raheiran. Like Tanta Bron. But the old healer never told her that. Only that her mother was the captain's daughter who left Cirrus Cove after Khamsin was born. And her father, an unknown Hill Raider. Did Tanta Bron not know? Or did she lie?

The sun settled behind the mountains in the west. The reflection of the candles on Ciro's table flickered in the windowpanes. Khamsin's own reflection was there, too, though vague and uneven, as if her identity were no longer sure.

She swung back to face Ciro. The world she knew was falling apart. She needed answers, for suddenly she had hundreds of questions.

"Was my father a healer?"

"It's possible, but I can't say for sure. And before you ask, no, I don't know who he was. Only that you are Raheiran by your father's blood."

"But, there must also be others with Raheiran blood. Yourself for one!"

"I wasn't born eighteen years past in the midst of a storm."

"But someone else was! There are many Cove towns, dozens of inland villages. Surely . . ."

"More wrong keys, Khamsin?" He sighed loudly. "I can't answer your questions, child, and not because I don't want to. But my powers aren't what they once were, it seems. And all this turbulence from this constant battling!" He waved his hand through the air. "It interferes with my readings."

As it interfered for a long time with hers. She gazed at the mage circle in Ciro's hearthside floor and wondered what kind of power lay behind this knowledge that was now being so carefully guarded by the gods themselves?

As if in answer, the candle on the table suddenly sputtered, then extinguished itself as a draft chilled the large room. Khamsin shivered. She and Ciro exchanged glances.

"Ciro?" she questioned, seeing a concern on the lined face she thought was inappropriate. After all, this was an old warehouse and one often buffeted by winds from the Great North Sea.

He shook his head. "Strange times," was all he said, cautiously.

Three nights later, however, Khamsin returned after sharing her evening meal with Queenie and the captain to find Ciro's comments considerably more expansive.

"Those ill-mannered, interfering bastards!" He paced feverishly in front of the long table, and the sound of glass, crunching underfoot was heard. "Meddlesome sons of bitches!"

Khamsin drew in her breath, sharply, and stared at the floor near Ciro's boots. Someone, or something, smashed the last few bottles of Ciro's favorite wine over the mage circle. The thick, red liquid now flowed over the etched surface like streams of blood.

"What happened?"

"What happened, what happened?" The ancient mage puffed. "Damned if I know. Go out for a stroll, I do. I'm allowed, at my age, to do such things. Come back and see this!" He waved his arm over the mess on the floor, his long sleeves billowing with the force of the movement.

"Desecration!" He spat out the word. "But worse, such a waste of good wine. Those bottles were over fifty years old, child. Fifty years old! The last of the harvest. Damn, impudent fools!"

Khamsin poked gingerly at a piece of green glass with her foot. "Pranks, maybe? A healer who . . ."

"Healer, you say? Child, show me a healer who can gain entry to Master Ciro's, and I'll show you a healer who isn't a healer, but a wizard. Or maybe," and he let the words halt there as he considered whether to voice his speculation. "Or maybe, even a Sorcerer."

This time Khamsin shivered, and there was no draft whistling through the cracks in the brickwork. "Surely, Ciro, not . . ."

"No, no. Well, this kind of thing is not his style, that's for sure. Still, these are strange times." He sank down into a nearby chair. His shoulders sagged under the thick fabric of his robe as if his four hundred and fifty years weighed very heavily upon him.

"I don't know what to make of this, Khamsin of Cirrus Cove. Truly, I do not know."

CHAPTER THIRTEEN

"When?" Khamsin bolted upright in her seat in the corner of Queenie's Tavern. She dropped her spoon into the steaming bowl of vegetable stew the captain just placed before her.

The dusky man eased onto the bench across from her and put his own bowl on the mottled surface. The line of his mouth was grim. The news he brought disturbed him greatly as well. He shook his head.

"Yesterday, or perhaps the day before, best I can tell. Heard it from a trader ship, a fast vessel that docked this morning. They saw the smoke and fire from where they were, off the coast. Their captain took a look with a spyglass, and it's as I told you. Browner's Grove's near been destroyed. Taken by Hill Raiders. And demons, some say."

"That's impossible. It can't be!" Her hand dropped to Nixa, seated by her side. The cat rubbed her ears against Khamsin's cold fingers.

"I'm sorry, lady. Did you have kin there?"

"Not really. A friend, a very dear friend, often had reason to travel through there, and I hope . . ." her voice trailed off, as a numbness crept over her. Perhaps Rylan hadn't returned because he couldn't. Perhaps he'd been in Browner's Grove. Trapped.

She should have been there. She should have gone with him. She could have used elementals. Her sword.

She stood abruptly. "I have to go."

"Go?" Queenie had ambled over, a basket of hot, braided breadsticks in her hand. "Go? But, child, ye ain't et nothin' and . . ."

"I'm sorry, Queenie. But I have to. I have to talk to someone about this."

She threw her cape over her shoulders with a quick movement, then gathered Nixa into her arms. She hurried out into the light rain that had been falling since midday. Any other time, she would've walked the few short blocks to Ciro's warehouse, even in the rain. She enjoyed the sensation of the mist on her skin. And Nixa liked to prance around the puddles.

But not tonight. She stepped down a side alley and, under the cover of the thick shadows, whispered the spell that would transport her and the cat immediately back to the room on the top floor.

She blurted out the news as she materialized in front of the fireplace.

The old man sighed heavily. "The Witch Melande's been known to cause trouble in Browner's before. But

I thought, after the last time, well . . . perhaps we should've tried to interfere. But I'm wary, so wary of tipping my hand, as they say in that palace. If he realizes . . ."

"But he knows!" interrupted Khamsin. She released Nixa. The cat sought the warmth of Ciro's hearth. "He didn't complete the assignation but he knows I'm in Noviiya. The demon he sent, it knew my name. The time had passed for a calling, but I *felt* it, Ciro, when it said it!"

Ciro pondered her words before speaking. "Time is growing short," he said, just as Tanta Bron had many times told Khamsin. "You know as well as I do that in less than two months the Land will begin its turn toward First Thaw. That means it must pass through Wintertide. And you know what that portends."

She knew Wintertide, and all the tragedies it brought, only too well.

"I've no right to ask this of you, child, but that name, the one you guard so carefully. It may be the key we need to find the answer we seek: how to put a stop to this infernal war before all the Land crumbles under its hatred."

"How can my name make such a difference?"

"It represents you as one of the chosen ones. Words have power; you know that. Names, especially a name given by rune sign, have even more."

"But Tanta Bron told me to keep it secret . . ."

"Until the proper time. Didn't she also tell you that?"

167

Khamsin nodded slowly. "I always thought it had something to do with the claiming when I was born. Or the assignation he placed on me. I didn't think there was any other purpose."

"Just because the assignation never happened before your eighteenth birthday, doesn't mean you can put aside your destiny. Your life path as one of the chosen ones, as a Raheiran, is still there. Following that path starts with acknowledging who you really are."

Khamsin started to open her mouth, but the old mage jumped from his seat.

"No!" He moved quickly round the room, warding, touching his hands to the doors and the windows, closing books and receptacles. He even re-corked the wine bottle lest something slip in, or out.

Lastly, he took a piece of embroidered black satin and placed it over the circle. He nodded to the young girl in boy's clothing.

"Kiasidira," she said softly. "I'm Kiasidira."

The north wind, which had been blowing against the windows steadily all afternoon, suddenly stilled.

Ciro closed his eyes, and his hands began to tremble.

The sight shook Khamsin. "Ciro, what does my name mean?"

"You don't know, child?"

"No. Yes. I mean, I understand I'm the one he would seek. The chosen one. Tanta Bron told me that. But you said there have been others, in the past. I don't understand why my being Kiasidira . . ."

"Then, it's best I don't tell you until it's time."

He worked feverishly on her instruction after that, testing her skills by creating mock-demons and fiery elementals that barraged her at random. Time and again she was forced to draw her sword and strike out at her "enemies," vanquishing them with the words that rolled easily off her tongue. Khamsin and the sword were one now, and she cast spells with it, into it, and through it.

Ciro also taught her to create a perfect visual duplicate of the sword, advising her to always leave more than one sword lying around when she didn't have the enchanted weapon strapped to her side. Woe be the wizard who was undone by the fingers of a petty thief!

Then there came the day she materialized at Ciro's table, and for once, nothing came screaming across the great room after her. There was just Ciro and Nixa and a square, wooden, jewel case, metal-strapped and locked.

He pushed it toward her. "Open it."

She touched the lock lightly, springing it, and prepared herself for any manner of banshee that might come howling from its interior. She lifted the lid slowly. There was only a rolled piece of parchment and some trinkets of a base metal inside.

"Go ahead." He nodded.

She pulled out the parchment and laid it carefully against the table as she unrolled it. It was a map of the Land, and she read the names of towns she knew: Wallow's Cove and Dram, Bright's Cove, and her own, Cirrus. There were the Hill towns of Favon and Flume and their most recent conquest, Browner's Grove. There was Noviiya, much larger in the northern corner, and graphic notations of mountains, forests, and swamps.

There was also the Khal, the bottomless lake of black waters. And on the mountainous peninsula that penetrated its darkness, Traakhal-Armin. The castle of the Sorcerer.

Ciro laid his finger on the accursed name. "There is where you must go, Khamsin of Cirrus Cove. To Traakhal. There is the lock that only you, as the key, can open."

He splayed his hand over the map. "In the east tower of the castle, there's a room that no mortal has ever entered. In the center of this room is a mage circle carved into the floor of polished marble and inlaid with pure gold. In the center of the circle is a crystal orb within a pedestal.

"It's this orb that's the center of the war that now scars the Land, with rapes and burnings and senseless death. And you are the key to this orb. Possession of it grants unlimited knowledge."

"The Sorcerer has this orb?"

"Yes. He states it's Tarkir's gift to him. But Lucial and Melande say it's theirs, also. They stole it once. That was before Traakhal was built. And, in a way, why Traakhal was built. To protect the orb."

She shook her head. "If it's safe from them in Traakhal, then why . . ."

"It's not Traakhal that's stopping them. Not even that fortress castle can withstand their combined powers. Something much stronger than the castle protects the orb."

Ciro pointed his index finger and traced a circle on the tabletop. "The circle around the orb is fused with impenetrable wardings. It took the Sorcerer twenty years to create it under Tarkir's instruction. Twenty years in which it's been said he never left the tower room, so intense were his incantations."

He stabbed at random points in the circle he'd traced. "Now, there are twelve rune stones in a mage circle, as you know. In his, every rune stone is a carved gemstone. And each gem alone has the power to destroy a city larger than Noviiya."

"But then, how could I gain access? I'm just . . . I don't have those kinds of powers."

"Perhaps you don't. Perhaps you do. But you are Kiasidira. It is written that only two beings can cross through the golden mage circle around the orb and live. One is the Sorcerer. The other," and Ciro looked directly at her, "is Kiasidira."

She sat back in her chair, her eyes wide.

"You could take control of the orb, Khamsin. No one could stop you, if you can gain entry to that room in the east tower. And you could settle who could use it, and for what, right then and there. Or you could choose to destroy it. So that it no longer is the center of this war.

"But no matter what your choice, know you'll be faced with the powers of Lucial, Melande, and the Sorcerer. The Sorcerer is in control now. But Lucial and Melande want it badly. Enough to cause this turmoil around us."

"And I have to decide who rightfully controls the orb?"

"Yes. The orb should guide you in this. But know that if you choose one to share control with you, you will leave behind two others who will be very angry. And very powerful."

Khamsin sat for a long time, her eyes blending from silver to blue to deep green as they remained fixed on a point on the map.

Traakhal-Armin.

"Why didn't he kill me when I was born? Then he'd be the only one who could cross the circle. The only one to use the orb." She spoke as if the very act of speaking drained her.

"Because I believe he knows that Kiasidira could also be a powerful ally. You understand that Lucial and Melande represent one side. He represents the other. Of course, he's the more powerful. Firstborn, he always would be. But perhaps they're wearing him down. He's reaching three hundred and fifty or so, you know. Began to feel a bit peaked myself at that age."

"So all this, all this death, is about possession of the orb?" She didn't try to hide the note of anguish in her voice.

"And power. Isn't that what they're all about, child? Power. Really, I could guess this is nothing more than a common case of sibling rivalry. Except that the siblings are anything but common."

The thought of sorcerers and demigods having tantrums like petulant children could almost be an amusing one to Khamsin, were the situation not so serious. And now, so personal.

"But if he seeks an alliance, as you say, then why not do so openly? With you, Ciro, or with us?"

"He and I have met, on occasion," Ciro admitted. At Khamsin's interested glance, he continued. "But understand that I represent the Temple of Ixari. He is Tarkir's son."

Khamsin frowned. Ixari and Tarkir were husband and wife. Why would Tarkir's son not view Ciro as an ally?

"He is Tarkir's son," Ciro explained, seeing her confusion. "But he isn't Ixari's."

The gods, too, had their bastards.

"I was raised to pray to Merkara and Ixari," Khamsin noted, answering her own earlier question. "My circles, like yours, carry their symbols."

"Perhaps that's what kept the assignation from occurring."

Khamsin had a fleeting vision of a peak-faced, white-haired man in gold-embroidered black robes suddenly appearing within her circle, a claw-like hand held out toward her, thin lips parting into a sneer. Would she ally herself with that? She shuddered.

"But that's only a supposition." Ciro nodded. "Hopefully, you'll learn more as you approach Traakhal. The Land, I would imagine, fairly bubbles with intrigue there."

"When?" It was the question she dreaded.

"Ah, now that's one of the few things I do know for certain. Before Wintertide. Yes, it must be before Wintertide, though why I don't know. Only that the timing is important. That gives you a little more than a month, Khamsin. And you have a ways to travel. I recommend you prepare to leave Noviiya sometime in the next two days."

She was stunned. "Two days?" She glanced around the attic. "But what will I need, what do I take with me? How?"

"Easy, easy, child. All this I'll tell you before you go."

"You're not coming with me?"

He looked sad. "Oh, but for the adventure of it! And to be in the company of a lovely, young lass, again. Truly I would if I could. But it's not written that way.

"No, it's you, alone. Nixa, though, would not be considered an interference." And he scratched the gray cat's ears whose eyes were now as wide as her mistress's.

CHAPTER FOURTEEN

Khamsin unrolled the long, brittle chart Ciro handed her and shook her head. There was no making easy sense of this! She followed a few of the lineages and tried to match the names and the towns.

The chart represented the genealogy of the Hill Raiders. There were three main tribes: the Magrisi, the Fav'lhir and the Khalar. These tribe names long ago became synonymous with great regions of the Land upon which they staked their claim.

The Fav'lhir originated to the south, centering upon a small town there known as "Favon." The Magrisi ruled the plains southeast of the Khal. It was Magrisi tribesmen, with their red-bordered leather vests, that had ridden into Cirrus Cove eighteen years ago at Wintertide.

The Khalar had the largest landholding. Their camp-sites, called "nests," were sprinkled throughout

Darkling Forest, west of Noviiya, and through the mountains surrounding Traakhal-Armin. And, as the name implied, the Khal. The Kemmons within the Khalar held the hills and forests from Browner's Grove to the Black Swamp. And there was no doubt as to their allegiance to the Sorcerer.

However, as often happens through generations, bloodlines become mixed.

"Interfamily feuds sparked dissension and dissatisfaction." Ciro paced in front of the long table as he proceeded with his lecture, sounding more like a learned professor than an ancient wizard. His knobby fingers stabbed the air as he made each point. "Further rivalry among the Hill people created factions. From the Fav'lhir came Kemmon-Fav. You may find them often carousing with their stockier cousins from the Mid-Lands, the Magrisi. And from the Magrisi we now have Kemmon-Magri, who are known to ride with the Khalar."

In truth, only an expert could distinguish one tribe from another, and even Ciro, after studying all the Land had to offer for four hundred and fifty years, admitted he had trouble telling the lesser Kemmons apart. A rededged vest, he warned Khamsin, whose chin was now propped tiredly against one hand, was no longer irrefutable proof of a Magrisi lineage.

She hoped to ride west from Noviiya and attach herself to a Khalar tribe, disguising herself as a traveling, young mercenary. It was not unusual for a poor farmer with too many sons to send off his youngest as such.

Inlanders didn't have the prejudices against the Hill people that the Covemen did.

"But how can I hope to be accepted, when I can't even tell the Fav'lhir from the Kemmon-Magri?"

"Since I don't recommend your traveling south that shouldn't be something to worry about." Ciro poured himself another glass of wine, holding it up before the candle to inspect its clarity before continuing. "The Fav'lhir rarely ride north of Flume. They have no great liking for the Black Swamp, you see. Not that I know anyone who does. And this far north, it should only be the Khalar and their Kemmons in the hills. Maybe the Magrisi."

That was three too many, as far as Khamsin was concerned.

"But your ability to differentiate lineage concerns me less than your final lessons. Come, Khamsin. Let's try it again." He waved her over to the far corner of the cluttered attic.

Khamsin waited until Ciro closed his eyes before starting with the spell. It was a protective warding, a shielding of her identity.

It was the same form of incantation that Ciro had used in changing himself into the simple-minded dog in the bell tower. Only Khamsin didn't yet have his shape-shifting abilities.

"Not to worry," Ciro advised on the subject. "Only picked up that little trick myself in the past hundred years."

Still, the shielding was the more important part of

the two. Khamsin felt the old mage's mind probing hers. She moved around the attic, constructing a mental wall. She watched Ciro's face for his reaction.

Good. She could see his confusion. He had lost her.

"Excellent, child," he said, turning to where he believed she was. But she wasn't. He craned his neck around in the other direction until her voice, directly in front of him, made him jump and almost spill his wine.

"Here!"

"My, my, young lady. Well done. Let me see. You shielded then dematerialized, am I right?"

"On the money!"

"Good, good. Well, still would feel better if you could make yourself into a hawk or something. Would do away with this nasty business of the Khalar. Would also save time." He sighed. "But, over the years I have learned that one must work with what one has."

They practiced the spell a few more times. The final test came that night with an appearance by Khamsin before a local healer who, Ciro informed her, was the most talented of all the supposed healers in the city. And he was still more of a trickster and a thief than a mage.

Khamsin stood before the greasy-faced man with fabricated questions regarding an offer of marriage. Should she or shouldn't she? The healer surveyed Khamsin's plain green dress that did little to hide her slender waist and full breasts. Then turned his quick scrutiny to the face framed by her dark scarf.

She eavesdropped on his mental appraisal. And was

flattered at his belief that where this "little lady" was concerned, there would be no lack of ardent suitors.

He tossed his stones over a small, tabletop mage circle and, seeing nothing unusual, proceeded to give her some very general advice.

She thanked him with more enthusiasm than the situation called for, her elation coming from the fact that she knew she was successful in her deception. Even the powers within the circle had not known her for what she was.

It was just after midnight when she reappeared in Ciro's attic and threw the borrowed scarf across the back of a nearby chair. She pulled the dress over her head. The last time she wore it was to dinner with Rylan. She pushed the memory, and the ache, away. The clothes she would wear tomorrow, a pair of dark brown trousers, white, high-collared shirt, and thick over-tunic, lay on the low table at the foot of her bed. It was a standard outfit for an Inlander.

There was just one other thing to be attended to. She donned her bed robe and sat on the edge of the table before Ciro, closing her eyes as the sound of scissors snipping filled her ears.

❊ ❊ ❊

Khamsin left Noviiya before dawn the next morning. Her steps took her through the Old Quarter into the center of the city, where the cobblestone streets were lined on either side with identical, two story row houses; their walls were made of gray stucco the same color as Nixa's fur. Candlelight flickered through closed windows, an occasional door slammed, and a voice called out in the early morning stillness. A dog barked. The smell of the sea was prevalent and a damp, cold mist clung to her face. Even when the sun rose to its full height, she knew it would not get much warmer. The Land had already crossed the threshold into winter.

She passed through the back end of Courten's Square, sniffing at the aroma of freshly baked bread wafting down the alley. The memory touched off a small spark of pain. Rylan the Tinker never returned for her. She hoped it was her warnings about her ties to the Sorcerer and not the invasion of Browner's Grove by the Hill Raiders that had prevented him from doing so. She could accept his rejection far more easily than she could accept his death.

She paused for a moment and gazed up at the window of the room that had been theirs. It was closed now, locked. In the same way, she let herself shut the portals of her heart.

The market was empty at this hour. The ramshackle wooden stalls were lined up in uneven rows, filling the large, square plot just steps from the west gate. Within the hour, however, it would be jammed with farmers and vendors and journeymen, hawking their wares, squabbling with customers over prices. Nixa sniffed at a forlorn-looking, half-rotten head of lettuce and, declaring it unfit even to swat at, trotted back to her mistress's side.

At the west gate they saw Ciro with the reins of an unimpressive, brown horse in his hands. Khamsin threw her small satchel over the horse's back and adjusted her sword on her belt before hoisting herself on top of the beast.

"This is Cinnabar," Ciro told her, while Khamsin stroked the glossy head and found an intelligent mind within. "He will do well by you."

She accepted her cat from Ciro's hands and settled the feline in front of her. Cinnabar seemed to mind not at all.

"Ciro . . ." And there was suddenly a sad look on her face. She held her hands out to the old wizard, who clasped them in both of his. "There'll be much to tell when I return."

He smiled. "Be worth a good bottle of wine or two, no doubt."

"No doubt."

"Blessings of the gods upon you, little Khamsin of Cirrus Cove."

"And forever upon you, m'lord. Forever upon you."

She dug her heels into Cinnabar's lean sides and galloped into the diminishing darkness, tears streaming down her face.

❄ ❄ ❄

She rode for two days through the thick forest that covered the land west of Noviiya. There were more pines here and less leaf-bearing trees, so the forest floor was clear of the clutter of dead leaves found in the wooded regions to the south. When she stopped for the night, it was to rest on a bed of pine needles, their aroma fragrant and pleasant.

The road west was wide and well-traveled. There were several small Inlander villages within a two-day ride of the city, and she passed farmers' carts and family wagons as she rode, nodding politely in greeting as was custom. She watched young people on their way to Noviiya for the winter, now that Last Harvest was through and the parties of Fool's Eve behind them. Noviiya meant schooling for the children of the wealthier landowners; shop and store apprenticeships for the poorer ones. They would return right after First Thaw.

Khamsin prayed silently that she would be with them.

The morning of the third day was cold and overcast with a white sky hinting at frost. She longed for a mug of something warm to drink, and when the main road appeared to split at a crossing, she chose the narrower path that led to a nearby village.

It was a village unlike Cirrus Cove, for where Cirrus had been a straight line of houses and shops bordering the shoreline, this small inland village was laid out in a square with nothing at the center but a large pine. She dismounted and led Cinnabar to a watering trough. He ducked his long head into the rough-hewn wooden trench. Nixa balanced pertly on one side and lapped delicately at the water.

Her hands on her hips, Khamsin scrutinized the

buildings for a tavern or inn.

"You in need, lad?" It was an old woman, her eyes milky with age. She wore a heavy, dark woolen dress and short shawl and carried a small covered basket in her hand.

"Just of something warm to drink, Tanta."

"Young 'un to be out on your own."

"Had to be."

The woman nodded understandingly. "No tavern here nor the likes of one for many miles 'round. But Mistress Elsy at that house at yonder corner might have a bit of bread and some hot tea, if you've small coin."

Khamsin thanked the old woman and headed for the corner house with the wooden fence in the front. The weathered gate creaked as she opened it, and she followed the stone path to the back. There was no one in sight but a young girl about ten or eleven years of age, her auburn hair braided and hanging halfway down her back. She sat on the stump of a tree, shelling nuts.

"Blessings of the day, young lady," Khamsin called, and the girl looked up. "I've been told to ask for Mistress Elsy."

"I'm Elsy." The girl put the handful of nuts into the basket at her feet and stood. "Can I be of assistance?"

The girl's manner and mature phrasing took Khamsin by surprise.

"I'm called Camron," she told her. "And I'm traveling north to meet with my uncle. It's been a cold morning, and I was told I could purchase some hot tea and maybe some bread." She held out her palm. Several coins glinted in the light.

Elsy choose two of the smaller ones and motioned to the long rear porch. "Take a seat, traveler. I'll bring something out for you."

The tea was hot and an excellent, rich brew. Khamsin sipped it appreciatively and was offered a thick piece of sweet bread laden with raisins.

"You Kemmon?" Elsy openly studied the sword at Khamsin's side.

"No. But I'm not much of anything else, either."

"My Pa's Kemmon-Ro." There was an unmistakable pride in her voice.

Khamsin had the good sense to look impressed, though the name of the faction was unfamiliar.

Encouraged by Khamsin's nod, Elsy launched into a monologue of her father's accomplishments: how strong he was, how fast he could run, how he rode the wildest stallions. Her small face beamed with love. Khamsin regretted that she could only stay for a few minutes, as time was pressing. Elsy reminded Khamsin of young Lissa and of better times at Cirrus Cove.

She handed the empty mug to her chattering companion as a male voice spoke out from behind.

"Talking some poor lad's ears off again, eh, little Elf?"

Khamsin spun around. She stared up into the gray eyes of a Kemmon-Ro Hill Raider in full riding regalia of dark leather breeches and vest. Involuntarily, she shuddered as she forced herself to remember that to Inlanders, the Hill Raiders were often their local heroes.

And the man before her looked the part, the boyish grin on his well-tanned face contrasting with the visibly lethal knives strapped to his thighs and the dagger on his wrist. His shirt was of a coarse material with black bandings on the cuffs and high collar; his vest was also trimmed in black.

" 'Tis all right, Pa. He's just a traveler, looking for his uncle up in North Country."

The man eyed Khamsin. "Your uncle, lad? He's Kemmon, I take it."

Khamsin's mind worked quickly. "To be truthful, sirrah, it's been years since I've seen him, or he, me. He's my ma's youngest brother, 'bout your age, perhaps. And, as I am her youngest . . ."

"Babes takin' to the hills," the man muttered and pulled at the downy beard covering his chin. It was a recent growth and was lighter than the chestnut color of his hair, which was pulled back and tied at the nape of his neck. There was no doubt as to the source of Elsy's auburn locks.

"You're not fifteen if you're a day, lad."

Khamsin glanced down at her boots.

"Things that bad at home?"

She nodded silently.

He gestured to her sword. "Where did you get that?"

"Was my grandfather's, sirrah. My only inheritance."

"Best learn how to use it before you try it out on someone."

"Yes, sir." She knew she could use it very well, thanks to Ciro. "I'll be on my way now. Thank you for your kindness, Mistress Elsy, sirrah. Blessings of the day upon you."

As she mounted Cinnabar, she glanced back toward the small, corner house. The chestnut-haired Hill Raider had grabbed his daughter around the waist and lifted her up, twirling her around. A burst of childish giggles reached her ears. She watched with envy as father and daughter shared a love that she had never found in her own life.

She stroked Nixa, and the small cat purred her disagreement.

"Of course, I love you, too, Nixa." Khamsin rubbed the cat's whiskers and focused on the forest path opening before her. And not on the hole in her heart she tried so hard to keep closed.

DARKLING

CHAPTER FIFTEEN

The road leading toward the East-West Pass rose sharply under Cinnabar's hoofs. Khamsin felt the horse strain as they picked their way around large boulders strewn in their path. They were in the mountains that separated the tranquil forest villages west of Noviiya from the wilds of Darkling Forest. The pass was the only way through the high ridge that ran from north to south. Khamsin kept alert lest they veer off in error onto one of the lesser pathways and find themselves lost.

And many side trails there were, too, as the region was dotted with Hill Raider nests. But the trails were as treacherous as those who'd carved them. Several times Khamsin was forced to dismount and stare at a crossroad, seeking signs of the most well-traveled way.

The closer she came to the East-West Pass, the more difficult traveling became, as few ventured this far into the Land. The pass led to Darkling, and Darkling bordered the Khal. She wondered if she were the first of the Cove people to willingly set foot on this part of the Land.

A chilling wind whispered through the pines. She drew her cloak more tightly around her, the hot tea of the morning now just memory. Tonight, perhaps for the first time, she'd build a fire. She hadn't done so before. Traveling alone, she'd avoided attracting the attention of those who roamed the forests at night.

Suddenly, Cinnabar reared. Khamsin clasped the reins in one hand and Nixa with the other. The horse's great front legs pawed the air.

"Whoa, Cinnabar, whoa!" The quiet horse wasn't easily spooked. She glanced to her right. Something dark slithered across the road and out of sight.

A snake. A long, black, shiny-scaled snake. But in winter?

The hairs on the back of her neck prickled. She transferred Nixa to her left hand. Quickly she reached down to her boot top and pulled out her short hunting knife.

She longed to draw her sword. A black snake this time of the year wasn't natural. The flash of the blue spellbound metal would be a reassuring sight. But Ciro warned her to use her magic sparingly. And only when absolutely necessary, lest the Sorcerer or his siblings pick up on her whereabouts. What was the use in shielding her identity, if she then broadcast it loudly through the powers of a spell?

She waited, listening, her gaze flicking left and right. She heard only the sigh of the wind and Cinnabar's soft breathing. And nothing more came crawling from the rocks.

She urged Cinnabar onward, but slowly, her eyes keen to every movement around her.

The path narrowed through a small grove of bristling pines. Their scent was almost sickeningly sweet. It stuck in the back of her throat. Nixa sneezed.

Then she heard an almost imperceptible scratching sound over her head. She jammed her heels hard into the horse's side. Cinnabar bolted. Khamsin turned just in time to see the snake drop from an overhanging branch. Its two-inch long fangs almost grazed the horse's flank. She yanked him around as she threw the short knife with deadly aim. It pinned the snake in the center of its flat head, splitting the skull. Green ooze and a foul smell gushed from the opening. A familiar unworldly, foul smell. The body spasmed and disappeared.

Slowly Khamsin climbed down from the horse, her boots touching on the graveled surface as if she feared a flood of more reptiles at any moment. But no such scaly, black creatures sprang from the stones. She snatched her knife from the ground, which was bare and dry with no sign of the snake. Just Cinnabar's hoof marks in the dirt.

She shoved the knife back into her boot and rode on for over a mile before her hands stopped shaking.

There were stories, legends about those who attempted the East-West Pass into the Darklings. Tales told around the hearth fire late on Fool's Eve night to scare little children and timid adults. Tales of horribly deformed creatures that crawled out of the Black Swamp and into the hillsides, seeking the flesh of innocent travelers to feast on. Was the black snake such a creature, a poisonous vampire seeing her as something warm and blood-filled? Or was it something more? An omen, a message-bearer, a warning? Did its jeweled eyes see her as Camron the traveler or Khamsin the healer?

Without her magic, she couldn't even begin to guess.

High, bare cliffs rose on either side of her. Her progress was slowed by the unevenness of the road. Without the protection of the forest, it was badly rutted from furrows dug by driving rains. Small boulders cascaded down from the heights, leaving a crumbling trail that was almost impassable. Finally, she was forced to dismount and, in the waning light of the setting sun, led Cinnabar carefully around the obstacles in their path. She hoped to clear through the pass before nightfall. But the lengthening shadows around her told her that wouldn't be so.

Darkness settled quickly. The moons had yet to rise. The pale light from the few stars overhead did not help. Again, Khamsin longed to use her magic, to cast fiery elementals to light their way. But she feared the power of the Sorcerer more than she feared the pass at night. She settled for sending Nixa on ahead and keeping a light mental contact with the feline, who had the natural ability to see in the dark.

They were on the descending trail for more than an hour, when the moons finally rose pale into the sky. But it was an overcast night, and their glow diffused into the clouds. Everything was deathly still. No owls hooted; no mountain wolves bayed. Even the wind seemed to have vanished. The steady clop-clop-clop of Cinnabar's hoofs took on an eerie resonance.

Finally, the trail widened and small clusters of trees cropped up again, sparse and thinning. Nixa darted on ahead and came back with the news of a grove of pines on the left.

With Cinnabar tied to a low branch and Nixa snuggled in the safety of her arms, Khamsin fell into an exhausted slumber on the bare ground, foregoing even the promised pleasure of a fire.

❅ ❅ ❅

Twice Cinnabar snorted softly. The sound carried through the early morning mists of lavender and gray, rising from the frost-covered ground.

Khamsin stirred and rolled over on her side, her knees curling up against her chest, her eyes tightly closed. She stretched out one arm in the languid, clumsy movement of someone in a deep sleep. Then she slowly edged her fingers toward the hilt of her hunting knife and, feeling the coldness of the metal, laid her hand firmly against it.

Nixa twitched her ears and relayed back to her mistress what she and the horse sensed. Intruders. Men. In the pines around them. Coming closer.

How many?

An image of three forms flashed into her mind. From the perspective of height, she knew the information came from Cinnabar.

Nixa?

The cat lazily opened her eyes, slit-like.

One. She saw only one.

That made four. Only Nixa's approached her, the other three were fanning out through the small grove. Khamsin felt a man's touch on Cinnabar's soft nose. The horse held still at her instructions, though the desire to rear and strike out at the intruder was strong within him.

No. Khamsin didn't want either of her animals injured.

At her signal, Nixa scampered into a nearby bush. It was a normal reaction as the intruder knelt down beside Khamsin and stretched his hand out toward her. She waited until he was only inches away. She sprang into action. She grabbed the outstretched wrist and forced it backward. The man fell on one elbow with a loud grunt, collapsing onto his stomach as Khamsin wrapped his arm in back of him and yanked, hard. She knelt on his back, her meager weight not as much of a deterrent as the sharp point of her knife just under his ear.

"Stay where you are or I'll slit his throat!" She yelled her warning out into the pine trees. The three men moved toward her, their own knives drawn.

"I mean it!" She nodded to Cinnabar, who with two quick shakes, unwrapped his reins from the tree limb and reared up at the closest man, snorting and whinnying.

Had the men carried spears, she wouldn't have allowed the horse his glory.

"Druke, hold up!" came the muffled command from the man beneath her. He spat dry twigs out of his mouth. The men stopped, and Cinnabar shook his head pridefully.

"Damn it, lad, didn't mean you no harm!" It was her intruder again.

Khamsin looked down at the point of her knife and saw the soft beginnings of a downy beard on a well-tanned, square-jawed face. Chestnut-colored hair fell across his cheek and over one ear.

She had almost killed Elsy's father.

She stood up abruptly and shoved the knife back into her boot top.

The Kemmon-Ro Hill Raider rolled over into a sitting position, ruffling the pine needles out of his thick hair. He glared up at Khamsin but with more amusement than anger in his gray eyes.

"You're pretty quick for a light weight." He offered her a crooked grin.

"I could've killed you."

"Aye, I know, lad. My mistake. I thought you were still asleep, or I would've hailed you, proper. As I said, I mean you no harm."

Khamsin nodded. "My apologies, sirrah."

"Egan!" A stocky man with a fringe of black hair surrounding a bald spot on his head stepped out of the brush. He was clothed in the same manner as Elsy's father, but his black-edged vest barely covered the plumpness of his stomach. He eyed Khamsin warily, a thin dagger still in his grip.

"Put your knife away, Druke. The rest of you too." Egan waved at the other two coming into the small clearing. They were clean-shaven and looked as if they'd not yet seen their twenty-first birthdays. Their hair, like Egan's, was a deep reddish-brown, and their faces had the same strong lines hinting at a blood relationship between them and the older man.

Daggers slid from sight.

"You have business in Darkling?"

"My uncle." It was the tale she'd told him in the small village. She hoped it would be adequate now.

"So you said. But my daughter told me neither he nor you are Kemmon. What makes you think you'll find him here?"

"Because that is where I was told he was." She answered as a fourteen-year-old lad would, stubbornly, but with a trace of respect.

"Perhaps he is, then. Give me his name."

"Aric. Aric of Tynder's Hill." She borrowed her late brother-in-law's name and combined it with an Inlander town from Ciro's chart.

Egan looked at Druke then back to Khamsin. "I know of no man who calls himself such."

She shrugged. "Perhaps he's changed it, then. Hilma and her family were none too pleased when he left. Though she did name the child after him."

Egan only raised one eyebrow, but Druke chuckled knowingly. "Wanted the milk but not willing to buy the cow, eh?"

"So you seek him now in the Darklings? Well, lad, many a man has hidden out here for the very same reason. Your uncle has lots of company."

As Khamsin adjusted her satchel on Cinnabar's back, Egan laid a hand lightly on her shoulder. "Where are you headed now?"

"West, as the main road goes."

"We go that way as well. Ride awhile with us, if you like."

"Thank you, sirrah." Khamsin was surprised at his offer. Hill Raiders weren't known for their generosity toward travelers, though in truth, she'd never heard of any North Landers attacking a young farm lad traveling alone. Only old, fat, wealthy merchants and land barons were considered prey. No doubt they surmised from the cut of her cloth, she owned nothing worth stealing.

She snapped her fingers. Nixa sauntered out of the bushes. She placed the cat on Cinnabar's back before she grabbed the horse's strong neck and, with a practiced jump, flung herself onto his back.

"You travel with a cat?" Druke voiced the question that was also evident in Egan's mind, from the look on his face.

"A gift," she explained, having only moments before concocted the story. "From our village healer. For luck, I was told."

"Guard him well, then." Egan stroked the short fur on Nixa's nose. Khamsin wasn't sure if he had spoken to her or her cat.

CHAPTER SIXTEEN

Khamsin told enough of herself and her make-believe family so as to appease Egan's well-meaning inquiries. But not so much that she might get caught later in some minor detail in her lies. She also turned the conversation, with very little difficulty, to the subject of the man's daughter.

"Ah, little Elf," he smiled warmly.

Druke groaned. "Ach, Camron, lad, now you've done it. Got ol' Egan started on the subject of the little lass of his. There'll be no peace now for many a mile!" He spurred his roan horse ahead of them, the younger men at his side.

Khamsin and Egan kept up their steady pace behind.

"She's the star of my sky, she is," Egan told her. "Lost her mother when she was still a babe. Dena, my sister—that's who has the house in the village—she and her husband take care of her for me. Not proper to raise a girl child in the wilds, like this."

"You're fortunate to have your sister there."

"I get back to Pinetrail as much as I can. And in the winter, we have good times, she and I. Dena taught her to read. Now Elsy swears she'll teach her old pa before Wintertide!"

Khamsin chuckled. Egan's description of himself as old was far from accurate. She judged him younger than Tavis. Clearly, he felt fatherhood, not the passage of years, granted him his elder status. And yet he looked forward to letting his daughter play teacher.

For a moment, listening to Egan's words, Khamsin forgot it was a Hill Raider riding next to her. She saw only a young father, who loved his daughter and delighted in talking about the child. Just like Aric had. Or Mikhail the Chartmaker back at Cirrus with his three daughters. They were men who could love. That was something she'd never before thought a Hill Raider could do.

Maybe there were more differences amongst Hill Raiders than just the names of their Kemmons, the color of their bandings. All Cove people weren't alike. Craft that sailed from Cirrus Cove were longer and sleeker than the squat, shallow draft boats that came from Wallow's Cove, far to the south. Their captain and crew were different in temperament as well.

She'd never known Hill Raiders with black bandings like Egan's to have appeared in any of the Cove towns. And Elsy had bragged of her father as a skilled horseman, not a marauder. Khamsin hadn't sensed the fear, or distrust, she'd expected in the small village. Or from the red-haired child.

"Elsy seemed very bright, the little time I spoke to her."

Egan's face glowed at her compliment. "She's a smart one, all right. Knows her figures and her letters now. And she's good with the animals. Cats or cows, it doesn't matter. 'Course, all the people like her too. Got a nice way about her, she does."

And it went on from there until they came to a small clearing in the thickness of the pines. Druke slowed and motioned for Egan to come to his side. They exchanged a few words and with a nod to one of the younger men to accompany him, Egan rode on ahead.

Druke turned his horse to face Khamsin. "Tried to warn you, didn't I?" he teased. "Bit of a one-sided conversation when you get him talking."

"Where's he going?" She watched the riders fade into the shadows.

"Been trouble here before. Fav'lhir."

Ciro said they never came this far north! "Why would the Fav'lhir cause trouble here?"

" 'Tis a good question." Druke didn't sound as if he meant to be sarcastic, but there was a note of frustration in his voice. "There was a time, well past, when all Hill people shared a bond, a respect. But a blood lust, an unholy taste for death and destruction is part of the way of life for the Fav'lhir these days. You can thank Lady Melande for that." There was a derisive note in his voice. "They ride in that witch's service, you know."

That she did. "And Kemmon-Ro?"

Druke eyed her with surprise. " 'Tis plain as the name itself, if you think on it. Why, we're the only ones who carry his name in ours at all! Kemmon-Ro, lad. We ride for the Master of Traakhal."

Khamsin sat in stunned silence. She should have known. Kemmon-Ro. It was the first part of his other name as Kiasidira was hers. She knew it, though it was a name she'd only read. She forced it from her mind, fearful of even mentally voicing it. But the thought that filled that vacant space was just as disturbing.

She rode in the company of the enemy.

Egan returned at that moment.

"Best not to chance it, Druke." His expression was grim. He reined his horse around to face Khamsin. "Camron, the main road ahead could hold trouble, more for us than for you, as you bear no Kemmon. Still, there's always a chance."

He nodded over his shoulder to the break in the pines. "We're going to take the south trail toward the Khal to get around. You're welcome to come, if you like. Unless you think your uncle's Fav'lhir."

Khamsin's mind worked furiously while he spoke. What better place to hide from the Sorcerer than in the midst of his own riders? They were not only protection but a source of information as well. The Land here, as Ciro foretold her, fairly bubbled with intrigue.

"Unlikely," she replied to his comment. "Unless the Khalar, too, work with the witch."

A disparaging snort was all she received from Egan,

as he waved the younger men on ahead. "Skeely, Wade, we'll take the lake road. You know the way."

And in a flurry of pine needles and dust, they were off.

Having already admitted her ignorance about Egan's tribe, she questioned him further on Kemmon-Ro as they rode, jostling along the narrower trail to the south. The forest thinned out. She saw the first signs of marshland in the patches of mossy grass interspersed with thin, stick-like reeds.

Kemmon-Ro, Egan told her with a strong note of pride in his voice, were a faction of the Magrisi, though the split took place over two hundred years before. But they were forest and plains people. The mountain-bred Khalar accepted them with reservation, suspicious at first of these newcomers who perhaps thought to usurp their position in Traakhal. But the Kemmon-Ro were content with their forests. The Khalar soon realized no threat existed, and an alliance was formed.

The Kemmon-Ro dealt with the Khalar on equal terms now. Both wore the black band of the Sorcerer on their tunics and vests. Khamsin had seen the striping on Egan's clothing when he played with Elsy in the yard. Now, she understood what it meant.

Their saddle blankets, too, were bordered in black. Even horses had their affiliations.

"Are there any other Kemmons the Khalar deal with?"

Egan nodded. "A small tribe north of Darkling called Kemmon-Drin and another called Kemmon-

Nijar. But you don't see much of them here."

"None from the south?"

"No. The south wears the red and the yellow of Lucial and Melande."

That, at least, was as Ciro told her.

The road widened when they came upon the marsh. The riders fanned out. It was dusk, and there was an icy chill to the damp air that blew across the wide, flat expanse. It came, Khamsin knew, from over the Khal. Though they were still a ways from the shore, she could smell the musky scent of the lake around her.

The ground underneath the horses' hoofs was hard, frost-frozen. The shallow pools of water on either side would no doubt have a thin layer of ice on them by morning. Khamsin rode with Nixa tucked into her cloak, for the cold was biting and bitter.

She saw Skeely spur his horse and ride on ahead in search of a place to spend the night. It was several minutes before they came upon him again at a fork in the road.

He waved them on to the right. They followed, the trail narrowing so they rode in single-file. Marsh weeds and swamp brush of a grayish-green filled the ravines on either side of their pathway. The glistening of small pools of water shone through the thin stalks. Some clusters of the weeds were so large they appeared solid. That was deceptive, Druke pointed out, for they grew on top of each other's roots. Finally, they came upon a small island of true land in the middle of the marsh, not much larger than the great room at the inn at Courten's

Square. A few sparse trees clung to its west bank.

Their horses cleared the short distance between the trail and the island with a jump. They dismounted, crowding the horses into a circle. Druke and Skeely started a fire, while Egan opened a pack and withdrew some provisions. Khamsin sought out her own small satchel, then released Nixa who returned shortly with a marsh-rat in her mouth.

"Your cat found dinner." Egan offered Khamsin a slice of bread and a small meat pie. She waved away the pie, but took the bread and brought a short twine full of dried figs from her satchel. The sweet fruits were a treat, saved for last, and Druke enjoyed his with such relish that Khamsin wished she could create more, but knew to do so would attract questions. And attention. Those fruits she made while still in Noviiya.

Wade pulled a deck of cards from his pack. He cleared a small patch of ground then dealt a hand for Egan and himself. Khamsin watched the progress of the unfamiliar game in the firelight. The shouts and laughter of the Kemmon-Ro Hill Raiders resounded across the vastness of the frozen swamp in the dark.

She was the first to see the odd movement. She tensed and caught the sickening smell just as Nixa did. The cat's whiskers twitched. Her ears lay back flat against her head, her small muscles tensing under her thick fur. Neither she nor her mistress knew what was out there; only that it was demon-spawn. And it was coming toward them.

Khamsin rose swiftly to her feet.

"Egan!" Her voice was strained. The bearded man quickly looked up from his cards.

She snatched her blade from her boots and pointed. "There!"

Two red orbs glowed in the darkness, swaying with a peculiar rhythm as they moved closer.

"By the jaws of hell!" Wade rose, thin daggers in both hands.

Druke eyed the hulking form in the darkness. "One of Melande's toys." His words held a mixture of caution and disgust. The creature approached, swaying. A wheezing noise came from its direction. The sound was strained and guttural, unnatural.

"Aye, one of the witch-lady's playthings," Egan said roughly.

The creature stopped just short of the island. It stared through the firelight, directly at Khamsin. They could all see it now with the lipless cavern of its mouth dripping slime and its huge, claw-like hands flexing spasmodically. Its body was covered with dull, yellowed scales. Wade shifted nervously in his stance. The creature's red eyes darted in his direction, only to return to the firelight. And to Khamsin.

"Must be drawn to the fire," Druke said.

"If we put it out, will it go away?" Skeely asked nervously.

"Don't know."

There was such calmness in Druke's voice that Khamsin had to question. "You've seen these things before?"

"Aye, but not loose like this. In Traakhal. Master Ro has a few in the dungeons."

"Well, damn it, Druke, we've got to do something!" Wade rasped.

"Easy, boy," Egan said but he, too, glanced toward the balding man. "You seem to be the one with the knowledge, Druke. What do you say?"

The demon swayed hypnotically before them.

"Why doesn't it attack?" Skeely took a step in Egan's direction. But this time the demon's eyes remained fixed straight ahead.

"Do you want it to?" Egan answered.

"Hell, no, but, damn it! It's, it's . . ."

The demon moved slowly sideways around the perimeter of the island, not touching the dry land but keeping right to its edge. The horses whinnied nervously. Khamsin heard a low rumbling from where Nixa crouched.

The men turned in the firelight as the demon stepped into a murky pool of water. A foul stench rose up in the tendrils of steam at its feet. Khamsin heard Skeely gag.

She passed the hunting knife into her left hand and laid her right on the hilt of her sword. Ciro had said to use her magic only in the direst of circumstances. If the demon charged, she felt the situation would qualify.

But it kept its distance and seemed to study the group from all angles. As if it were looking for something it couldn't quite find.

Khamsin increased the thickness of her mental shield. If it was seeking her, as she was sure it was, perhaps it was only a matter of time before it lost interest and departed.

It completed the circle of the island and now faced north, again. Egan tested the balance of the daggers in his hands.

"Druke, I'm going after it." He spoke through his teeth, obviously no longer able to bear the tension of being stalked by the hulking form.

"No." Khamsin took her hand from the hilt of her sword and laid it against Egan's forearm. "It's going away."

The uneasy feeling that had been with her since they entered the marsh faded. As it did, so did the demon. It took a few steps backward then dissolved before their widening eyes into the murk below its feet.

"Son of a Nijanian bitch!" Skeely's words came out in a hoarse rush, and he turned to Wade. But the other man had already dropped to his knees and was vomiting his supper over the edge of the island.

"You know, Druke, I think I would've preferred to face the Fav'lhir in the forest, rather than that." Egan moved away from where Skeely bent over his suffering sibling.

"I won't argue that point with you, Master Egan." Druke glanced at Khamsin. "You're made of solid stuff, lad. Help me with the horses, will you? Don't think any one of us is in the mind to spend the night here now. Think we'd best just keep on riding."

CHAPTER SEVENTEEN

They rode into the darkness, the sound of the horses' hoofs crisp on the frozen ground. They rode faster than was called for, pushing their steeds as if every moment they could put between themselves and the demon was another day added to their lives. Overhead, the moons bathed them in a sickly light. It was as though all the marshland suffered from their encounter.

At daybreak they were on the shore of the Khal. Khamsin looked out over waters that glistened like polished onyx. There, perhaps a few miles away, was her destination. The castle of the Sorcerer. The rising sun in the East played across the expanse. She could've sworn, in the glimmerings, she saw the towers of the fortress rising, crested with snow. No banners would unfurl from its parapets. No such decorations were necessary. There was only one castle carved from the very heart of the mountains and jutting out into the lake of eternal night: Traakhal-Armin. She could feel the pulsations of power even at this great distance.

At Egan's signal, they reined in their horses and made temporary camp for breakfast. Khamsin spoke the first words uttered since they departed the small island.

"How did you know the demon was Lady Melande's?"

Druke looked up from the fire he tended, a thoughtful expression on his round face. "First, because it was a varl. One of Melande's favorites, as I hear tell. But second, because it made as if to attack us. The Sorcerer would never send a demon out after his own. Lest we'd displeased him in some fashion," he added after a moment.

"You're sure?" Skeely didn't seem convinced.

"You've not been to Traakhal, as I have." Druke sat back on his haunches and studied the young man. "Ask your uncle. He's been there as well, though not as often."

Dena's sons turned toward Egan.

"It's true." The chestnut-haired man pulled a small loaf of bread from his pack. He handed it to Skeely, who speared it onto a thin branch. "Druke first brought me to Traakhal after I was named Kemmon Rey. I spoke with Master Tedmond, Lord Chamberlain of Traakhal. He instructed me on the duties for Kemmon-Ro and what was expected of us. He also told me what to expect from the Master of Traakhal."

"And what was that?" Khamsin's curiosity about the

Sorcerer overrode her self-imposed reticence.

"Protection from foes. Instruction when necessary. Retaliation and vindication from wrongs." Egan repeated the words as if he'd memorized them.

"Says nothing in there 'bout demons," Wade replied glumly.

Egan only glared at the young man. He pulled the dagger strapped to his thigh from its sheath then retrieved a small flat stone from his vest pocket.

"And what's 'Kemmon Rey'?" Khamsin asked, as Egan worked carefully on the short blade.

This time it was Wade's turn to cast a disparaging glance. "Don't teach you much in Tynder's Hill, do they? Kemmon Rey is the Kemmon leader." And with that he turned his attention to the piece of bread Skeely had just handed him, warmed from the fire. He bit into it hungrily, his appetite returning now that the demon was only a bad memory of the previous night.

"But maybe the demon, this varl, escaped," Skeely said.

"From Traakhal? Not likely," Druke answered. "Nothin' gets into the castle that isn't supposed to be there. And nothin' that's meant to stay, gets out."

"But if that demon was Lady Melande's and if the master was keeping it . . ."

"Captured it," Druke corrected, "so that Lady Melande couldn't use it."

"Then why keep it? Why not kill it?" Skeeley pressed. "Isn't the master powerful enough?"

"Powerful enough?" Druke snorted. "Lad, he could

reduce you to ashes with a mere glance. But these demons," and he waved one hand aimlessly in the air, "they're ensorcelled. You don't kill them things. You just . . ."

"Send them back to the nearest available hell," Khamsin said softly.

Druke heard her. "Aye, that's about the size of it. And only a wizard or a witch can do that. Or the Sorcerer. Which is why I know the varl didn't come from Traakhal's dungeons."

"Why would Lady Melande send a demon so close to Traakhal?" Khamsin didn't want to believe that Melande's monster was looking for her. For if it was, she had more than just the Sorcerer to fear.

"That witch and the master have been at odds for some time," Druke said. "Surely you've heard that, even in Tynder's?"

Khamsin hesitated. She wasn't sure how much she could admit. But she also knew she had much to learn. She shrugged. "I've heard lots of stories. But I don't pay much attention to what people say. I mean, witches and wizards aren't things you worry about every day."

Egan put down the dagger he'd been sharpening. "You do when you're Kemmon-Ro."

"It's over the orb, isn't it?" Wade asked his uncle.

Egan nodded. "Melande and Lucial both want it. But there are spells protecting it. Keeping it safe. Just as it's our job to keep these forests safe."

He rose, sheathed his dagger. "So we'd best be at it, lads."

No more was said. Within minutes they were back
on the road, cloaks and outer-tunics drawn tightly
around them. Winter had finally arrived. Khamsin
felt Nixa's reassuring warmth against her legs and
thought of the times the cat had snuggled against her
when they'd sat in the crook of one of the great trees
surrounding Bronya's cave.

Cirrus Cove, and Summertide, suddenly seemed
very far away, indeed.

Finally, they turned and headed north, back toward
the forest. They made an early camp at the first thick
pine grove they encountered, having had no sleep at all
the night before. Supper was light, the better to sleep
on. Then with Wade volunteering to take first watch,
they settled in for the night.

Khamsin awoke a few hours before dawn. Egan
nodded before the glow of the embers, his beard fuller
than it was when she met him in his sister's village of
Pinetrail. She was afraid of him then, seeing only a Hill
Raider. Now she saw Egan as a man, a good friend to
Druke and the boys, and good father. In many ways, not
unlike Tavis.

She appraised the strong profile. He was also a
handsome man, his features more even than Tavis's.
But he wasn't as handsome as Rylan. And he didn't
have the tinker's sharp mind or quick wit.

She was comfortable with Egan. But Rylan had the
ability to fascinate her. He had depths she knew she
could spend years exploring. He would never tire of her
questions and seemed to know just how to open her

mind to the answers.

And her heart. Abruptly she halted her thoughts.

She could no longer focus on Rylan, but on her other losses. That of her husband and friends. For as long as she lived, she'd never forget the sight of Tavis's lifeless body hanging from the tree. Or the bodies of Rina's children by the hearth. Anger burned inside her. And it was anger that fed her determination to reach Traakhal-Armin.

No other emotion was of use to her. She'd learned that much in Noviiya.

Egan turned his head, his gaze meeting hers through the gray light of morning. He motioned with his hand.

"Had enough sleep, lad?"

It took Khamsin a moment to realize the Kemmon Rey was speaking to her. "For now. A soft bed would've helped, though."

Egan chuckled. "Can't argue with you there, as Druke would say."

"You've been friends long?"

"Eleven years. Ever since I married his sister."

Khamsin tried to envision Elsy's mother from Druke's plump features but failed. "How long were you married?"

"Little less than two years. Elsy was born that first year. The following year, Maryse died giving birth to our son."

Khamsin could hear no pain in his words and assumed time had healed the wounds.

"When did you become Kemmon Rey?"

"When Maryse's father died, six months after Elsy was born."

She made a quick mental calculation. "You were young . . ."

"Probably younger than you think, Camron. I'd just turned twenty."

"Is that unusual?"

"To be chosen to lead a Kemmon? A bit. But I'd ridden with the Kemmon since I was younger than that. I knew the forests. I certainly knew how to fight. And after the Fav'lhir raid, there weren't many men to choose from. We lost more than Agard, my father-in-law. All that was left were the women, the farmers, and the boys."

"So your family wasn't Kemmon?"

"My father was a grain farmer. There was just Dena and I and ten years difference between us. When she married I let her and her husband take my share of the farm. I've never had the feel of the land that my father did. Guess your uncle Aric felt the same way," he added.

Khamsin thought of Rina's Aric, a Coveman, a fisherman. "No," she said truthfully. "He never did care much for the land, either."

"And you, Camron. What do you seek, lad? Adventure? Riches? A willing wife and a warm hearth?"

"Knowledge," she said, staring at the fading embers. "Experience and answers." And that, she knew, was also the truth.

"We'll be back into Darkling before noontime." Egan rubbed his hands together, feeling stiff from the cold. "But we won't be continuing north from there. Wintertide approaches. Once I meet with the nests at the foothills of the Nijanas, we'll be heading back to Pinetrail. You think your uncle's out here, some-where?"

Khamsin nodded. "Though maybe not with any Kemmon, since you say you've never heard of him. Perhaps with the Khalar?" If Egan could pass her on to the Sorcerer's tribe with his recommendations, it would make her mission easier. It was beginning to sound more and more difficult to gain access to the castle.

"Not an Inlander, I doubt it. Though I've nothing against your uncle," he said quickly. "It's just that they don't recruit from outside. Inlanders join up with the Kemmons, if they make it this far.

"Lad, I hate to think of you wandering 'round in the wilds here not familiar with the Land and all. 'Tis not a place for a solitary traveler."

"So I've heard from many," she acknowledged, wryly admitting to herself that her traveling companions were the very ones she was warned away from.

"Aye, well of late there's been more than the usual trouble with the Fav'lhir. And now with Lady Melande and her pets." Egan's brows furrowed at his own thoughts. "I could take you myself to Kemmon-Nijar. Perhaps there?"

"I've no wish to trouble you, Master Egan."

" 'Tis no trouble. Been a time since I've spoken to

Radclough or old Gilane. Druke's well skilled in watching after the boys. Besides, 'tis pretty country and you might like to see it, different as it is from your home."

"I'll take each day as it comes," Khamsin replied, touched by the concern in Egan's voice. "A friend once told me that was the best way to proceed."

"You must keep wise company." He stood up and stretched. "Still, don't refuse my offer just yet. I'd be glad to help to you, in findin' your uncle."

He eyed the finely featured lad before him. "You wouldn't happen to have an older sister, a pretty one, back at Tynder's, would you? Someone I could share a cup of tea with, if I happen to travel that way? With news of you and your uncle, of course."

Khamsin suppressed a smile. "I'm told I have a cousin in one of the Cove towns. A young widow."

Egan shook his head. "Don't think I'd get much of a warm welcome riding east. The Fav'lhir have tainted all Hill people's names with their actions. Still," and he considered something for a moment.

"Would you be up for a ride now, Camron? We can cover some distance while these sleepyheads break camp."

"I would, yes!" Khamsin saddled Cinnabar, while Egan woke Druke and informed him of their plans. They were to meet again at the nest.

They set off with the sunrise at their backs, the cold air feeling suddenly crisp and refreshing. The sky cleared and the sunlight promised warmth later in the day.

Khamsin secured Nixa against her and dug her heels into her horse's side, answering Egan's challenge for a race.

For an unimpressive-looking, brown animal, Cinnabar kept pace with Egan's Hill-bred, black stallion with ease. Even the Kemmon Rey looked at the horse with more respect, when they stopped near a small stream and allowed the horses to drink. But it wasn't only Cinnabar that caught his attention.

"You surprise me, Camron," he said after he dismounted.

Khamsin had been watching Nixa stalk through the underbrush. She turned. "Sirrah?"

"You play the timid lad very well, when it suits you. Like in Dena's yard with my daughter. But there's more to you than that."

She'd known the gray-eyed man for almost five days. Did he see through her deceptions? Ciro clipped her hair short, shorter than the tinker had. And she kept her form cloaked in a heavy outer-tunic and concentrated on lowering her voice when she spoke. No one else, not Druke or Skeely or Wade, gave the slightest inclination they suspected she was anything other than a slightly-built, fourteen-year-old, farm boy. But since this morning she was aware of Egan studying her. And his comments back at the camp, about a sister. Was there some feminine mannerism Egan saw, perhaps because he had a daughter?

"I bear no ill." The confusion in her face was genuine.

"I'm not saying you do. It's just that I see the makings of a fine warrior within you." He stepped up beside her.

217

"You've a strength not visible to first glance, as they say. A calm under fire. Perhaps your pa knew more than he allowed, when he told you to take the traveler's road."

"I've much yet to learn. I know that."

"And the family farm wasn't the place to do that, eh? You're not a farmer, Camron. Like me, you never could be. You learn quickly, I'd wager, but are always looking for more to learn."

He let his broad hand come to rest against her shoulder. "Would you consider bearing the black band of the Kemmon-Ro?"

His words stunned Khamsin. Egan offered her the highest honor a tribesman could extend an Inlander: that of bearing the colors of his Kemmon. She never expected the bearded man to respond to her so strongly. He had said he had lost a son at his birthing. Perhaps this is what he sought in the lad he called Camron. And, in spite of the hard shell around her heart, part of her wished she could accept his offer. And that her answer didn't have to be couched in lies. If only in regard for the sense of loyalty she knew ran deeply in the man.

"Master Egan, I'm truly honored. And undeserving of your kind words. But I can't, in all honesty, answer you at this time. I have a matter of family to rectify. If I joined Kemmon-Ro without first seeking further for my uncle, it would foster bad feelings. I must give my search for him more time."

Egan told her he respected her decision. It was the same one he would make given the circumstances. "But when you resolve the question of your uncle, know that my offer still stands."

Khamsin's eyes shone brightly in response.

"I was rather hoping, too," he admitted with a smile, "that as part of the Kemmon, you'd come to know my Elsy better. You'd be a good friend, a good guide for her, I think. And welcome in my own family."

Khamsin felt the emotions underlying his words. A sense of friendship, no. Kinship. Egan looked upon her as something between a younger brother and, as she suspected, the son he never had a chance to raise.

His innocent kindness overwhelmed her and reminded her too strongly of another man's kindness. And gentle touch.

And painful absence.

She picked up Nixa and nuzzled her face into the cat's neck. "And my cat, too?" she asked, peering over pointed gray ears at Egan.

"Of course, the cat! Having your Nixa around, I think, would please Elsy more than anything."

CHAPTER EIGHTEEN

The flatlands gave way to the foothills, but they were low, rolling, and richly forested. There was a light cover of snow on the ground. Only under the canopy of the pines did the brown grasses still raise their heads upright. Egan stretched out his hand as he passed beneath a low-hanging pine branch. He grabbed a handful of wet snow, fashioned a ball, and chucked it over his shoulder at Khamsin.

She shrieked in delight as it caught her unawares, showering her and the unsuspecting Nixa in a light frosting of white crystals.

The next handful was hers. Her aim was good, but he expected the retaliation and ducked just as the missile whizzed past his head.

"You need practice, Camron," he teased and rode on ahead of her toward the next clump of low-hanging pines.

She held back, slowing Cinnabar to a canter. She

gave Egan time to prepare his ambush. She found she enjoyed the game.

There was little levity in her life as of late. Not since Rylan amused her with stories of the princesses of Noviiya. She'd laughed with him until her eyes watered. Now thoughts of Rylan brought water to her eyes for a different reason.

She watched Egan disappear into the shadowed grove ahead and waited for a count of fifty before proceeding, expecting at any moment to be caught in a barrage of cold, wet snowballs.

The expected never came.

The unexpected, however, did. Fav'lhir Tribesman. Six of them, mounted and armed. And one slashed open Egan's chest and shoulder with his sword.

Khamsin screamed his name. Two of the Fav'lhir jumped down to the ground. Egan staggered between them, blood spattering the snow at his feet. One grabbed the Kemmon Rey by the arm, his blade poised over his heart. But Khamsin had already pulled her knife and, in a swift motion, threw it. It found a home in the attacker's throat. He reeled backward, gasping and gurgling.

Egan turned immediately and, in spite of his own wounds, wrenched the blade from the lifeless body.

"Camron!" he called, but she couldn't get to him. The other four horseman crowded around her. They taunted her with their daggers. She reined Cinnabar in circles, holding Nixa tucked against her with one hand.

"Kemmon-Ro have a liking for young boys," one said, and he spat in her direction. Another laughed cruelly. His hands made lewd motions.

Suddenly, the horseman who'd spat at her gasped and fell over his mount, his arms flinging outwards. He tumbled into the snow. A familiar hunting knife protruded from his back.

But the maneuver had cost Egan dearly. He stumbled in the drifts, the Fav'lhir almost on top of him.

"No!" Khamsin reined Cinnabar in with all her might, secured her cloak around Nixa. She whispered an incantation and then gave the horse the command to jump. The horse was airborne immediately, clearing the two riders in front of them. They landed a few paces away from where Egan struggled with the other Fav'lhir rider on the ground.

Cinnabar reared again and chopped at the Fav'lhir's back with his hoofs. Stunned and bleeding, the man rolled into a snow bank. With a quick movement, Egan slit his throat.

Khamsin reached down. Egan leaned against Cinnabar's flank, grabbed two of his daggers from his boot and thigh straps. He passed them quickly into her hands. She turned and threw again. Two riders fell with the hilts of Kemmon-Ro weapons protruding from their chests. Their horses bolted into the forest.

Two riders were left. Khamsin kept her horse between them and Egan, who lurched weakly at her side. Dark bloodstains covered the front of his tunic.

The Fav'lhir pulled back, obviously confused by the aggression on the part of the young boy. They exchanged hushed words. One reached for an amulet hanging from his neck chain. And a cold, sickening terror crept up Khamsin's spine.

The thing rose from out of the snow as if it were created from the crystals themselves. A demon with yellow eyes churning, but unlike the demons in the bell tower and on the marsh. This demon was twice the size of the others and hairless, almost man-like, pale gray and naked. Its skin was slick and slimy like a snake, but with no scales. Three horns protruded from its bald head. Its snout was like a wolf's. Long fangs jutted from its mouth. It curled back its lips, hissing. Khamsin could see the flames that roiled within its body.

It was the essence of hell itself.

Nixa's low growl rumbled against her leg.

"Camron, run!" The weak voice was Egan's, behind her. "Go back. Find Druke. Tell him, tell him the nest has been taken. Get the Kemmon. But go, lad! Save yourself."

"I'm not leaving you!"

"Don't be a damn fool. No mortal can fight this thing. It's a mogra. It's got the power of Lucial *and* Melande behind it. Camron!" And she felt him clasp her ankle, his hand shaking.

"No!"

"For love of Tarkir, go!" His voice was hoarse.

He tried to push her away. She reached for him, her eyes still on the demon that slowly advanced in their direction. "You come with me."

"I won't make the ride . . . child."

She glanced into eyes full of pain and love. His face was pale as his life's blood dripped onto the snow around his boots. Something greater than fear of the demon welled up inside her.

"No," she said, softly this time. She let go of Egan's wrist, then quickly secured Nixa more tightly into her cloak. Squaring her shoulders, she unlatched the sheath and drew out her sword. It pulsed with a blue light, faintly at first, but then stronger as she raised it over her head. She cried out in the ancient tongue of her people.

"*Tal tay Raheira!*" She dug her heels into Cinnabar's side and charged the thing spawned from the depths of hell.

The blue glow of her sword infused the air around her, encompassing her like a haze. Khamsin and Cinnabar cast no shadows against the whiteness of the ground as they quickly covered the short distance toward the mogra. The creature straightened its stance as she approached, sniffing the air. The scent of magic hung heavily in the stillness between the pines.

The Fav'lhir stepped back, reining in their horses, the animals skittish and trembling. Their tails whipped feverishly at something that prickled against their hides. But nothing they could see was there.

Suddenly the demon screamed, a high-pitched, hideous howl. It lashed out with its long arm. Thin streams of fire, blood-red, flowed from the tips of its black claws. Khamsin struck down with her sword, deflecting the flow that sputtered and sizzled as it rained down on the snow. Again, the mogra threw its hell-fire

224

and again Khamsin slashed out, first right, then left, then right again.

Cinnabar shifted from side to side as his mind worked in conjunction with hers. But these were defensive movements. Movements that would soon tire her and the horse, and gain nothing except a little more time for Egan to die. So as the mogra cast another slash of liquid flames in her direction, she let the blaze roar past her and into the base of a pine. She spurred Cinnabar. The horse reared up, its hoofs now equal with the demon's grotesque face.

It raised its arms, as if to grab Cinnabar's hoofs. Khamsin struck out, lunging forward with her sword. The sword caught the side of the mogra's face, ripping its cheek in half, leaving a gaping chasm from its left eye socket to the corner of its mouth. A bubbling, putrid froth flowed from where spellbound metal touched infernal flesh. The demon clawed at its own face, half-blinded.

"T'cahra fie di raheira!" she cried. Cinnabar reared again, forcing the demon back toward the Fav'lhir. It growled as it stumbled, its left arm whipping out just as Khamsin brought her sword down against it. She severed the arm just above the wrist. The clawed hand dropped, exploding as it touched the cold snow.

The mogra's visible form wavered, pulsing, its slimy body throbbing as it sought to shift its form. The trunk shortened, the arms lengthened, and a thin layer of a translucent hide flowed out of its sides. The snout became beak-like with ridges of sharp teeth. Cinnabar snorted warily.

Quickly, Khamsin grasped the cat tucked securely against her legs. She touched the hilt of her sword to Nixa's gray head, murmuring the words Ciro had taught her. She dropped her to the ground. The small animal grew, doubling then tripling in size until she was the length of the horse and half his height. Nixa roared at the featherless winged creature before her. She was no longer Nixa, but a sleek-furred, silver panther surrounded by the pulsing blue glow of Khamsin's spell.

The mogra lifted its wings but too late. The panther's lightning speed brought it on top of the foul creature. Nixa sank her teeth into its neck, ripping at the tough hide. The froth-ringed head lolled to one side. Nixa spat out a large chunk of flesh distastefully then bounded to stand protectively by Egan.

Khamsin kicked Cinnabar's sides and charged again. Her sword sliced through the center of the demon's body as easily as if it were made of silk.

The demon's wings spasmed. A hideous, shrieking sound shook the snow from the pines. The ground beneath the mogra churned, the air around it thick with a suffocating stench. Khamsin abruptly urged Cinnabar back as the demon's body throbbed. A cold wind rushed past her, then wrapped around the mogra, spinning its lifeless form.

The Fav'lhir screamed in terror. They gouged their horses with their boot heels in vain as they were sucked into the infernal cyclone. Bodies and beasts spun madly until all was a blur of brown and yellow and red.

Then there was nothing but the whiteness of the

untouched landscape before her. And the whisper of light winds through the tops of the pines.

Egan leaned feebly against a cracked and weathered boulder, his breathing labored and ragged. Eyes full of pain and confusion regarded her, unwavering. He slid to the ground, barely conscious.

A delicate coldness prickled Khamsin's face as she dismounted and ran to kneel by his side. She glanced up at the gray sky between the branches. It was snowing.

CHAPTER NINETEEN

With his good arm draped around Cinnabar's neck and Khamsin's arms wrapped around his waist, Egan allowed himself to be dragged to the mouth of a small cave at the base of the foothills. Nixa, now just Nixa again, guided them to her find and stayed with the injured man while Khamsin returned to the horse for her satchel. It was snowing harder. Cinnabar wedged himself under a wide overhang near the cave, content to chew on a few sprouts of dry grass growing in between the rocks.

She stripped Egan of his heavy outer-tunic. She pulled the remains of his shirt down around his waist, then examined the deep wound that crossed over his shoulder and chest. Handfuls of snow washed out the debris. She pulled cleansing herbs from her pouches, mixing them with the snow, and applied the mixture to the wound as Nixa paced nervously nearby. The Kemmon Rey had lost a lot of blood. His eyes burned bright with fever, his body fighting infection in its own way.

Twice he slipped from consciousness as her hands lay against his shoulder. The healing wasn't without its share of pain. She took as much of his pain into her own body as she could bear and transmitted to him what strength she could give, knowing she worked against time.

She had to stop the flow of his life's blood and stave off infection before he lapsed beyond the reach of what medicines she could conjure, given the meager supplies she brought with her. She lacked merris root and tislain, and there was no time to search for them. So she used more magic than was prudent. Ciro's warnings about using her powers so close to Traakhal were no longer valid. She had drawn her sword and battled an ensorcelled demon. The time for caution and timidity was passed.

Besides, Egan's life was at stake. And though he was Kemmon-Ro and a Hill Raider, he also proved to be a friend. And she was, before all else, a healer. The supernatural abilities of her craft knew no political boundaries.

Finally, she did all that she could, all she knew how. She stripped her cloak from around her shoulders. She laid it over the wounded man and touched his forehead with a slumbering incantation. He closed his eyes. She listened to the sound of his breathing. Hearing a normalcy return to its rhythm, she curled up on the rocky floor next to him, her heavy-outer tunic a pillow for her head and Nixa warm against her legs.

She woke from a deep sleep into darkness and

stumbled to the mouth of the cave. It was snowing heavily, the low-hanging clouds obscuring any light from the moons. She guessed it was near midnight or shortly after, a supposition confirmed in her mind when she touched Cinnabar's sleepy one.

She used a small spell to make some lifesweet for her horse, then returned to the depth of the cave, shivering, gathering a few small rocks as she went. She piled them in the center, a foot or two from where Egan lay. She drew her sword from its sheath and placed it on top of the stones. Soon, a reassuring orange glow seeped through the rocks. She removed the sword, returning it to its covering, and let the heat from the stones warm her body. The stones grew hotter and the interior of the cave brightened. She turned to find Egan's eyes open, regarding her with an odd mixture of gratitude and fear.

"Who are you?" His voice cracked as it passed through his dry, parched lips. A fever burned within him.

Before she could answer, he added, "You're a healer?"

This time she nodded. "Yes."

"You saved my life. Thank you."

"Did you think I'd do otherwise, Egan?"

He studied her profile in the glow of the stones as if he were seeing her for the first time. "No," he said. His gaze followed the feminine lines of her form beneath her thin shirt, lines previously obscured by the bulk of a thick tunic and shapeless cloak.

"You're not Camron."

"No."

He stared at her for a moment longer, then his eyes closed again, his head turning slowly to one side. There was still much healing his body had to do.

He woke a few hours later. She was changing the poultice on his chest. His left arm moved painfully until his hand lay on her wrist.

"I thought I dreamed you." His voice was stronger. And his eyes clearer, Khamsin noticed with some satisfaction.

"Nightmare, more like it. Are you thirsty? Do you think you could sit up and take water?"

He nodded.

She bundled her cloak and outer tunic under his back as he propped himself up on one elbow. She had filled an empty wineskin with fresh snow and herbs. She held it to his lips.

"Slowly," she cautioned. When he finished, she touched his face. His fever was receding but still higher than she liked.

"How long . . ."

She glanced over her shoulder to the mouth of the cave where Nixa sat. It was as gray as the cat's fur outside. "Five, six hours. There's been a bad storm. Makes it seem worse than it is."

"You've been here. The whole time?"

She nodded.

"Then, I don't remember. I asked you, didn't I? There is no lad called Camron."

"No." She offered him a smile. "Just myself. And yes, I'm a healer. Lest you fear I don't know what I'm doing," she added, as she scooped a fresh mixture of herbs and oil from a small bowl. She dabbed it carefully into his wounds.

"Why did you pretend . . ."

She shrugged. "It's a safer way to travel. Few question a young farm lad out after adventure."

He shook his head slowly. "Adventure? You came here looking for adventure?"

"No."

"Then, what do you seek?"

"Knowledge. Experience. Answers."

"And your family permits this?"

"My husband was murdered." Her voice went flat.

Egan closed his eyes for a moment. "But this uncle . . ."

She drew a deep breath. "That was just part of Camron's story."

"There's no one else?"

She thought of a pale-eyed man with hair the color of ravens' wings and a mist formed in her eyes. "No. Everything I've ever had is gone, save for my cat. And my horse."

He seemed to consider this information. "Lady, everything is *not* gone. You have Kemmon-Ro as your family. And Egan, Kemmon Rey, by your side, if you want him." He reached for her hand.

She clasped his fingers in her own. "I don't know how Elsy will take to having a sister."

"My offer isn't one of adoption."

Khamsin heard the emotion in his voice and remembered the strong feelings of kinship, and love, she had sensed in him. Her fingers slid through his. She turned toward the glowing pile of stones, as if the heat could burn off the water threatening to spill from her eyes.

"Thank you, Master Egan," she said finally, ignoring a familiar ache that resurrected again in her heart. "But I've loved truly only once in my life. And I've no further desire for anyone to take his place."

"I understand, lady." She glanced back at him. His face was full of compassion. "And I envy, then, what you and your husband had. For I've yet to find it in my life."

But it was not Tavis that Khamsin held deep within her heart. It was Rylan the Tinker.

Egan closed his eyes. Khamsin gently pulled her garments from under his back, folding her outer tunic again for his pillow. His breathing was steady as he slipped into sleep. She tucked her cloak around him.

She returned to her place by the warm stones. Egan offered her his name, his protection, his family, and his love. But she could never marry again, could never share a bed with a man and not think of the soft bed in Courten's Square. And the man who had taught her about love within it.

Neither could she brew tea and not see Rylan's hands holding his own cup out to her, as she lay weak and bruised on the forest floor.

Nor could she walk down a cobblestone street and not feel him, tall and strong, by her side.

Suddenly she could no longer hold back the tears. She lay her head against her knees and sobbed, the knowledge Rylan was indeed her very soul, her very life—and that which in her heart of hearts she knew she truly sought—coming much too late.

❋ ❋ ❋

Egan slept through the morning, waking once to accept the potion Khamsin gave him. His fever broke and the infection subsided. He only needed time to regain his strength.

She dozed herself but didn't sleep, fearing her dreams and what she might learn from them. Her presence had been felt, she was sure, yet she was reluctant to draw a mage circle and seek answers. If he was coming after her now, best she didn't know. There was little she could do about it, anyway.

The snow hadn't subsided and now drifted in great piles along the pine groves. She hoped Druke, Wade, and Skeely managed to find shelter before the storm hit.

She heard Egan stir and left her post at the mouth of the cave.

"You're better this afternoon."

"Is it that, already?" Painfully, he pulled himself into a sitting position and stared at the whiteness in the distance. "I wondered if you'd still be here when I woke. Now I see why."

"I'll stay until I can trust you on your own. Or until Druke finds us."

"Druke's got more sense than to attempt any traveling in this. Besides, when it snows this hard, it rarely lasts long. Things should clear shortly."

She nodded, knowing as soon as it did, she'd make preparations to depart.

"Lady?"

She turned.

"I . . . I know I said this last night, at least, I think I did. But thank you, for saving my life."

She smiled. "Elsy would never forgive me if I didn't."

"Is there a reason I can't know your name? I don't feel right calling you 'Camron.' "

"Khamsin. My name's Khamsin."

"It means 'child of the winds.' "

"I know." Bronya had told her, many times, the story of the day she was born, in the midst of a maelstrom.

"Will you travel back to Pinetrail with me, Lady Khamsin?"

"I can't, though be sure that my prayers will be with you on the road."

"Then there really is an uncle you seek, from home, from Tynder's Hill?"

Evidently his fever wiped some of their earlier conversations from his memory. "No. Aric wasn't my uncle but my brother-in-law. But he was killed several months ago."

"When your husband was killed."

Some things he did remember. "Yes. In a raid."

Egan was quiet for a moment. "Tynder's Hill is north of the Fohn and, though not Kemmon-Ro, is in our region. Am I right in guessing what you seek is revenge, Lady Khamsin? As the Master of Traakhal promises: protection, retaliation, and vindication?"

She wouldn't be the first to call upon a higher power for such ends, and as the story seemed one that Egan could comfortably accept, she let him think her reasons were so. The Kemmon Rey had enough problems to deal with. Disillusionment over his lady wasn't one she wanted to add. Besides, he was still Kemmon-Ro and as such would scarcely approve of her real reason for seeking out the castle of the Sorcerer.

"Do you know who murdered your people?"

"No," she lied. "They were killed in a raid outside the village. They'd gone hunting."

Egan sighed. "I could have the Kemmon bring you justice if you knew. But without that knowledge," he shook his head, "the answers must come through other sources."

"Other sources?"

"Yes. Protection, retaliation, and vindication. The Master has ways to know who planned that raid."

Khamsin had little doubt in that. The Sorcerer had many ways at his disposal, not the least of which was the Orb of Knowledge. And Egan's belief that his master was the provider of not only knowledge, but protection and vindication as well, gave Khamsin the opportunity she needed to admit Traakhal was now her destination.

"But the mountain trails will shortly be impassable," Egan said. "So, it's best you return with me to Pinetrail. We can make inquiries through the nests. If nothing more is known about the raid near Tynder's, then I'll take you to the castle after First Thaw. I'll be all healed then, as well."

She glanced at the deepening snow outside. "But isn't this the first storm of the season?

"Here, yes. But not in the mountains."

It was a difficulty she hadn't considered.

He saw the disappointment on her face. "Druke and Wade might be able to guide you there, lady. But there's no way you could return until after First Thaw."

Return? She wasn't the least bit concerned with returning; her only thoughts were on gaining entry to the Sorcerer's room in the east tower and destroying the orb. Wintertide was still a few weeks away.

"Elsy needs her father, Egan. She's looking forward to teaching him to read. It's best if you return to Pinetrail without me. What I have to do, my friend, should be done alone."

"You're going on to Traakhal?"

"I have to."

"But, Lady Khamsin . . ."

She shook her head stubbornly. "No."

"But?"

"Egan, please. I appreciate your offer but I'll not change my mind. This is something I, alone, have to do." She thought of how she had told Rylan almost the same thing, knowing the dangers that sought her out. Dangers he may already have met in Browner's Grove. Perhaps if she'd been with him, she could have saved him from Lady Melande's riders.

No. She wouldn't expose Egan to the wrath of the man he called his master. She wouldn't lose him too.

"I have to go," she said finally, and even the softness

of her tone could not hide the stubborn note in her voice.

❋ ❋ ❋

Druke, Wade, and Skeely found their cave two days later, amid much shouts and cries and backslapping. Khamsin returned to her disguise as Camron and made Egan promise not to tell the truth, or the story of what happened with the mogra until after Wintertide. He was puzzled by her request, but admitted he owed her. He agreed, asking only that he be allowed to accompany her to the beginning of the mountain trail that would eventually lead her to the peninsula in the Khal.

He was much stronger now, so this she granted him. They left the men from his Kemmon lounging comfortably in the cave. Egan traveled almost until sundown by her side, reaching the foot of the trail just as the last light of the day bathed the peaks before them in a pale yellow glow.

There was a traveler's nest just an hour farther, he told her. She thanked him, letting a silence fall between them for a moment before spurring her horse onto the trail.

Years later, though, when Elsy the Rey's daughter would gather her children around her on a warm night in Last Harvest, and recite the tale of their grandfather and the magical lady, she would swear that before Kiasidira faded into the twilight, she first kissed Master Egan good-bye.

TRAAKHAL - ARMIN

CHAPTER TWENTY

Khamsin rode west into deepening snows for a full day. The sky overhead was clear. The deeply rutted path turned sharply just after she set out the next morning, and for a while the rising sun shone on her face. Gradually, though, the trail wove in a southerly direction. By noon she entered the peninsula.

She was high in the mountains above the tree line. The cliffs rising upon either side of her were stark and gray. Having resumed her shielding, she saw no one and sensed no one. He may be expecting her, but she would not aid him as to when.

Her hood covered her short-cropped hair. Gloved hands held Cinnabar's reins. A Kemmon-Ro blanket lay across the horse's back, a gift from Egan.

Progress was slow as the bare sections of the trail were rocky and treacherous. Those areas blanketed in snow hinted at dangers that could cripple her horse. She was forced to dismount again and lead Cinnabar on foot, while Nixa emitted displeasure at being deprived of the warmth of Khamsin's cloak. The icy winds ruffled her fur, and the gray cat tucked her paws beneath her as she balanced on the padded saddle on Cinnabar's broad back.

The cold sterility of the landscape affected Khamsin as well. Her young face took on a more determined mien, her heart again hardening where emotions rubbed it raw. She had lost the warmth and security of Tanta Bron only to make her home with the smith, in Cirrus Cove. Until that, too, along with Rina's bright laughter and Aric's teasing smile, was abruptly taken from her. She'd given up then, been willing to die, to release her hold on life when the tinker found her, healing her first with his words, and then with his touch. Of all of those she'd known in her eighteen years, only he hadn't sought her with questions but instead, taught her how to find answers. And he hadn't taken or demanded, only offered his love and understanding.

And she'd lost him, too.

Ciro was her teacher. She accepted that her purpose in his life was only that of an obedient student. Still, she was fond of the mad wizard. She had hoped he'd accompany her on her journey, for companionship, if nothing more. But that, too, was denied her.

Of all the most unlikely hurts she carried within her, it was that of Egan, the Kemmon-Ro Hill Raider. He was, in all reality, her enemy to be hated and feared. Or at least, she at one time believed that was true. Just as she believed it was true that all Hill Raiders were wanton murderers.

Now, she knew the destruction she'd seen were the acts of the few: the Fav'lhir, under the command of Melande the Witch. The Northern Kemmons protected their own territories, but never invaded the Cove towns.

She also now knew Egan as a man who loved his daughter and his people and was capable of loving her. But she had nothing to offer in return. When the tinker left Noviiya, he took Khamsin's heart with him.

All she had now was her purpose, the reason Bronya the Healer sheltered her for so long. And that was the only thing that kept her moving, trudging through the heavy snows, ignoring the icy sting of the winds on her face, as she made her way through the mountains of the peninsula toward Traakhal-Armin.

She pushed herself to the point of exhaustion, gathering only a few hours rest, aware that in the four days since they had turned south, they had made as much progress as she and Egan had in four hours across the marsh.

Cinnabar's sides were thinning out. The horse existed on the dry, flaky patches of moss that were the only life in the bleak mountains, other than the half-dead spiders and occasional, pitifully meager, gray mice Nixa found in the cracks and crannies of the cliffs. Khamsin had the last of the bread and shared half of her dried apple with Cinnabar when she was sure they were still a few days from the castle's outer walls, since the trail hadn't yet started to descend.

At the rate they traveled, it could take them another week to cross that distance. It was only the thought of her animals starving that made her break her self-imposed mystical silence and conjure a few small items of food: a meat-pie for Nixa, a small bag of rich grain for Cinnabar, and some carrots and figs for herself. As she drew the objects out of the mage circle, the first one she etched since leaving Noviiya, she tensed and waited for the inevitable to appear.

But nothing did. She flattened herself against the depression in the cliff's surface and watched the light dusting of snowdrift down from the slender ledge above, coating their rations with glistening crystals.

The trail showed no signs of descending toward Khal after two more days travel. With a sinking heart Khamsin accepted that perhaps they were lost. They must have gotten off the main trail during one of the small, snow squalls that temporarily blinded them, and they now traveled in circles, up and down the mountain, but getting no closer to their destination. She looked in vain for something familiar in her surroundings, but all the stark landscape looked the same. She gained no guidance from the stars at night either, as they weren't visible through the thick overcast of clouds around her. So she urged Cinnabar onwards, judging Wintertide now less than a week away.

The trail ended so suddenly, that, blinded by the snow, they almost stumbled over the edge of the cliff. Cinnabar skittered backward, nickering as Khamsin plunged, her boots finding nothing solid beneath them. She clung to the reins in her hands for dear life as the horse dragged her backward, ignoring Nixa's claws in his neck.

She lay panting in the snow, her heart pounding. Then she kneeled on the edge of the cliff and peered over through the snow swirling around them. It was a sheer drop of hundreds of feet into a white-crested valley. In the distance, the lights from signal fires glinted, beckoning, and she could just make out the outlines of a great fortress. And the darkness of a lake beyond. Traakhal-Armin lay before her.

A turn-off or a fork. They must have missed the turn-off, a trail leading rapidly downwards. They retraced their steps, finally coming upon a narrow gap in the mountainside. It was a slow descent, narrow and awkward. She wondered how the Hill-Raider's slim-hoofed horses ever made it down the trail. There must be other trails, she surmised, that would be uncovered after First Thaw. This one was no doubt used only in emergencies, as it was also undoubtedly the most treacherous.

Then there was forest around them again, and the smell of the pines assailed her like the aroma of bread baking, warm and reassuring. There were sounds, too, sounds that had been absent in the mountains, of winds rustling branches and the occasional calling of a winter bird. Nixa's ears perked at this last sound, her stomach interpreting what it meant. She bounded ahead, ignoring Khamsin's remonstrations, and only returned after she feasted on her kill. It wasn't polite, she knew, to eat in front of others when she had nothing to share with them.

The distance between the cliffs and the castle seemed short as she gazed down from the trail's end, but it was a trick her eyes played on her due to the height of the cliffs. So it wasn't until late the following day, with the cover of dusk to aid her, that an exhausted and half-frozen form was carried up to the castle's outer walls on the back of an equally weary and decrepit nag, the colors of the Kemmon-Ro clearly visible in the torch light.

The Khalar guard assessed the situation quickly and, calling for aid, allowed the great gates of the walls to be opened, admitting the unconscious, young boy.

Khamsin groaned weakly, as she was pulled from the saddle.

"Easy, lad," a man's voice said.

She tried to stand and had to lean against him for support.

"Tedmond, Lord Tedmond," she rasped. "I must speak to him. I bring a message of urgency, from Master Egan, the Kemmon Rey."

The guard nodded as he held her meager weight. She let her head drop forward, covering her face with her hood.

Go! she told Nixa. She stumbled against the guard, drawing his attention. The gray cat, secreted in her unlatched saddlebag, jumped to the ground, and scurried toward the stables. She would find her mistress later. But at the moment, her existence might elicit unwanted questions.

"Bring him to the hearth room," someone called out.

She let herself be dragged into the castle and up a flight of long stairs.

She was guided into a well-padded chair before a small table, a blazing fire at her back. Only then did she allow herself to raise her eyes and examine her surroundings. The hearth room was just as its name bespoke: a large room with a hearth at one end that filled almost the entire wall. Over the hearth hung two swords, crossed and encrusted with jewels. An adjoining wall made of gray granite had windows draped with heavy curtains and richly woven tapestries. The table beneath her hands was of a polished wood in a deep color.

A silver goblet was placed before her, full of wine. She was instructed to drink. She gulped at it thirstily, aware of its heavy bouquet and well-aged taste. What was offered to her might not have been found in even the best of taverns in Noviiya.

She thought wistfully of Ciro.

Kindly hands made as if to remove her cloak, but she shivered and said "not yet," and they complied.

The door at the far end of the room swung open. A thin man, not much taller than Khamsin, strode through the entryway, his slight form draped in robes of deep burgundy trimmed in black. His hair was white and pulled severely back from his angular face. His mustache tapered in two, long tendrils down the side of his mouth. Small, intensely dark eyes regarded her critically.

"Lord Tedmond, this lad brings news from the Kemmon-Ro. At the risk of his life, as you can see."

The Lord Chamberlain nodded. "Thank you, Witton. You may go. Tell Fenella to prepare the guest room in the south wing for our friend. I don't think, from the looks of him, or the storm, he'll be going anywhere for quite some time."

"Thank you, m'lord," Khamsin gasped weakly, lowering the pitch of her voice.

"Now, lad, first, your name. Then, whatever needs you may have, wounds to be tended to, before we require your story."

"My name's Camron, m'lord, Camron of Tynder's Hill for that's where I was born. But I am Kemmon-Ro now, and I follow Master Egan. The news I bear comes from him and Druke."

Tedmond nodded. Khamsin knew the sound of the familiar names gave her story the needed credence. She continued. "And I have no wounds that require tending any longer, sirrah, other than I haven't eaten in days and am half-frozen. But those things I'll survive. Those in my tale have not, for they've succumbed to a creature the likes of which has not walked through the Darklings before. It attacked Master Egan, and as I speak, I don't know if he still breathes. It also attacked a Drin nest, and no one there lives to tell the tale. It was Druke, sirrah, who sent me on my way, along with Skeely and Wade, Egan's nephews. We became separated in a storm. I'm grieved to learn from your guard that they haven't reached Traakhal before me."

"What manner of thing did you see, Camron?"

And Khamsin described the mogra, adding to her

story and embellishing it as she felt was necessary. She wove a dire tale of battle in the foothills, drawing on names and attributes of other Kemmon-Ro gleaned in the fireside conversations in the swamp. It was a convincing tale, and as she finished, Lord Tedmond knotted his hands together.

"You'll be given a place to rest and heal, boy, and I'll send some of our best out into the mountains to search for your companions, as soon as the storm abates. Don't give up hope. They may be safe in some cave, yet tired and cold, but alive.

"As for the creature you describe, it's a mogra, under the command of Lady Melande. We hadn't thought she'd be so brazen as to come this far north. But it looks as if we underestimated her. What I fear now is those tales that haven't yet reached our ears. Where else she has struck and to what devastation."

"But, sirrah, couldn't Master Ro tell you?"

Lord Tedmond hesitated. "He could if he were in residence, lad, but he isn't. The master's been absent from Traakhal for some time now, dealing with the very problems you've encountered. He has much to tend to these days, as Tarkir's youngest are keeping him busy. I've no doubt he already knows of these demons. And will return shortly with the news that they're no longer a threat."

Tedmond smiled tiredly at Khamsin, and she was aware of the weight of the responsibilities he carried on his slight frame.

She also knew something else: the Sorcerer wasn't

here. That meant the Sorcerer's room would be empty. And if Tedmond was right, if the Sorcerer really was aware of the existence of the mogra in the Darklings, perhaps he was too busy dealing with Melande's pets to pay attention to the security of his home. For who would ever suspect one small, fourteen-year-old, farm boy of being capable of invading the castle Traakhal-Armin at Wintertide?

CHAPTER TWENTY-ONE

Khamsin lay on the soft bed with the warm, woolen coverlet pulled up over her ears and listened to the footsteps approach her door. Someone knocked softly and, receiving no answer, entered, along with the aroma of hot stew. Footsteps became tiptoes, and there was the sound of a tray placed on a table. Then the door closed again.

Khamsin counted to thirty before throwing back the coverlet and springing out of the bed. She'd removed her cloak and heavy over-tunic and couldn't risk being seen in just her thin shirt, which impugned her identity as a boy.

She ate what she could of the bread and the vegetables. The wine she avoided, settling for water, since she needed a clear head about her tonight. When she finished she laid the bowl of stew on the floor. Nixa's small head popped out of her satchel. The cat willingly finished what her mistress kindly left to share with her. She scampered under the bed as Khamsin pulled the coverlet up around her neck again. Within minutes, the door opened and the same tiptoeing footsteps that brought her meal, retrieved it.

Now she had to wait. She let the darkness creep through the comfortably furnished room without stirring. She and Nixa took turns dozing. While one slept, the other kept watch on the position of the moons, knowing that in the waning hours of the night, most of the castle should be asleep.

It was only then that she again slipped from the bed and strapped her sword about her waist. With Nixa in tow, she stepped cautiously for the door.

She listened for sounds before opening it and, hearing nothing, pulled it only as far as was necessary to slip through. She closed it quickly and laid her hand against the lock, sealing it with a small spell.

Her back to the wall, she crept silently forward. She was at the end of a long hallway in the south wing, a sole, lighted torch just outside her door. Quickly, she moved into the shadows, sending Nixa ahead of her as sentry. Her footsteps were noiseless on the stone floor.

The castle had three wings: north, south, and east, radiating out from the large square of the main hall. She had glimpsed as much from the end of the mountain trail. It was with this image in mind that she traveled swiftly down the stairs, knowing she had to pass through the back of the great room to gain access to the east wing. She moved with a stealth learned in the woods around Cirrus Cove, where she and Nixa had set up ambushes for each other on its winding trails.

She reached the last step and found not one great room but several, large gathering halls, capable of housing an entire Kemmon in each. There was a noise. She darted behind the thick drapery. Nixa described to her the sleepy-eyed guard that strode by.

It took her several minutes to find the east stairs; they weren't adjacent to any of the common rooms, but then, she hadn't expected they would be. The east wing was the private sanctuary of the Sorcerer. Few had had reason to seek this section without specific invitation.

She found the great staircase with its carved railing through a small room that led to a library and then another room. There was a peaked archway at this point with no light beyond. It was through this Nixa led her. Taking a deep breath, she followed the cat up the stairs.

The fact that no one interrupted her wanderings, that doors were not kept locked, or rooms cordoned off only attested to the power the Sorcerer exercised over those who resided in the castle. The price one would pay for violating his property far outweighed whatever meager gain the thief might, for a few seconds, grasp in his hands.

There was a chill apparent in the air as she entered the east wing. She remembered the Lord Chamberlain's words. The Sorcerer hadn't been at the castle for some time. Evidently, no one kept the hearths burning in anticipation of his return either. Still, Khamsin quickened her steps, urging Nixa onward in search of the final staircase that would lead to the tower and the room with the golden mage circle.

The cat darted ahead, only to come back with the news that this hallway, too, came to an abrupt end like the two others they had traveled on below. The south wing had five levels and no tower. The access they sought had to be somewhere on the next two floors.

They climbed and they groped through the darkness. No torch lights here cut into the gloom. Rooms, unlocked, were empty of anything resembling a staircase or an irregularly shaped wall signaling that such an addition lay within. Khamsin was aware of books and map charts on walls and tabletops, carved figurines and vases and urns and just about anything else that could have been collected over a three hundred year span. There were musical instruments and costumes such as those worn during a Fool's Eve Ball. In another room, a collection of weapons: swords, spears, and things so foreign she couldn't even recognize them, except to understand their placement in this particular location designated them as lethal.

The last room she came upon was lavish but its furnishings unfamiliar, save for a few items. It was a games room, like the palace in Noviiya, with card tables and game boards, wheels of fortune and games of skill. Several decks of cards had been laid out on the tabletops in various patterns, as if the Sorcerer moved from one game to another at whim. She thought of the card game played by Egan and the others that night on the marsh. She wondered against whom the Sorcerer played, and if he ever lost.

Quietly, she pulled the door of the games room back into place and leaned against the wall, puzzled and dejected. Nixa sat on her haunches, her tail swishing, her eyes on her mistress. They found no staircase, not even a hint of one. But there had to be some way.

Of course. The answer was so obvious, she almost laughed out loud. Of course there was no staircase. For what would a Sorcerer want with stairs? And what better way to insure he wouldn't be disturbed during his conjurings than to build the circle room with only one means of entrance or exit. Ciro had said no mortal man had even been there. For no mortal man could dematerialize and materialize at will.

But Raheiran blood ran in her veins. And weeks of preparation with the aging mage in Noviiya had taught her how to use that gift, if nothing else. She swept the cat up into her arms, as she had so many times on the street in front of Ciro's lodgings, and stopped.

There was a slender window at the far end of the hall. Now the first rays of the morning sun slipped through its meager slot. Soon, the rest of the castle would awaken. Already, she surmised, the cooks and kitchen help bustled below. Someone might come to check on the lad, bring word of a hot breakfast awaiting him. If Camron were not to be found . . .

Involuntarily, she glanced upward. She was so close. She knew it, could feel it almost as if the walls around her throbbed. But she needed time . . . time.

Well, she had locked her door. Perhaps just one quick look.

With an audible sigh, she dropped her shielding and transported herself into the large round room directly over her head.

For all that Ciro had told her, for all that she had seen in her trespassings this very night, nothing prepared her for the opulence that fairly glittered from the walls and floor around her. Khamsin gasped and truly believed, for the moment, that she had fallen into an immense treasure chest.

The room was round and had four tall arched windows, one facing east, one west, one north, and one south. A waist-high mantle ringed the wall. On it sat those objects long associated with the manufacture of magic: amulets and charms, tokens and chalices, wands, and mortars and pestles. The striking thing about the collection, though, was that all of the objects were cast of the purest gold or platinum, encrusted with jewels and edged with feather-light filigree. Khamsin counted seventy-five chalices before she turned her attention to the center of the room.

The mage circle inlaid into the floor was just as Ciro had described it, though words did it no justice. At each outer rune point was a blue diamond; a smaller circle, inside, was made of rubies. The signs of the heavens formed even a larger circle outside the mage circle, and Khamsin stepped carefully around until she found the month of her birthing. It was here she reached out and felt, rather than saw, the tenuous fabric that ran from floor to ceiling, through which only two beings could pass.

She ran her hands along its surface, sensing the spells and incantations woven together like threads. The skills it took to create something of that nature were beyond even her comprehension. For the first time a small knot of fear formed in her stomach. This was no shaman or trickster with whom she was dealing, like the one she had fooled in Noviiya. This was the Sorcerer of Traakhal-Armin.

The Orb of Knowledge beckoned from within the circle of rubies, its smooth, round surface reflecting the pale light filtering in through the high windows. It was secured inside a cabinet fashioned of silver bars on top of a high, six-legged pedestal. The orb rested on a thin, silken scarf strung between two carved handles, the way a large jug of water was often carried down from the stream. Khamsin stared, perceiving something liquid beneath its surface. But the light outside was increasing. She was wasting time.

She motioned quickly to her cat, and as the soft animal snuggled in a familiar way in her arms, she allowed herself one last indulgent glance around the magnificent room before dematerializing.

The next thing she saw was the broad, wooden back of the door of her room. And someone knocked loudly against it.

Quickly, she shoved Nixa under the small bed and draped her tunic over her shoulders, thankful she had remembered to lock the door earlier when she set out on her explorations.

"A moment, a moment," she called out in answer to

the rappings, her voice carrying the thickness that comes with sleep.

A matronly chambermaid stood on the other side of the door as Khamsin opened it.

"Thought we might've lost ye, young sirrah." The gray-haired woman fluffed the short, white apron bound around her thick waist. "But then, I allows ye've had a troublesome few days, out there in the cold. Overslept, did ye?"

"Aye." Khamsin bowed her head slightly, ruffling her hair as she'd often seen Tavis do in the mornings and yawned. "Feel much better, I do now, ma'am. Sorry if I gave you a fright."

The older woman chuckled and, reaching out, poked at Khamsin's ribs through the hastily donned tunic. "A good hot meal 'tis what you need, lad. Fill up them skinny bones of yours. Come downstairs when you're ready."

Khamsin leaned against the doorjamb, as the chamber-maid ambled down the hall. She had been lucky, so lucky, in returning when she did. If the castle staff discovered an empty room, a locked, empty room, she might not have fared so well. As it was, she had nothing more now to worry about than the good-natured chiding of the kitchen-help at having overslept.

At least, that was all she had to worry about until nightfall. Then, she would have to return to the room with the golden mage circle and take the Orb of Knowledge into her hands.

Her thoughts traveled no farther than that.

❄ ❄ ❄

After breakfast, she made the expected inquires about her supposed traveling companions, lost in the mountains, feigning a believable concern. The lean-faced guards she spoke to were well trained to keep the optimism in their voice, encouraging the young farm lad that all was not lost and, by the grace of Tarkir, his friends would soon be found.

A twinge of conscience poked at her during the exchange. She knew that on her words alone, several Khalarian guards would have ventured out into the mountains, seeking lost travelers who did not exist. But more than that, she was bothered by her newfound ability to lie, to fabricate events and existences so completely that even the Sorcerer's highly trained staff were unable to see through her deception. She found herself expressing emotions she didn't feel and reacting to events that didn't exist until she began to question her own veracity.

What had she become, what happened to young Khamsin of Cirrus Cove? She was the one who was gentle with animals, upon whose outstretched hand wild birdlings rested. She was the one who had helped birth babes and healed the sick and cared so deeply for those in her small coveside village that she had risked all to further her knowledge, in order to protect them. Even when they had shunned her and, at the worst, had tried to kill her, her only thoughts had been of them, of her village, of her people, and what she owed them. It was why she was here now, to avenge the atrocities that had given her life, and her friends, death.

It should be more difficult, she admonished herself, as she sat in the window well of her small room in the castle, watching the late afternoon sun cast long shadows across the wide courtyard below. Her physical discomfort, her personal losses, her tribulations in the mountains, were slight compared to the devastation upon which she was now prepared to embark. To be the one responsible for the destruction of the Orb of Knowledge should carry more of a price than she paid. For all that the Sorcerer stood for, she still respected his wisdom and his skill; *had* to respect it. She'd touched the protective shielding at the perimeter of the mage circle and knew that this was something so far beyond her capabilities, so far beyond her imagination that she found herself in awe of the power that created it.

Almost . . . almost she wished she wasn't the one to cause its end. Of all of those born in the Land in over two hundred years, Ciro had told her she was the only one besides the Sorcerer who could gain access to the Orb of Knowledge. The protective veil surrounding it insured that. But she was perhaps, also, the only one who could appreciate it, understand it, revel in its depths and intricacies. She felt like a musician in a room full of deaf mutes demanding the death of the orchestra.

Khamsin closed her eyes and let her head rest against the stones behind her. This wasn't the time for such soft and sentimental thoughts. Those were allowable when she was no more than Khamsin of Cirrus Cove, wife of the smith, and healer of the village. But the smith was dead and the village, her village, was burned and abandoned. And she was just Khamsin now. No. Perhaps no longer even Khamsin, but Kiasidira.

Kiasidira had only one purpose in the Land.

And it was to be found within the Orb of Knowledge.

CHAPTER TWENTY-TWO

The hours of darkness this time seemed to move more slowly than they had only a day before. Khamsin prowled restlessly around the confines of her room, as she waited for the castle noises to cease. The night before, much of her fatigue was genuine. She slept, confident in Nixa's watchful eyes.

Tonight, though, she was thoroughly rested and well fed. Sleep wouldn't come. Even the gray feline seemed more agitated than usual. Khamsin wondered if the same thoughts plagued the smaller mind as well, but was reluctant to share her concerns with the cat. To do so wouldn't be reassuring to either of them.

The Sorcerer was due to return. Lord Tedmond said as much at Khamsin's first and only meeting with him in the hearth room. And judging from the attitudes of the guards and the servants, it was their opinion as well. The only problem was when.

The few discreet questions Khamsin laid upon the kitchen help gave her little information with which to work. It was not unusual, it seemed, for Master Ro to be absent from Traakhal for extended periods of time. It was also not unusual for him to reside in the great castle for months, even seasons on end, without leaving. Khamsin began to realize that after three hundred years, any display of behavior was considered within reason.

But she had only tonight. The longer she delayed, the more questions would be asked about Camron of Tynder's Hill. For now, she had enough to worry about with the comings and goings of the castle staff. The inexplicable appearances, and disappearances, of the Sorcerer could not even be taken into consideration.

If only she could convince herself of that! She winced now at her foolhardiness of the previous evening, when she had blithely traipsed around the east wing of the castle in the dark. Her shielding may have protected her from him, if he sought her whereabouts. But it also hid the Sorcerer from her.

There was one other constant she learned in her conversations with the kitchen maids, as she had helped herself to a thick slice of freshly baked bread earlier that evening. It was that the castle—save for the aging Lord Tedmond—seemed to operate on a much more efficient level when the Sorcerer was absent.

Not that it was said he ever interfered. In truth, there were those in the lower stations of service who admitted to having never even set eyes upon their master. They were also the ones more willing to gossip about the Sorcerer.

The problem lay with those who had seen, or knew, their master. They were the ones who said very little, who drew an almost inaudible breath when his name was mentioned.

Khamsin was familiar with the single-minded devotion and respect often accorded the lord of the manor by his people, as was his due. But at Traakhal, she wondered if it weren't more than that.

If it weren't unembellished fear.

And in the day and a half she had lived amongst them, that same fear crept up into her spine, too.

She splayed her hands out in front of her in the darkness, raising them toward the window until they came between her face and the twin moons, now cresting high in the winter sky. The pale light filtered through, glistening in the depths of her eyes. She allowed herself to be drawn by the silvery ribbons, slowly, carefully, still maintaining contact with the nervous, gray feline that was her watchdog. She sought out any strong emanations of power nearby. If he traveled, perhaps by horseback, or boat . . .but no. The emanations from the walls of the castle itself were too strong. Too much magic had been cast here over the centuries. The residue from the spells and incantations now laced through the air like smoke from an ever-burning fire.

When she first learned her magic at Tanta Bron's side, she came up against the same problem. The old woman's cave would seem to pulse with the power of ancient spells. In time, she'd been able to overcome that interference, even use it to her advantage.

But try as she might, there was no way she could overcome the presence of the Sorcerer now.

And he wasn't even in residence. Of that she was sure.

"There's nothing more I can do," she said softly to her cat, though the comment was unnecessary. It made little difference to Nixa. She would do as Khamsin requested, out of love.

Khamsin knelt on the floor, taking the small feline into her arms.

"Now," she whispered again, into ears as soft as an evening breeze in summer.

And they were gone.

❋ ❋ ❋

She placed the cat on top of the mantle that ringed the room and, her hands now free, unlatched the clasp on her sword. It was strictly for precaution. To draw it would shed more light in the darkened room, for a cloud had temporarily obscured the moons. But to draw it would also signal that something of power entered the chamber, more than the dropping of her shielding or the use of her minor spells to transport herself here. And that was something she didn't wish to do.

Besides, she knew her eyes would adjust in a few moments to the darkness. And the moons should come out, again.

Nixa high-stepped fluidly over a series of large amulets, her whiskers twitching at the pungent odor of the perfumed oils that coated their surfaces. She relayed her opinions back to Khamsin, but her mistress wasn't interested.

Not now, she chastised silently. She followed the intricate carvings on the floor until she stood in the same place she had the night before, when the first light of dawn filtered in, urging her to return to her chamber.

But it was now a hair's breath of two hours past midnight and hours before daybreak. And this time she had no intention of returning to her room, daybreak or not.

This much she knew: When she smashed the orb, it would send a searing signal to any and all of the powers. Other wizards, like Ciro, and mages and alchemists would feel it like a rent in their flesh; village healers would start and gasp. What the Sorcerer would do, she chose not to imagine. But she accepted that, at that moment, he would return to Traakhal.

But it would be too late.

Trembling slightly, Khamsin held her hands out until she felt the spellbound curtain before her. She stepped toward it.

"Kiasidira," she said in a hushed voice. The curtain parted, closing behind her as she came inside.

❖ ❖ ❖

Many hundreds of miles to the east, in the cluttered attic rooms in the top of an old warehouse, a black-cloaked figure felt the parting and stiffened. The parchment in his hands drifted to the floor.

❀ ❀ ❀

Nixa stirred restlessly underneath the north window. Khamsin heard the sound but ignored it, her eyes now fixed on the churning of brilliant colors inside the orb. She reached through the wide, side opening of the cabinet, fingertips barely grazing its surface. She felt a tingling travel through her.

On either end were two large handles of wood. They weren't attached to the cabinet but rested on a cross-piece. The orb could be removed from the pedestal in order to facilitate its use.

Or its destruction.

She grasped the handles firmly and slowly lifted the orb from its cradle, testing its weight and balance as she did. It was bulky but not as heavy as she expected. She wove her fingers around the thick handles. The position was awkward and cumbersome. It might slip but not break. It could roll through the protective curtain. She released the handles, but only momentarily, so as to change the position of her hands.

There. That was better. This was no more difficult than lifting a heavy laundry basket. In spite of her circumstances, or perhaps because of them, the thought struck her as oddly amusing. She rested the handles again in the crosspiece. A soft giggle rose in her throat. Then died abruptly.

A pulsation of power shot through her. She choked back a scream, her fingers flying from the handles as if they'd touched molten metal. She collapsed in half, her legs buckling.

Her world exploded inside and outside of her simultaneously. Her conscious mind reeled. She could see nothing but a swirl of colors before her eyes. A stabbing brightness, a searing brilliance. She tore her gaze from the orb as if the translucent object itself was the source of her torture.

But it wasn't. That much she sensed, as she clung to the thick silver bars of the cabinet. Nothing was coming from the orb, but rather was building around her, through the very air of the mage circle.

The searing energy intensified. She slid to her knees. The mind-deafening pulsations continued.

She grasped one of the pedestal's thick wooden legs and tried to pull herself to her feet. Her fingers slid numbly down the ornate posts. Then a second wave of searingly hot energy rolled over her and through her, tossing her like flotsam in the tide. She dropped to one knee and clung to the pedestal, fighting for air, struggling to breathe. Her head fell forward. She buried her face against her arms. But there was no protection, no cessation. The pulsations grew stronger until she felt them come to a focal point burning directly into her back.

Weakly, she knelt next to the wooden column. She'd waited too long. There was only one being, only one entity in the Land who possessed that much power, that much force that his mere presence alone was capable of crushing the strongest of men to the earth, flattening them into the very dust they came from.

That being was the Sorcerer.

The Master of Traakhal was home.

Suddenly, the incessant pinpricks against her skin disappeared. And, save for her breath that was still coming in great gasps, it was as if nothing at all had happened. She raised her face and peered through the pedestal. The stars in the dark sky outside still twinkled through the narrow window before her. The night air was still.

Then she heard the soft rustle of cloth like the sound of long robes or a cloak behind her. Trembling, she inched her body around in her crouch until she faced the source of the sound.

And there, clad in the night-black, riding regalia of the North Land Hill Raiders, with a long, black cloak secured by a platinum clasp at his throat, was Tarkir's first born. The Sorcerer of Traakhal-Armin.

She leaned back against the pedestal and breathed a name in disbelief.

". . . Rylan."

CHAPTER TWENTY-THREE

He stepped quickly toward her, hands outstretched.

An icy blade of fear ran through her body. Khamsin struggled to her feet. "No. Stop!" Her voice, hoarse, broke as she called out the words. "Come no further or I'll . . ." and she fingered the hilt of her sword but suddenly changed her mind. She wrenched the orb from its case. She held it in front of her. It swayed in its cradle of silk.

"I'll destroy it." Her voice was stronger now. She adjusted her stance like a fighter, squaring off to face her enemy.

He stopped, an odd expression on his face, a mixture of anger and confusion. "Khamsin, I'm no threat to you."

"But only if I do what you want. Bend to your will."

"How can you believe that after . . ."

"Because you're the Sorcerer. Rothal-kiarr." Hatred burned in her voice. His own was flat by comparison when he answered.

"Yes, Kiasidira, I am."

Still, his voice, saying her name, shocked her.

"Then you must be stopped. This," and she held the orb away from her body, "will tell me how."

"It will provide you with information. But it won't make decisions for you."

She studied his face, so familiar in so many ways, seeking some glint of malevolence in his eyes, steeling herself against expected wrath. But she saw nothing: not hatred or suspicion or fear. He was just Rylan, dressed in black, with Hill Raiders' daggers strapped to his thigh. A blue-white diamond, like the ones in the mage circle, glistened in his ear in place of the small gold star he'd always worn. From his belt dangled a small, familiar, favored amulet.

He was the tinker. Yet she knew he wasn't. Incomprehension mixed with fear.

"I'll take what I learn back to Ciro."

"Ciro's dead."

Her arms shook, the orb momentarily feeling almost too heavy to lift.

"Why?" her voice cracked. "Was he such a threat to you? He was just a mad, old wizard, he . . . he . . ."

"I'm not the one responsible for his death. Believe me. It wasn't my doing, or my wish." He took another step toward the curtain. "Khamsin . . ."

"No! Stay where you are or I will drop this. If I can't use it, then you won't, either."

"You can use it, *we* can use it together."

Ciro had said the Sorcerer would seek Kiasidira as an ally.

"And what is it you wish to teach me, Master Ro? How to kill innocent children, slit their throats and the throats of their mothers? How to burn villages, destroy farmlands, steal babes from their cradles?"

"Those aren't my methods."

"They're Hill Raiders' methods." She pushed thoughts of Egan and Druke from her mind. Now was not the time to question the feasibility of her actions. She had been born for this day. She tried to focus on the charred embers of Cirrus Cove, and not on the memory of the soft smile of a man called Rylan. Or one called Egan. "The Hill Raiders follow your commands."

"Only the Khalar. The Magrisi pay no allegiance to me and neither do the Fav'lhir. The Khalar are not wanton murderers. I wouldn't tolerate that."

"But the day the riders attacked the Cove, you were there. They killed my husband. They hanged him and burned my house. And you didn't stop them!"

For the first time since he entered the room, he pulled his gaze from her and stared out at the dark slit of a far window.

"No, I didn't stop them," he said finally, turning back to face her. His voice held a heavy note of resignation, as if the admission pained him.

"But you could have."

He clasped his hands behind him. "Those were Magrisi riders, under Lucial's command. So in that sense, I had no part in his death. But I admit it served my purpose. I wanted you too much."

She gasped in horror. "You wanted . . . you . . . you allowed death to claim an innocent man to serve your own ends?"

"Lucial sent riders after some of my people in the Nijanas, first, as a diversion. I didn't know of the raid on Cirrus until his riders were already in the village. I did what I could to make sure Tavis and the children didn't suffer. But I was more concerned with keeping you safe, getting you away from there."

"Why? So I could lead you to Ciro? Is that why you sent that deformed, hell-spawned creature to the bell tower that night? Or the one in the marsh? Your pets in the dungeons, Rothal-kiarr!"

He looked perplexed, but only slightly. "What creature in the bell tower?"

She almost screamed at him. "The one that called my name. Said 'Kiasidira' with a mouth that had no lips! And looked at me with sockets that had no eyes! Ciro saved my life that night. And even he didn't know my name until I told him. Who else but Rothal-kiarr knew to call me Kiasidira?"

"Lucial and Melande," he replied, and his voice was quiet. "They knew."

"You lie!"

"Ask. Place the orb back into the pedestal and ask it." He pointed at the translucent orb wavering in its silken cradle. "Let me show you how. It can't lie."

She hesitated, then, "No. You're not interested in the truth. You're only interested in controlling the orb."

"I am interested in the truth. As well as in the proper balance of power."

"So you thought to kidnap me, is that it? In Noviiya, with all your pretty words and pretenses, to make me do what you want. You thought to deceive me. You . . ."

"No, Khamsin. There was no deception."

"But you knew who I was!"

"For many years, yes. I even knew on the road outside Cirrus when you healed my horse."

She frowned as her mind raced over past events. "What was it, m'lord," she asked, her voice now strangely quiet, "that kept you from claiming me on the road that day? Or in my own house? Why the game of being Rylan the Tinker? The lies? You could've claimed me the day . . ."

"I did. As you said, on the road when we met. I offered you my blessing. You accepted it."

"You . . ." She was shocked. She had no knowledge of any claiming. Just of soft words. And a chain of brightpinks wrapped around her wrist. All innocent, harmless gestures. "But I've come here on my own. If you'd claimed me, surely you would've . . ."

"Taken you forcefully?" He sighed. "Khamsin, you have much to learn and know nothing of the claim you received by accepting my blessing. By claiming you I placed my mark on you, so that as you learned who you are, you'd understand what you mean to the Land. And to me.

"But by claiming you I couldn't force you to do anything against your will. If you came to me—just as you did in Noviiya—it had to be of your own volition."

She remembered their first night in Noviiya. She'd slept alone in the small trundle bed. But not before Rylan had given her his promise.

"Do you recall what I told you?" he asked.

"Yes. No!" The memory held too much pain.

"I told you," he said softly, "I'd never take anything from you that you weren't first willing to give. And I'd never force you to do, or be, anything, other than what you want to be. And I said that in this, if in nothing else, you may now and forever, place your faith."

Khamsin's throat tightened as tears pricked the backs of her eyes.

"If you also remember," he continued, "I asked you in Noviiya to seek out your answers at Traakhal, and you refused. And when I left, I again asked you to come with me. And again you refused. I didn't force you, but neither did I intend to ever stop asking. Khamsin, I hoped as you learned more, you'd . . ."

But he never finished his statement. There was movement in the room to his left, a wavering of light, a liquid motion. Suddenly a woman stood under the south window. Her hair was dark and fell like a glossy drape to her waist. She wore a golden gown patterned like rich brocade, with chains of gold wound around her slim waist. At her throat was a solitary ruby, the size of a hen's egg.

Khamsin thought she was the most beautiful woman she'd even seen.

The Sorcerer, however, was greatly displeased by

the sight. "Melande! This is none of your affair!"

Khamsin had never heard him speak in anger before. Never knew how much hatred could be portrayed in a tone until now. A chill of fear shot through her as the Sorcerer growled out his words at the figure in gold by the window. Perhaps this was the way his servants knew the Master of Traakhal.

Melande seemed not to notice at all.

"Well, Ro, it's nice to see you, too, love." She held slim hands out toward her brother, her fingers laden with jewels. Then with a loud sigh let her arms drift back to her sides. "There was a time, you know, when he would've kissed these same hands. He can do that so very well. When he wants to."

She smiled knowingly at Khamsin, who suddenly felt a dull ache throb inside her. No wonder the tinker had been anxious to leave Noviiya and reticent in returning. Even the princesses parading through the city's tea rooms could not compare in beauty to the woman before her.

Khamsin was barely aware that the Sorcerer was speaking, only hearing the harshness in his tone.

"You're not welcome here, Melande. Now, will you leave or must I do that for you?"

"What, sweetest, banish your little sister again?" She pursed her lips into a moue. "Is that how you reward all the pleasure I've shown you?"

"You pervert any pleasure." He spat the words at her.

"Well, if I do, darling, it's only because you were my teacher." She walked around the room toward him, trailing a jeweled finger along the mantle, her rings glinting as she passed under the east window.

"Melande, I'm warning you for the last . . ."

"At it again, Ro?"

Khamsin spun at a voice behind her and almost lost her hold on the orb. It swayed dangerously. She was forced to clutch it against her, her thoughts on the man now striding in the direction of the Sorcerer. He matched him in height and features, but not in coloring. The man had hair as pale as lightning.

Her question was answered before it fully surfaced in her mind. He was Lucial. And he was her father.

Khamsin gasped and thrust the orb away from her body.

The man, clad in deep red robes, turned in her direction. "And good evening to you, lady. Tell me, do we have here who I think we do?"

Melande stopped in her meandering. "Lucial, you don't think . . ." She scrutinized Khamsin more closely, her dark eyes narrowing.

"Of course," she breathed. "It's little Kiasidira. My, she's grown, hasn't she? Child, what happened to your hair? Is that what they're doing now in Noviiya? The latest fashion?"

"You've known all along who she is, damn you!" The Sorcerer pointed at Melande. "You were the one who sent the mogra after her in the bell tower. That's why you sent your riders to Browner's Grove. To draw me away."

"I haven't the slightest idea what you're talking

about, Ro, sweetest. Why, I've never seen her before in my life. I only know of her because of what Lucial has told me and well, she does look like her father, you must admit. The last I heard she was growing up sweet and charming in some little backwater cove."

"Then how did you know I was in Noviiya?" Khamsin spoke out clearly.

Melande and Lucial looked at her in shock, as if unaware she could do such a thing.

But the orb granted her more than Lucial's identity, when she inadvertently held it against her. It had shown her who she truly was as well. Khamsin now understood why she had to be the one inside the circle. She saw what she meant to the Land, and the Land to her. Not to possess it, but to heal it.

She held her head a little higher, met the gaze of the beautiful witch with more confidence than she'd even known existed in her heart before.

"Why, I just guessed you'd been to Noviiya." Melande's hands fluttered as she spoke. "Doesn't everyone go to the city at some time in their life?"

"Kiasidira." Lucial stepped toward her. "Child, bring the orb to me. Before you drop it. Or someone who shouldn't have it, grabs it." He glared at Melande.

Khamsin turned to her right, toward Melande, then left, at Lucial. "She can't get in here."

"Someone has taught you well, daughter." His gaze shifted for a moment to his half-brother as he emphasized the final word. "Bring the orb to me."

278

"I think I'll keep it for now, thank you, m'lord."

"Kia, Kia, you can trust your Tanta Melande," the witch purred. Khamsin glanced in her direction. "Your father, he abandoned you! Why, I remember saying to him when he told me about you, 'Lucial, let me raise the child if you've no love to give her.' We could've been friends, Kia, you and I."

"You don't need friends like that, daughter."

Khamsin turned again.

"Khamsin." The Sorcerer said her name quietly. Yet she heard it as if his were the only voice in the room. "Put the orb back in the pedestal."

"No, Kia. Bring it to me!"

"Daughter, listen to your father. Come here. I can . . ."

"Lucial, shut up! Kia, don't listen to him."

Khamsin spun dizzily under the barrage of voices.

"Khamsin!"

"Kia!"

"Daughter . . ."

"No!" She thrust the orb over her head. It jiggled precariously.

All were silent.

"Now," she said, her voice suddenly firm. "It's over. There shall be no more fighting. No more burning of villages, killing of children, raping of women. There shall be no more summer snows or poison rain. It stops now. Or I smash this."

Melande's face hardened. "You halfling bastard, how dare you dictate terms to me! Rothal, go in there and take it from the bitch." She swung one arm out toward the Sorcerer. "You can do that, can't you?"

"Take one step and I drop it!" Khamsin shook the handles slightly.

The man in black did nothing for several heartbeats, then raised his arm. Khamsin tensed, knowing what the movement could signal. But he only ran his hand wearily through his hair. "Smash the orb, Khamsin. It's the only way. They're not going to listen to anything else. Believe me, I know. I've tried."

"Are you mad?" Lucial spun on his brother, his hands coming up in a threatening gesture. "That'll kill us! We'll all die!"

"Just a bit sooner than expected, in sixty or seventy years. As we should have, three hundred years ago. We've lived, Lucial, too long. Much too long."

"But we'll get old!" Melande's hands went up to her face.

The Sorcerer chuckled dryly. "You passed your two-hundred and twenty-fifth last Summertide, Melly. I wouldn't call that young."

"Your humor, Ro, is ill-timed, as usual," Lucial snapped.

"I'm tired, Lucial. Tired of three hundred years of fighting, of deceit, of treachery." He paused, his words now for Khamsin. "And of emptiness."

She knew. The orb had shown her that as well. Rothal-kiarr had been on a journey of his own, not unlike the one she'd just experienced. But his had been crueler, more frightening. Until he turned his back on the beckoning darkness of the ultimate power that consumed Lucial and Melande. They abandoned him, then joined forces against him. Sibling against sibling.

Until a child was born in the midst of a maelstrom.

"Well, maybe you're tired but I'm not!" Lucial lashed out at his older brother, grabbing him by the arm. "Go in there and take the orb away from the little tramp, or I swear I'll . . ."

"You'll what, Lucial?" There was a deadly note in the Sorcerer's voice.

The younger man tensed visibly and snatched his hand away.

"Weakling!" Melande hissed, the venom carrying across the circle. "Kiasidira, now listen to me. You've carried on your foolishness long enough. You're meddling in something you don't understand."

"Don't be so sure," came the Sorcerer's smooth reply.

"But this I will promise you," she continued, over-riding her eldest brother's tones. "You will gain nothing and lose all if the orb is destroyed. You can't take away the powers we already have. Or the knowledge. That's past. The past can't be altered. You can't destroy us. You will simply shorten our time for revenge. But a lot can be accomplished in seventy years, Kiasidira. A lot . . . can . . . be . . . accomplished."

The threat was there.

Khamsin lowered her aching arms until the orb swung before her, swirling, pulsing, like a whirlwind full of rainbows. She gazed into its depths before holding it out toward the man before her.

"Rylan," she said, almost shy in using the name she had whispered night after night in her dreams. "I'm tired, too. But I'm not yet ready to die."

And she passed the orb to the Sorcerer as he stepped through the curtain.

CHAPTER TWENTY-FOUR

"Khamsin, you're sure? You understand?"

She nodded hurriedly, the tears trickling down her cheeks as the weight of the past few months flowed over her. Cirrus Cove, the deaths of Tanta Bron, Tavis, Rina, and Aric. The pain of being physically beaten by the Covemen. The pain of loving and losing the tinker. And then there was Egan, so concerned, so caring. Yet he was a Hill Raider, like those who had killed Rina's children. Like the man who stood before her.

She found herself stripped of all illusions of what she had assumed life was supposed to be. Yet, in an odd sort of way, she understood it all and knew she understood nothing. She was finally open for the truth. She raised her tear-streaked face to the man in black.

He gently pulled the orb from her grasp and slid it back into the cabinet. She watched his movements as if mesmerized, as if she were here and yet not. But when he turned toward her, she let herself reach out and touch him, laying her hand on his sleeve. He drew her against him, wrapping his arms around her as he kissed the dampness on her face.

She brought her mouth up to his, no longer shy, knowing he was the answer to her questions.

"Kiasidira!" She heard Lucial's whining voice.

Khamsin ignored her father, having more important things to tend to.

"Rothal!" It was Melande and she, too, received no response.

Finally, Khamsin pulled away. She studied the face just inches from hers. Nothing had changed. He was still the man she knew as Rylan the Tinker and always would be. But many changes now beckoned to her.

"What will you do," she asked him softly, "in eighteen years, when I'm older than you?"

He touched his fingers to her lips. "In eighteen years, child, you will still be eighteen, as you will also be for the next five hundred. You're Raheiran, and to a true Raheiran the orb grants unlimited knowledge, and a limited immortality. It's the price we pay for the duty that befalls us.

"Unfortunately," he said with a sideways glance toward Lucial, "some of use choose to ignore and abuse that duty."

"Some of us," Lucial shot back, "aren't muddled by weak sentimentality."

"No. Just greed. When a Raheiran comes into his or her power, it's easy to be tempted to want to control, instead of guide. Sometimes the gods have bred a little too finely," he added, his mouth twisting slightly.

Khamsin remembered what Ciro had said: The Sorcerer was Tarkir's offspring, but not Ixari's. Lucial and Melande were.

"That's why Merkara told my mother to keep you safe from us for all that time. He knew, just as we all did, what you'd learn, what you would become. It was important you reach that day without any outside influences from us."

"Your *mother* kept me safe?"

"Merkara's half-sister. You called her your Tanta Bron."

Khamsin opened her mouth as if to speak, then closed it.

"She was keeping you away from us until you could make your own decisions. Bronya knew the mistake she made in allowing Tarkir and Ixari to raise me in their temples. She saw what Lucial and Melande had become, knowing only priests and priestesses, who jumped at their every whim. She didn't want to repeat that mistake with you.

"And she refused to let me near you, until she could be sure I wasn't like them . . ." he motioned with a dismissive gesture toward the witch and the wizard, ". . . anymore."

He lifted his gaze from her face and looked at his siblings. "Kiasidira has decided. And she has the power to enforce the decision."

Melande stepped to the curtain, her mouth a tight line. "My riders . . ."

"Your riders will cease, Melande. As will yours, Lucial. You may not have wanted to listen to me before.

But you will listen to us, now."

"I'll see you in hell, Rothal-kiarr!" For a moment Melande's eyes burned with an intense fire, a look that had been known to reduce mere mortals to ashes.

The Sorcerer merely raised one eyebrow in a quizzical expression. His voice, however, was hard as stone.

"Be ye gone, witch."

And Melande disappeared.

Nixa trotted over to sniff the spot where the witch had stood, and sneezed.

Lucial eyed Khamsin warily. "You may have a winning hand, Ro, but the game's not over. Not yet."

Tarkir's sons stared at each other through the curtain, Lucial dropping his gaze only seconds before he, too, disappeared.

And then there was a silence in the room. Nothing stirred, not even Nixa who crouched down on all fours until her paws were invisible. She stared at a nonexistent point in the distance.

Rylan, too, stood motionless, his hands resting lightly on Khamsin's shoulders. His own sagged ever so slightly with a hint of tiredness. The eyes that studied the small form in his grasp now lacked the brazen confidence that shone in them, only moments before.

But Khamsin saw none of this for she stared where the gray feline stared, at nothing, as it was often in nothing that it was easiest to find what you seek.

He waited for her to turn her face back to his.

"I know you're angry with me. You've a right to be, no doubt. So say what you will. Or ask what you need to know."

She paused thoughtfully. "What constitutes a 'winning hand,' Rylan? I don't know. You see, I've never played cards before."

She could tell by his expression that wasn't the question he was expecting, but then, she had no intention of doing the expected. Or of facing, at the moment, the very serious issues she knew they'd have to deal with soon enough. She was exhausted, emotionally and physically, and suspected he was as well. She needed, more than answers right now, to see his smile.

He responded with the genuine warmth her heart sought.

"Well, then, my lady, you still have a lot to learn," he teased lightly and grasped her by the elbow. He guided her out of the circle of the circle, the curtain shimmering like a silver veil in the wind as they stepped through.

She paused at the mantle near a trio of platinum chalices but touched a gilt-edged deck of cards instead. She withdrew a card from the center of the stack. With a shy smile, she handed it to him and he turned it over.

The first light of the new day filtered through the east window of the room and caught the brightly gilded colors on the card in the Sorcerer's hand. On its face was an artist's rendering of two figures, one male and one female, intertwining in a passionate embrace.

It was the card of the Lovers.

"An omen?" she asked, her hand resting on his arm.

"A promise." He drew her against him, sealing his promise with a kiss.

FIRST THAW

CHAPTER TWENTY-FIVE

They came after First Thaw, up the winding trail through the Nijana Mountains. Their slim-hoofed stallions stepped carefully over patches of ice-crusted snow, splashing through mountain streams and rivulets of clear, cold water that flowed from the crevices in the gray rocks. The sky was clearer than it had been since Wintertide, though not the sapphire blue of summer. Still, it no longer blended with the snowcapped peaks in the distance. The brown-clad Hill Raiders, their vests and saddle blankets edged in Kemmon-Ro black, saw the pale azure canopy overhead as a good sign.

They crowded into the great halls of the castle with the other Kemmons: Kemmon-Drin from the northwest and Kemmon-Nijar from the foothills of the northeast. The deep burgundy and greens of their bandings soon intermingled with the black banding of the last to arrive from the region of the Darkling Forest. All drank and caroused and gambled under the watchful eyes of the Khalar–the castle's own Kemmon—who wore no bandings, for their vests and tunics and leather trousers, like their cloaks, were solid black. The color of the Master of Traakhal-Armin.

Like their master, the Khalar were tall, broad-shouldered, square-jawed, raven-haired men. Their large hands wielded the longest swords as easily as they fingered the feather-light reins of their stallions. For Khalar horsemen were the best in the Land, outriding even the flamboyant, but now less powerful, Fav'lhir whose speckled steeds were legendary in the South.

The four Kemmon Reys, or leader-chieftains, of each faction were finally led to the hearth room that lay directly above the great halls of the castle. The rumble of men's voices and occasional burst of deep laughter followed them up the wide, stone stairs. They took their places at the long, polished mahogany table in front of the hearth, with burly Tahan of Kemmon-Drin and round-faced Potro of Kemmon-Nijar on one side, chestnut-haired Egan of Kemmon-Ro and dark Humbert of the Khalar on the other. Their backs were to the tall arched windows draped with heavy, brocaded curtains, now drawn back to let in the strong rays of the late afternoon sun setting in the West.

At the foot of the table stood Lord Tedmond, a frail, white-haired, old man whose thin mustache drooped past the sharp point of his chin. He was clad in robes of rich burgundy, having once hailed from Kemmon-Drin in his youth. But the title he now bore was Lord Chamberlain;

his allegiance was solely to the man who had reigned in Traakhal-Armin for over three hundred years.

"Master Ro" as they called him—and it was only with the greatest of respect—didn't appear at this meeting, or the two that followed, having no interest in the minor negotiations of the Kemmons that took place at the Council of First Thaw. Tedmond handled that as he had for seventy years, since he came into Master Ro's service. He inherited the position from his wizened father, who likewise had borne the responsibility of Lord Chamberlain for the master for nearly three-quarters of a century before he died.

There was the traditional oath of allegiance pledging fealty and loyalty, followed by the offering from each Kemmon as proof of their faith: a new contingent of highly trained scouts or trail cutters added to Master Ro's service or the gift of a finely bred stallion or mare of great bloodlines, all for the betterment of the tribe.

Minor grievances were aired as were territorial disputes, for even within the closely-knit loyalties of the tribe, the Kemmons often fought among themselves. Inter-family jealousies were traditional.

Master Ro himself wasn't above these petty jealousies, and there wasn't a man now present in Traakhal who didn't know the reason for their existence: They were the defenders of two-thirds of the Land claimed three centuries ago by their master and the Khalar. The other third was held jointly by Lady Melande the Witch and Lord Lucial the Wizard. It took the two of them and all their combined powers to attempt—for attempt was all they did—to keep Master Ro, their eldest brother, at bay. For he was Lord of Traakhal-Armin, first-born of the God of the Underworld, Tarkir, and the only one to bear the title and power of the Sorcerer. He was Rothal-kiarr.

The usual great hall gossip around who had transgressed whose nest, or who had the fastest steed or comeliest wench between his legs since Fool's Eve was not, at this council, the main topic of conversation. Two events had occurred over Wintertide. It was discussion and speculation on these subjects that flowed through the Great Halls as freely as Master Ro's excellent ale.

The first event was not an event at all but rather the lack of one. The almost constant confrontations between the Khalar-bred Kemmons of the north and the Magrisi and Fav'lhir and their Kemmons to the south had been visibly, noticeably absent since Wintertide. Border infractions were few, and none had occurred at all deeper in the Khalar region of the Darklings, where for three Wintertides prior, the red-banded Magrisi had struck. Neither had the Cove towns that lay against the Great Sea, villages like Cirrus, Nimbus, and Bright's Cove, seen any South Land Hill Raiders charging over the dunes. The Cove towns were neutral, aligning with none of Tarkir's offspring; their god that of the Sea, Merkara, or the Heavens, Ixari. Consequently, they were often used as pawns in the bitter game of sibling rivalry.

Even the trade city, Noviiya, set out on its finger of land, was unusually placid; the shopmasters, templemasters, and whoremasters carried on business as usual.

This tranquility, though a tense one, that had

descended upon the Land since Wintertide was directly attributed to the second event of Wintertide: the arrival of the Sorceress, the Lady Kiasidira of Traakhal-Armin.

She was now the subject of much speculation. An ethereal beauty, it was said, with hair as pale as lightning. Slender of form, but able to command the fiercest of stallions, wield the broadest of swords, and cast the most powerful of spells. It was her alliance with Rothal-kiarr that now tipped the scales heavily in the North Land's favor. And it was rumored that Lucial and Melande were more than greatly displeased and worrisome. For while Tarkir's youngest proved enough of a deterrent to the Sorcerer's acquisition of new territory, they weren't even remotely capable of stopping the combination of Rothal-kiarr and Kiasidira. For she was the only other one, besides the Sorcerer, who had access to the Orb of Knowledge, a gift from Tarkir to his eldest and favorite child.

Yet it wasn't Kiasidira's magical prowess that caused the raising of dark eyebrows as earthen mugs were drained, filled, and drained again of bright ale. It was speculation on her official position in the life of Master Ro that was argued from table to table and hearthside to hearthside. For not once in the Sorcerer's three hundred and thirty-three years was there ever a woman residing in Traakhal.

Not that his amorous adventures were not well renowned. It was said he had his own private stock of pleasures at Noviiya's infamous Games Palace where anything and everything that could involve pleasure could be obtained. And he had three centuries to sample the best that beauty had to offer, from the sloe-eyed seductresses of the Darklings, to the buxom blondes found in the south's Bright's Cove. But never, during that time, had any woman accompanied him back to the fortress carved from solid rock that was, it was said, as hard and as cold as the Sorcerer's heart.

Yet Lady Kiasidira was here, and had been since Wintertide. Though gossip said their relationship pre-dated even Fool's Eve. And from the most reliable of sources, the castle's chief cook, a jolly woman as rotund and brown as the bulging meat pies she baked, it was heard that Master Ro rarely let the pale beauty get farther from him than an arm's length. And most of the time he kept her much closer than that.

❋ ❋ ❋

"Well?"

Egan eyed the balding man whose dark fringe of hair had become increasingly ruffled from the hand-clasping and backslapping and boisterous mug-clanking toasts that echoed through the great halls on the final night of the First Thaw Council.

"Well, what, Druke?"

"Well, Egan my boy, did you hear of your little friend?"

He scratched at his downy, reddish beard, his winter coat, as Druke called it. It would come off shortly during his annual shearing. "Didn't see her in my travels, no, though to be honest, I've been only to the hearth room upstairs, the stables, and here."

"I'm well aware of where ye've been, boy." Druke only called his late sister's husband 'boy' when he was well into his cups. There was but a seven-year difference between them. "What I'm askin' is did you ask Tedmond if any 'justice rides' would be made?"

It was the last order of business in any council; the assignment of men, or at times whole Kemmons to retaliate for wrongs done by the Magrisi or Fav'lhir during the season. A family whose farmlands had been burned or livestock slaughtered or worse, whose children had been stolen by South Land Hill Raiders, had a right to petition the Master of Traakhal for retribution. And justice, when assigned, was swift. And deadly.

"Not involving a Camron or Lady Khamsin of Tynder's Hill, no." Egan answered Druke's question, his face expressionless. But there was a note of disappointment in his voice.

"Well, had she even been here? D'ye know if she even made it to Traakhal?"

That had been a deep worry of Egan's ever since he'd watched the young girl, disguised as a farm lad, ride off into the Nijanas just before Wintertide. A blizzard had blanketed the North shortly after, and not a day had gone by when he didn't find himself straining for the sounds of hoofs on the trail, hoping to see her come riding back to him on the large, brown horse she called 'Cinnabar,' for the road to Traakhal was rough in the winter and even the best of his riders were forced at times to turn back.

But she never returned. Or had news of either a Lady Khamsin, a healer, or a farm lad from Tynder's Hill named Camron been mentioned as seeking retribution for the death of a family during a South Land raid.

He assured himself through the worst of the winter, while sitting with his daughter Elsy in his lap before the hearth, that he would hear news of, or find his lady, when the Council of the First Thaw came around. But it was now the final night, and he had heard nothing.

Though in truth, he hadn't really asked.

"Why not?" Druke was, as usual, very direct.

"Because . . . because . . ." and the Kemmon Rey, who was by nature a strong and stalwart man, floundered in his reply. He could fight South Land Raiders, break the wildest of stallions, had even stood his ground against a mogra, an ensorcelled demon from the depths of Lady Melande's own private hell. But when it came to confronting the aging Lord Chamberlain Tedmond, well, it was almost like confronting the Sorcerer himself. And no man in his right mind willingly did that.

"Just be respectful when ye deal with the old goat and don't take up too much of his time. And ye'll get the answers to your questions." Druke peered into the bottom of his near-empty mug and, scowling, raised it in the air over his head. A well-rounded, serving wench sauntered by and, with a smile and a pat on his balding pate, refilled the mug for the sixth time.

"It's easier than not knowing at all, isn't that for true, Egan?"

Egan had to admit it was, for the worry caused him

to lose more and more sleep lately. And he had a full summer of riding ahead. Besides, he had held the position as Rey of Kemmon-Ro for fifteen years now. He had more than a small right to inquire, in ever so respectful a manner of course, regarding something of a personal nature of Lord Tedmond of Traakhal.

He found the frail old man about to enter a set of rooms he knew was off limits to any but those who resided in the castle on the Khal and hesitated. Perhaps this wasn't the best time.

But Tedmond already saw the broad-shouldered Kemmon Rey approach, a concerned look on his rugged face, so he turned and called after the man by name.

"Master Egan, is there something you require?"

Egan nodded and stared at the scuffed tips of his boots. "If it please your lordship, I would but request a moment of your time. In private. It concerns a matter of a personal nature."

Tedmond raised one bushy white brow, and for a moment Egan's heart chilled as if one of the icicles dripping from the castle eves had dropped through his chest. He, an outsider, was requesting to speak privately with the Lord Chamberlain. What could've possessed him to make such a request?

But then the frail man motioned to the interior of the room he was about to enter. With trepidation, Egan followed the Lord Chamberlain into the library of Traakhal-Armin.

CHAPTER TWENTY-SIX

The library was large and, like the rest of the main floor, high-ceilinged. Shelves packed tightly with leather-bound volumes in varying shades of green, gold, and brown lined two walls. Egan regarded the collection with awe. He'd only learned his letters this winter from his daughter, now turned eleven. Together they'd spent hours by candlelight just so he could write his own name. That any one person, or even persons, could fill up pages upon pages upon pages . . . it was beyond his comprehension.

"Master Egan?" Tedmond spoke evenly.

Egan took his eyes from the ornately carved staircase he glimpsed through the large archway, knowing the stairs led to the Sorcerer's own rooms in the east wing of the castle. Torch light flickered in the hallway, and Egan, embarrassed at being caught staring with his mouth open, felt a flush on his face as if the flame were within his cheeks instead.

"My Lord Chamberlain," he began, clasping his hands behind his back. "I had hoped that I wouldn't have to bother you with my questions, as I was sure the information I sought would be given out sometime during the council. But we're here on the last night, and I've heard nothing regarding a young . . ." And he stopped, suddenly realizing that he didn't know if the lady had presented herself as Khamsin or Camron, if she indeed did make it to the castle.

"A young what, Master Egan?"

"Well, that's the problem, sirrah. A young woman, disguised as a lad, was discovered by my patrol just prior to Wintertide. As I understood her story, she was on her way here to seek justice for the murder of her family. But since the last time I saw her, at the start of the trail, I've heard nothing and am concerned now she may have gotten lost. Or worse."

"She is kin to you, Master Egan?"

"No, sirrah, not exactly. That is," and he cleared his throat, knowing that a stranger's inquiring as to another stranger's business was frowned upon in Kemmons. "Well, I had tended her an offer of marriage, prior to her leaving."

"Marriage, Master Egan? To a young girl dressed as a lad?"

"I know that sounds odd, sirrah, but if you had ever met her, well . . ." Then Egan realized what had been said. And that his answer was plain. Khamsin never made it to Traakhal, or surely the Lord Chamberlain would've recognized her description and story.

He suddenly felt as if the knowledge he gained was something he could've lived without. Chances of a young girl surviving the harsh winter months in the mountains were slim. He damned himself for ever letting her out of his sight.

"I see now that she never made it to Traakhal, Lord Tedmond. I have no one to blame but myself if harm has befallen her. I should never have let her go on alone through the mountains at Wintertide." He lowered his head, but found little comfort in the worn spots on his boots or the elegance of the embroidered carpeting underfoot.

"It wasn't the wisest of choices, I agree, Master Egan." At the sound of an unfamiliar voice, Egan looked up. A man stepped from the hallway behind Tedmond; a man clad in black, like the Khalar, but who wore a cape clasped at his throat with an ornament of finest platinum. The daggers strapped to his thighs were of the same metal and encrusted with jewels. There was a small diamond in his left earlobe. It glistened a blue-white, matching the color of his eyes.

His hair was thick and dark as a raven's wing, his mustache full and straight cut. He regarded Egan without any noticeable trace of condescension, though his height was greater than the Kemmon Rey's.

Egan stared frozen for a moment before he became aware of an intense pounding that was his heart in his chest. He had never seen this man before, yet he knew; he knew from his manner and dress and bearing. He had no doubts that the man standing before him, towering over the frail Tedmond, was Master Ro. Rothal-kiarr. The Sorcerer of Traakhal-Armin.

Egan dropped to the floor on one knee.

"My lord!" he rasped, not daring to raise his eyes.

"Master Egan."

Had Egan had his wits about him, he would've been flattered that the Sorcerer knew his name. As it was, he was having trouble keeping his balance on the thick carpeting beneath his knee.

"You may rise, Master Egan. That's no doubt an uncomfortable posture for one who spends most of his time on a horse."

Egan stood, barely aware of where he found the strength.

"You were discussing, I believe . . ." The Sorcerer turned to Tedmond.

The Lord Chamberlain nodded. "An incident prior to winter, m'lord. A young girl, disguised as a lad, that Master Egan let ride off into the mountains alone."

"So I heard. And now you come seeking her?"

Egan nodded and found his voice. "Yes, your lordship. I've been concerned, you see."

"Then why did you let her ride off?" the Sorcerer asked.

"Because, because, well, your lordship, you would have to know the lady as I did. She wasn't like anyone you're likely to meet in the common. I mean, she saved my life. Battled a mogra in the foothills, and . . ."

"And now you're telling me a young girl dressed

like a boy killed a mogra."

"Aye, she did, m'lord, right before my eyes, she did. And mortally wounded was I. She healed me, m'lord and . . ." Egan realized he was rambling in his nervousness.

"So now she's killed a mogra and saved your life by healing you. And then you tell me you let her ride off alone."

Egan felt the color rise to his face for the second time that evening. His story sounded ridiculous. He was no doubt wasting Master Ro's valuable time.

"I know how all this must sound, like a story from some late night Fool's Eve celebration. But I swear on the precious life of my daughter that what I tell you is the truth! You would have to know the Lady Khamsin to understand why I didn't accompany her. She can be, you see, uncommonly stubborn."

"Aye, Egan, that she can," breathed Master Ro, as a noise from the hallway drew their attention.

A figure cloaked in a tan riding habit burst into the library, white mittens and riding crop in one hand and a long, fur-trimmed, white cape in the other. Her cheeks were rosy as if she'd just come in from outside. Her pale hair was pulled back into a netted snood. Her eyes glistened, first a pale blue then a deep green. She laughed, breathlessly.

"Oooh, you!" She pointed her riding crop at the Sorcerer and shook it. "You cheated! 'Twas to be a fair race, you said. A fair race! And when I'd given you my promise, what do you do but go . . ."

She stopped, as if suddenly aware of the other people in the room.

"Egan!" She dropped mittens, crop, and cloak to the floor as she threw her arms around the wide-eyed Kemmon Rey, hugging him tightly.

Egan clasped the young woman by the shoulders and held her back at arm's length, his eyes not believing what he saw. The short-cropped hair, part of her disguise as a farm lad, had grown; but, of course, it would have in the three months since he had watched her depart on the mountain trail. Her clothing was fur-trimmed, richer than the rough woolen tunic she'd worn in the Darklings. But the eyes, oh, the eyes that were palest silver or silver green or even blue at times, they were the same, long-lashed and mesmerizing. And the delicately featured face just as pretty. No, now definitely beautiful.

He found he could do nothing but say her name.

"Khamsin! Lady Khamsin!"

"You look well, Master Egan. But then you've had enough to eat and drink, I trust? Gleda has been frantic with the kitchen staff all Wintertide."

He looked at Khamsin again as she said the name of the castle's chief cook. Surely she wouldn't be attired so finely if she were a mere scullery maid? But even if she were, it wouldn't matter, for he'd found her and she was alive and well.

He smiled broadly. "You look well, too, lady, in truth, most lovely. I . . . I never thought I would see you again."

"No?" She glanced around at Tedmond and the Sorcerer, and suddenly Egan remembered whose company they were in. He dropped his hands from where they rested on her shoulders.

"But surely Master Tedmond told you I was here!"

At Egan's blank look she turned on the white-haired man. "My Lord Chamberlain, you know Master Egan is considered a friend. Why didn't you . . ."

"In truth, lady, because he didn't give me the chance."

"That's true, Lady Khamsin. I'm afraid I . . . I got a bit carried away in my story. You see, it's difficult to explain that you're looking for someone who might be a lad or a lass!"

Khamsin laughed. "And do you have so many friends, Master Egan, who fit that description?"

"Assuredly not, but . . ." And Egan was aware that, while they had been speaking, someone else had entered the room. A young boy, a groom or a page from the looks of him. He shifted nervously from foot to foot and seemed to want Lady Khamsin's attention.

But it was the Sorcerer who spoke to him. "You require something, Peppin?"

At the sound of the deep voice, the young boy started visibly. "M-m-my lord m-m-master. Just m-m-my lady's attention for a moment," he stammered.

"It's all right, Peppin." She held her hand out to the boy, who came to her side with a look of relief on his face. "Now?"

"Cinnabar, my lady. Will you be going out again

tonight, or shall I . . ."

Khamsin's hand flew to her mouth. "Oh, Peppin, I'm sorry. I was so intent on coming after Master Ro that I completely forgot to tell you. No, thank you, I won't be going out. And I'd be grateful if you tend to Cinnabar and take him back to the stables."

Peppin beamed. "With pleasure, my lady."

"Don't spoil him now, Peppin," she teased as he turned. But Master Tedmond stopped him, holding Khamsin's cloak and riding things out to the boy.

"Take this back to the tack room, Peppin and fetch Eldora to tend to Lady Kiasidira's cloak."

Khamsin reached for the fur-trimmed covering. "No, Tedmond, I'm perfectly capable of picking up after myself and putting my own clothes away. No need to bother Eldora. She has more than her hands full with the council in session."

Egan stared at the pale haired, young woman wrestling the piece of clothing from Tedmond. He seemed reluctant to let her take it, reminding her that that's what servants were for. She must think of her position, he told her.

"My position at the moment is in the library with half my cloak in my hands, Master Tedmond. And I'd be so very grateful if you would relinquish the other half to me so I can put it away!" Her tone was light, but firm.

"Lady Kiasidira." Tedmond frowned.

Egan heard the name again. This time it registered. Lady Kiasidira. The Sorceress. Lady Khamsin, his

Lady Khamsin, was the Sorcerer's Lady Kiasidira.

"My lady!" he gasped, and she turned, losing her grip on the fur-trimmed collar. With a victorious look on his face, Tedmond handed it to the waiting Peppin.

Khamsin started to open her mouth but stopped at a look from the Sorcerer.

"My lady," the dark-haired man said, in a softer voice than Egan would've ever thought was possible. "I learned a long time ago it's best to humor Master Tedmond. He can be unbearable when he doesn't get his way."

"But m'lord, it's so foolish when the staff is so busy, and I'm very capable of . . ."

The Sorcerer stepped up to her while she was speaking and placed his fingers gently under her chin, tilting her face up to his. He smiled down at her. "Very capable, my lady, very capable. But also," and he looked over the top of her head at Egan, who no longer knew what to say or do. "But also very, very stubborn."

CHAPTER TWENTY-SEVEN

Egan sat for a long time in the crowded, noisy hall, his elbows on the table, his eyes staring into his half-empty mug of ale. He seemed oblivious to the laughter and commotion around him. Even the sloe-eyed, serving wench who tickled his ear with the tip of her braid got no reaction. Miffed, she turned and searched out more willing prey.

"Damn it, Egan! You haven't said a bloody word since ye came back from talkin' to Tedmond. And a pretty, little tart flirts with ye and ye act like she's not even there. So now, for the hundredth time are ye goin' t' tell me what's the matter or not?" Druke leaned forward on the table, craning his head around. He tried to place his face in Egan's view. It wasn't easy.

"Egan!"

Egan groaned softly.

"Look, boy, if she's . . . she's . . . well, if she didn't make it, well there's nothing you can do. It wasn't your fault! Ye did all you could. Egan?"

"No, Druke, she made it." He wiped his hand over his face, then resumed his staring.

"Well, then, boy, if she made it here and out again, then we'll find her, won't we? You and I, together, right?"

"Don't have to find her. She's here. In Traakhal."

Druke looked confused. "And she didn't want to see you?"

"She saw me."

"But she didn't want to."

"No. Truth be told, Druke, she . . . she . . . hugged me."

"But, what is it? Now, you don't want her?"

Egan groaned louder this time, but when two nearby riders in Kemmon-Gar burgundy turned their faces he dropped his voice. "Want her? How can I not, how can I . . . Druke, I . . . I can't. Druke she's . . ."

"Beautiful? Ugly? Pregnant? What?"

He took a deep breath. "She's Lady Kiasidira. The Sorceress." The words came out in a rush.

Druke's mouth dropped open, and he stared. "Ye be daft."

Egan swirled the ale around in his mug. "I could live with that."

"Egan, boy, now this is no time for games. Ye not go sayin' things like that. Not here, boy. Why, that's blasphemy! I mean, what if *he* hears you, saying you think some little village lass is . . ."

"I don't think, Druke. I know. Tedmond called her Lady Kiasidira when he took her cloak, and then *he* did, too."

"Who he?"

"Him. Master Ro." Egan made an upward motion with his head.

"M-m-mast…! Egan, do ye know what you're sayin'? Do I hear ye right? You can't mean that *he* talked to you. That was Tedmond, boy, Tedmond. The old goat with the white whiskers. Not . . ."

"Tedmond was there, Druke. I know who Tedmond is." He shook his head. "Then the next thing I know there's a man, all in black, behind Tedmond. He said my name. 'Master Egan,' he said. And when I looked at him, I thought it was my time to die."

"One of the Khalar, that's all you saw. One of the Khalar. They know you; you're Kemmon Rey."

Slowly, he faced his brother-in-law. "I know who I saw. I know what I felt when I saw him. It was Master Ro. She even called him that."

"Who?"

"Khamsin. Lady Kiasidira."

"Egan . . ."

But Druke never finished his sentence, for suddenly there was a hush over the great hall. Heads turned in rapid succession toward the wide entrance. A young woman stepped into the crowd, a woman with hair as pale as lightning. She no longer wore riding clothes, but just a simple ivory-colored dress of a richly textured material with full sleeves and a modest neckline. Around her neck was a golden chain from which hung a golden, filigreed star with a single, blue-white diamond in the center. It was the symbol of the Sorcerer of Traakhal-Armin.

A name was whispered as she made her away around the long tables.

"Kiasidira. Lady Kiasidira."

She smiled, shyly, nodding to some of the serving girls, calling them by name, and they curtsied, eyes downcast. The last girl, though, had her hands full with a tray laden with wine goblets that tipped precariously as she attempted to bow. Khamsin grabbed the tray from her hands and, much to the surprise of the gathering, finished handing the goblets of red wine down the last side of the table. The girl smiled and giggled as the tray was returned to her. Evidently, they'd done this before.

Druke shot a quick glance at Egan who rose from his place. He clamped a hand on the younger man's arm. "That's, that's . . ."

"Lady Kiasidira," Egan finished for him, as Khamsin caught sight of him and quickened her pace. She arrived flushed and a bit breathless.

"My!" She dusted her hands together. "Thought I'd never find you, Master Egan. I've never seen so many people together in one place. Is it always like this at council?"

Egan saw that most in the hall were still standing. And most were still staring at the young woman before him. "Do you think you should be down here, my lady? I mean, we never expected, that is, it's not proper for . . ."

"Tedmond will have something to say about this later, mark my words. But until then . . ." She shrugged and smiled, widely.

He had no choice but to return it. "My lady, I think

you'd best sit down, or else they will not." He motioned to the crowd staring in their direction.

"Great heavens, I feel like I'm the main attraction at the market fair!" She looked behind her for an empty place. Druke moved quickly sideways.

"My lady," he began as she sat down next to him.

She looked startled. "Druke! Oh, Druke! I'm sorry. I was so busy looking for Egan I didn't see you!" She clasped his hand in hers.

"You look well, Master Druke. A lot better than when we saw the mogra out on the marsh!"

"Aye, my lady." Druke stared at her.

"But at least you knew what to say, then." It was Egan, and he couldn't resist teasing the older man.

"I was just getting used to Camron tagging along when next Egan tells me you're not Camron but Khamsin. And now we find out that you're not Khamsin, either."

"But I am," she replied softly, looking from one to the other. "Mostly, I'm just Khamsin. It's the only name I've ever been called, before now."

"My lady," Egan accepted two goblets of wine from the girl and offered one to Khamsin. "You could never be just Khamsin. Even when you are Khamsin."

They drank their wine while Druke had another ale. When the warmth had settled their nerves and calmed their fears, they talked to her as they had on the marsh, as a friend and companion. Khamsin glowed, happy to discuss the little memories they shared. Talk turned to Elsy, and Druke groaned, but she was anxious to hear of the little girl and promised to give Egan some books to take back with him for the child. Then they talked of Pinetrail, his village and Druke's, and other places in the North Land and Noviiya. She told them the story of the mogra in the bell tower. And how the old wizard, Ciro, had been angry because she never brought him a meatpie when he adopted the disguise of a stray dog.

They laughed, their laughter bringing others around them into the conversation, though timidly at first, afraid of Kiasidira. But not for long, as she was as excellent a listener as she was a storyteller.

Druke stood. A crowd gathered around them, seated on tabletops, kneeling on benches. He had all eyes and ears on him as he acted out the part of the mogra in the marshlands. He recounted the story of when he and Egan, Khamsin as Camron, and Egan's nephews, Skeely and Wade were trapped on a small island of dry land off the main, marsh trail at midnight. And a creature with glowing red eyes hulked out of the darkness, stalking them.

He played the part so well, hunched over and swaying that he drew the crowd into the story, designating one man as a tree and another as Khamsin's horse, Cinnabar. Druke moved stealthily around them, all the while offering a riotous explanation of what had been going on in his mind. So caught up in the scenario was the crowd that no one paid notice to a man, dressed like a Khalar Hill Raider, who threaded through them until he came to Lady Kiasidira's side. He leaned on the table and slipped his arm around her waist, for she was standing, playing herself in the scene. He pulled her back against him.

She looked up surprised, then smiled.

He kissed her lightly on the cheek.

"So there was poor Wade, losin' his supper. And Egan and Skeely lookin' like two scared rabbits on a rock. So I turned to the only sane one among us, the lad we called Camron, and said 'No use staying the night here'!"

There was a flurry of appreciative laughter.

"So he, I mean she and I picked up the camp *and* Egan and Skeely and Wade," more laughter interrupted, "and we got on our horses and left!"

Druke turned to where Khamsin stood. He took a step toward her, smiling, the smile fading from his face as he saw the black-haired man with his arms wrapped around her waist.

"Egan?" Druke breathed through half-closed lips to the man behind him.

Egan turned and saw what Druke saw.

The Sorcerer raised his eyebrow in amusement. "A very well-told tale, Master Druke."

It was a comment anyone would make. At first no one around them took notice of who spoke. Or in whose arms Lady Kiasidira now rested. It was the boisterous man's lack of response that made them take notice.

"Master Ro!" someone gasped. All heads turned as one in Khamsin's direction.

The Sorcerer waited until the murmur died down and all eyes were on him. "Well," he said, his voice carrying clearly through the crowd. "Did you really expect me to stay up there by myself, when all of you are down here having fun?"

There was a moment of tense silence. Then someone, whose loyalty to his Kemmon was stronger than his fear of his master, banged his ale mug on the table and then raised it in traditional salute.

"Master Ro!" he called out. Instantly the cry echoed all over the hall, with ale splashing and wine spilling as a fierce look of pride entered the eyes of those who, only moments before, were chilled with fear. For in his three hundred years as master, Rothal-kiarr had never come down to the great hall and joined the Kemmons. It was, and they realized it, the highest honor he could pay them.

The hall resounded with their appreciation.

Rothal-kiarr stood, though still not releasing his hold on Khamsin. He held one arm in the air for silence.

"Thank you," he said, "for your tribute. And your continued loyalty. But I assure you I am not half as interesting as the tales being told right here. The night is yet young. You've barely made a dent in my wine cellar. So if you'll continue, Master Druke . . ."

He settled back against the table with Khamsin in his lap as the cheering died down. Druke, on cue, stepped back into the center of the circle and gave what many say was his best performance in all the councils that night. A command performance for Lady Kiasidira, and Rothal-kiarr, the Master of Traakhal-Armin.